Fenella Fenton is a writer, poet, and blogger, now she is the author of the novel *Waiting for Alfie*.

Writing is in Fenella's blood, coming from an extensive line of American cousins who also have the writing bug. Her late father, Harry, inspired her to write after ill-health sent him on the literary trail with TV scripts, articles and short stories.

Waiting for Alfie has been a long time in the writing, but Fenella has ensured that her characters have palpable spark and come alive on every page!

Thank you to those who have supported me in my patience whilst awaiting this book's publication, your love and friendship are precious.

To my very dear friend and fellow author, Nikki Dee, thank you for your support, enthusiasm, help and friendship.

Finally, thank you to my late father, Harry Edward Fenton, for introducing me to the love of the written word and, lastly, the belief we all have at least one book inside us.

FENELLA FENTON

WAITING FOR ALFIE

AUSTIN MACAULEY PUBLISHERS™

LONDON • CAMBRIDGE • NEW YORK • SHARJAH

A CIP catalogue record for this title is available from the British Library.

ISBN 9781398446144 (Paperback)
ISBN 9781398446151 (ePub e-book)

www.austinmacauley.com

First Published 2022
Austin Macauley Publishers Ltd®
1 Canada Square
Canary Wharf
London
E14 5AA

A huge thank you to everyone at Austin Macauley Publishers and the exceptional support and advice from the teams who helped me so much in bringing Waiting For Alfie to life.

Prologue

Wrestling his lifeless body from the grips of ice-cold, pitch-black water, they couldn't tell if he was dead or alive.

"Tom, there's another one here." He heard a deep, hopeful voice in the distance.

Turning him over on his back, they stood as though they were observing a body in a morgue, wondering if the cadaver would spring to life; then, after they lay him on his side, a small trickle of dirty water escaped from his bluish lips. The trickle bought forth a huge gasp for air and the coughing up of salty seawater that suddenly flung him back into the world; but this was a new world, one that would give him opportunities, breaks and chances although, at that moment, he wasn't thinking about his future.

He lay there, soaked to the skin, covered in bruises; his mind began to wander.

"Son, what's your name?" The man whose face he first saw was speaking to him, his mind wasn't taking it all in.

"I don't know, um; I don't know…" The words sprang from his lips and trailed off; they then trembled in sadness. His mind darted to the reality he found himself in without even a name.

Why can't I remember? he asked himself.

"Look, son, you're safe now; it's going to be alright." As he looked up, he saw a sailor in uniform with a hat that had a White Star above the peak. He tried to make sense of it in the darkness, but it was futile. However, he did notice the same sailor had a long, jagged scar on his right cheek. Holding out his weather-beaten hand to steady him, the sailor watched as he staggered; observing everything around him, it was then that he realised he was one of only a few saved that night…

Part 1

Chapter 1

Patrick

Ireland, 1865, another rainy day on the green, lush land and several years after the Famine that decimated the population and had been the cause of mass migration to a brand-new world—America.

Patrick, the first-born, delivered at home to a typical Irish family by a large, rotund neighbour woman. This little boy blessed with a mother that loved and overindulged him, and a father that drank the weeks' earnings.

Growing up on a farm in a tiny, white-washed stone cottage that had a tattered sign hanging above the door, saying '*Failte*,' meaning *Welcome* in Gaelic, Patrick dodged the chores, as most young children did. He always made sure he couldn't be found when kitchen duties were being meted out though.

The carefree days of childhood were interspersed with witnessing the marital disharmony between his daddy and mammy, Paddy, and Mary Ryan, on a regular basis.

One night, when he was about seven years old, Patrick witnessed how his father treated his mother; he hid behind the peat turves near the chimney and watched with wide eyes. Already downtrodden by her husband through his drunkenness and lack of marital bliss, Mary would regularly have her clothes torn and be on the receiving end of a black eye, despite fighting back at him as best she could. Usually, it was after a session at the Bar where Paddy was full of beer, but he drank for a reason Mary knew nothing about.

He used the drink to help him cope with his boring, loveless marriage and the thought of being in it when he didn't want to be. His first love, Aileen had disappeared one night, running away with another man. Paddy was beside himself, he loved her but was unable to find her as, sometime after their passion, her body told her she had conceived Paddy's child.

Divorce wasn't an option in Catholic families so Paddy took to drink. It was only when he went to work that Mary could relax enough and have little Patrick sit with her whilst she prepared meals over the blackened hearth. She would sing children's songs to him, and sometimes songs of Ireland whilst Patrick listened, she held him to her breast and pacified him. He didn't understand a lot of the words, but he believed there was a love in them that was only for him.

Then, as years rolled by, Patrick revelled in the knowledge he was the only child and commanded attention from his mother every waking day, some months later, after Paddy fought with Mary one night, babies arrived.

This surprise came to Patrick in the form of his twin sisters, Colleen, and Marie, they made their entrance into the world when he was nine, and his introduction to them saw him ushered to their cribs where he looked at their tiny cherubic faces, beautifully formed and, after listening to their screaming, turned his nose up and walked away. Patrick was annoyed to learn he was not the only one now, it made him bitter, and in time, this bitterness became resentment towards his sisters and a total lack of respect for women.

The girls grew into two little beauties, both with shiny black hair in curls to their waists, they showed their brother unconditional love, but he just didn't feel the same about them. They came along when he should have had all the love and attention from his Mammy.

Growing up in a house full of females, Patrick had no desire to spend time with the twins but craved his Mammy's love. When Mary was breastfeeding them, he watched with big eyes and wished he were a baby once again.

At the age of sixteen, he spent most of his time in the fields cutting peat turves, eyeing the young girls at church on a Sunday morning and hoping to catch a glimpse of some flesh in one way or another. Witnessing his father's treatment of his mother, he began to believe that's how all women should be regarded. Growing into a handsome young man, with the bluest eyes, Patrick would go into the village sometimes making all the girls swoon with his good looks, cocky smile, and hair as black as an anvil.

One hot morning, a few years later, Patrick was working in one of the farm's fields cutting peat turves for the fire, he took off his shirt, the sweat glistened on his broadening shoulders and chest. As he stopped for a moment drinking the water he'd fetched from the small stream at the bottom of the field, he could see in the distance the form of a young girl no older than himself. His mind wandered.

14

No one would know it was me, he said to himself. *I heard it said it was easy, just threaten them into submission, and it will be the sweetest reward ever!* He wandered down the field having the most lecherous thoughts, his eyes were on the young girl, her hair was auburn, and her skin milky white, he walked quicker then suddenly saw a sight he wasn't figuring on seeing! It was the neighbour's daughter Beth, and she wasn't alone!

Chapter 2
The Visit

Patrick had never been with a girl before or even seen one naked, he had been preparing himself for his first time but found Beth sitting astride a man and both making noises he hadn't heard before. Patrick couldn't see who it was at first, but as he got closer, he could see what was happening, it then became apparent who was underneath Beth… it was his Daddy!

He ran back to the peat field, trying to erase the sight that was before him. His own Daddy, *how could he do that to my Ma?* But his mind was forming a plan, *maybe this situation might be a way of getting what I want?* He became jealous at the thought that Beth was being spoiled, and it wasn't his doing. He would speak with his Daddy that night.

Paddy came home sometime later that day, red-faced and looking dishevelled. He looked Patrick in the eye.

"Don't you say a word, you're not to tell anyone about what you saw earlier Patrick. I mean it!" Paddy was raging but calmed down a bit when Patrick turned it all around.

"Pa, I won't say a word, on one condition." Paddy listened as his son told him he wanted to share in the association with Beth when Paddy couldn't. On hearing his words, Paddy was unable to get mad as Patrick had a stranglehold over him, then nonchalance came over Paddy.

Well, this isn't the first time I've had my way with other women, let Patrick have her. He agreed and Patrick smiled knowing that his 'first time' would not be too far away!

A few weeks later, Patrick was out in the peat field again and saw Beth further down in another field, she was carrying milk buckets. *This must be my opportunity!* He casually strolled towards her, she smiled, his blood ran through his body giving him feelings he had never experienced but he liked it.

"So, Patrick Ryan, you are your daddy's boy for sure, it's the good looks and the rest, but I was expecting your Pa, but I guess you'll have to do."

She taunted him, his blood warmed, she beckoned him over to her. As she took his hand and placed it on her breast his stomach lurched at the touch and gave a message to him that she wanted something from him. He delivered, no sooner had she raised her skirts he threw her down on the grass and swiftly got on top of her not quite sure what he was supposed to do, she guided him, he took her breath away, and they made those same noises he had heard earlier. She took him to heaven and him her, he was hooked.

Chapter 3

Goliath and the Cowshed

Just before Patrick was born, Paddy took a job as a hired hand on a farm. He was given the tied cottage so he and Mary could live there ensuring he was starting work on time and would always be available should he be needed. He had known the farmer, Jonathan, for some years through his parents. With Jonathan having lost many of his workers through one thing or another, he jumped at the chance to get his business working again by employing Paddy to help him in the day-to-day running of *Shamrock Farm*.

Farm work wasn't lucrative enough for Paddy though, he wanted extra money for his other favourite pastime, drinking. This *hobby* allowed him to indulge himself, but he had only really taken up the drink since his first love, Aileen, had disappeared all those years ago. He moonlighted by working for the local blacksmith which helped to fill his pockets and left Patrick working harder on the farm with some of the other hired help. Unfortunately, after he had finished work for the week, Paddy spent most of his pay on whiskey in Doonhan's Bar, becoming more and more drunk and hooking up with any woman that would be agreeable to his advances.

One morning, Jonathan asked Patrick to take a package to Adamstown, about eight miles away, and deliver it to Jonathan's brother in *Begging Tree Lane*. There was money in this errand from Jonathan and the thought of it ensured Patrick set out in the early hours. As he walked down a dirt track towards the main road thinking about the long eight miles, he examined the package, it was roughly wrapped with waxed brown paper and string. *I wonder what's in this box?* The thought left him as quickly as it had arrived, he carried on.

It suddenly started raining heavily just after a mile or so, he quickened his pace, the farm eventually came into view. As he walked up to the heavy oak door, he had no idea what lay behind it, he stood with the package in his hand.

Patrick really didn't care what was in the box, the money for delivering it was his main concern. Giving a couple of hard knocks, he waited, the door creaked open, a giant of a man, sporting a full ginger beard and hair to his shoulders appeared in the doorway, almost filling it. He did not look like many Irishmen that Patrick knew, as normally they were quite small in stature.

This man is like Goliath! Patrick thought to himself. He handed the package over and proceeded to tell the man who he was, there wasn't a tiny bit of interest coming from Goliath, he took the parcel and quickly shut the door in Patrick's face. Unfazed by this, Patrick decided to find somewhere to eat and drink as he had had no breakfast that morning before setting out and was ravenous.

Meanwhile, back in the cottage, Goliath slowly walked to the kitchen muttering to himself. The package was well-wrapped, he ripped off the paper around it, opened it and found a small bunch of keys tied together with some dirty string and a note tied to them that said,

You own the farm now Brother, I'm leaving Ireland to have a better life in America, Jon.

Goliath knew this was likely to be true as they had agreed many years before that the farm would eventually become his should his brother decide he didn't want the bother of it and particularly since his wife had left him. Goliath was pleased with this news rubbing his hands together in anticipation. He wondered when he could get his hands on it and thinking about the possibility of living in the cottage tied to it too, *plans, plans*, he muttered.

Patrick walked down the dirt path away from the cottage and made his way in the direction of the village. As he strolled a few yards, a local bar loomed in the distance, getting closer, he noticed it had a small green stable door with the same welcome sign that hung above his own home. Two hours later he came out with a belly full of ale and some Bacon and Cabbage which, he was sure, would set him up for the day.

Slightly swaying, he walked back towards the farm looking for somewhere to rest as the thought of walking back to his home miles away didn't appeal at that moment and perhaps a little sleep would give him the stamina needed for the return journey. He walked further along the road seeing a small barn over on his left where he heard cows mooing. Pausing and walking closer, he saw a young girl sitting inside milking the cows, he reviewed the situation.

Now, I could just keep on walking, or I could further investigate? A smirk crept to his face as he belched from the beer. Getting nearer to the barn, he could see a young brunette girl with a white low-cut blouse, she looked up with innocent eyes from her milking stool to see him staring right down her cleavage in lust. His eyes saw every inch of her and when he looked at her, he could see that her skin was white like the milk she was extracting from the cow.

Patrick walked over to her slowly so as not to alarm her. His mind was full of anticipation at the thought of taking this girl as he felt a surge within him. *I'll use the excuse of being lost to take her mind off milking*, he thought.

As he got closer, she spoke to him.

"Can I help you?" her voice was soft and calmed him… for a few moments.

"Yes, you can, I'm slightly lost and not sure where the road is back to my village," he lied. Neither of them recognised each other.

The young girl went to stand up from the stool to help him, leaning forward, he saw her breasts jiggle, that was enough for Patrick; suddenly, he moved quickly and dragged her off the stool, she struggled and tried to grab his hair, he slapped her around the face that sent her reeling against the straw on the floor of the barn. Moving swiftly, Patrick put his hand over her mouth, she found she didn't have the strength to fight him off after being slightly winded from the fall.

He grabbed her and loosened his trousers, she struggled as best she could, but Patrick had built himself up over the years working on the farm and was far too strong for her. He took her innocence there and then. All this time she couldn't scream but just lay in shock with his hand over her mouth, and after he had finished with her… in the distance, he could hear someone calling a name, it sounded like 'Siobhan'…

––––––––––

The eight-mile walk back to the cottage was started with a skip in his step and a smile on his face, Patrick felt like the cat that had got the cream!

He whistled as he walked down the road knowing that that kind of activity in the cowshed was for him, he felt it was his right to take what he wanted, and no one could stop him. *Oh! It was grand that it was!* he thought, he had had a taste… he wanted more, Beth wasn't enough.

Chapter 4
Aileen

It took hours to get to the village where her Great Aunt lived, the kindly, wise woman helped her with the baby when the time came. The Aunt never told the family Aileen was with her, that same thing had happened to her many, many years ago when the father of a neighbour friend caught her in a shed looking for a lamb that had escaped from the field nearby, months later she realised she was in trouble, her parents wanted to send her to the local Convent, she had other ideas and vanished from the family home without saying a word.

When the baby arrived, Aileen saw she was the image of Paddy; black curly hair, blue eyes and perfect, she cried and held the little bundle to her breast with her tears baptising the little wisps of hair. After Siobhan reached two years old, Aileen met a Sailor one night when out with some friends. The Sailor showed her the deepest affection, she found herself wanting to know more about him after just one meeting. John told her everything she wanted to know, and Aileen found herself telling him about Siobhan but not Paddy, she would keep the baby's father a secret, so Siobhan didn't find out.

John went on to tell Aileen about his late wife and how she had been trampled by a horse and cart just outside the market. He had not only lost his wife but the baby she was carrying. Going back to sea two weeks later helped him cope with his grief.

Their first night together was special, he took her with the greatest tenderness, which made her remember Paddy, she ensured John was left happy and satisfied and put thoughts of Paddy to the back of her mind.

Aileen gave herself freely to John and knew he would be tender with her; just a few weeks later she moved in with him.

Marriage came along several months after moving in as she found herself pregnant with his child. She gave birth to a little boy, whom they called Andrew.

But, just after just three months of life, Andrew died of suffocation[1]. For John, there was no need for further children, he was heartbroken and never got over the loss of his son. On no occasion did he ever make love to Aileen again, they stayed together, she accepted this. Aileen so was content enough to go through marriage without intimacy, it was convenient for them both, their sadness at little Andrew's loss never left them.

John had accepted Siobhan without question and the little family unit got by with him at sea mostly with Aileen bringing up her daughter on her own. John loved Aileen, his life was complete and, as a sailor, knowing he had a home to come back to worked for him, he was a good man and treated Aileen well.

One hot July day, Aileen and Siobhan went for a visit to the farm to see Mary and Paddy, they were wanting to stay for a few weeks whilst John was away at sea. Aileen and Siobhan were true beauties, they inherited their genes from Aileen's and Mary's Mammy, Roisin. Siobhan was a beauty in the making though with striking blue eyes and the longest black hair hanging in curls over her shoulders, and at almost sixteen she could turn a boy to a heap of hormones!

Aileen felt the butterflies in her stomach as they walked along the path towards the cottage. Taking herself back in her mind to the time she had fallen in love with Paddy, she gave herself to him one night and when he took her with such tenderness her heart did indeed skip a beat, she was in love.

She kept this secret from her family, part of her felt ashamed for having sex outside of marriage, it was a burden she carried with love for hers and Paddy's baby. She felt it was right not to say anything... she called the baby *Siobhan*, which is the Gaelic version of *Joan* meaning 'God is Gracious.' Paddy never knew about the baby, she never told him. He had moved to another village miles away for work after she had left the family home that night. Sometime later she visited her family without Siobhan, still not wanting to tell them what had happened, and on that visit, her sister Mary announced she was marrying Paddy. Aileen hid her heartbreak well and only cried when alone that night. No-one guessed he was the father of her baby; *maybe one day I'll tell him*, she said to herself.

Paddy always had feelings for the younger sister, he wanted her, but she had disappeared from her home, no one knew where she was, he could only assume she went away with another man so resigned himself to being with Mary as he

---

[1] A seemingly healthy baby dying mysteriously in this way is what can be known as cot-death in later years.

had already made her pregnant too through lust more than love, but he still had strong feelings for her sister.

Aileen knocked on the stable door of the cottage.

"Come in, dearest sister." Mary smiled and was pleased to see her sibling and niece.

Mary was more worried about Paddy's drinking habits whilst having company, *I'll swipe him if he upsets her*, she was tense but relaxed in her sister's presence at the same time. She put the kettle over the fire and placed the best cups on the table, well, one had a little crack, and the other a chip but Mary kept them anyway; her mother had given them as a wedding present many years ago.

The siblings sat around the little wooden table with its rickety chairs whilst Siobhan preferred to stand and look out of the kitchen window nearby, Aileen leaned over and whispered to her sister.

"Mary, I'm worried about Siobhan, she has gone off her food and been sick these past weeks, I'm not sure what to do as I can't afford a doctor."

Siobhan turned around overhearing her mother, she bit her lower lip then turned back to the tiny kitchen window, her secret was almost out, she didn't know how to explain what had transpired a few months previously. The 'cow shed event' she called it, not divulging to anyone what took place, she kept it quiet; the bump wasn't quite showing though, but she knew she was at least five months gone. Mary made them tea, cut some freshly made bread and opened a jar of bright-red raspberry jam she had just made that morning.

They sat at the table chatting about old times in the family, they spoke with love when discussing their parents who had been long gone. Patrick was outside in the nearby fields cutting peat turves for the fire and unaware of the visitors, he was daydreaming of his conquest a few months previously which made him feel restless; *I may need to visit Beth again*, his mind wandered.

Waiting for a break in the conversation, and as Aileen sipped her tea, Mary had an uneasy feeling her niece may be pregnant, an all too regular occurrence in many Irish families and not by choice sometimes. She wondered how to broach the subject with Aileen without causing alarm, she thought up a plan.

"Aileen, I could do with some help around the cottage as with two small daughters, a growing son and husband, I hardly have time for all my chores."

She sat for a few moments and was about to speak; Siobhan spun around, "Please Mammy, could I stay with Aunt Mary just for a few months to help out? I wouldn't be in the way and will work hard."

Siobhan saw this as a way out of her predicament without hurting her mother *but what would happen to me when the baby comes?* Her mind was racing and then quietened when her Aunt Mary came up with the solution. Quickly Aileen agreed, Mary hadn't thought how Paddy would take the news of an extended-stay house guest, and *one that was pregnant;* she would handle all of that later that evening after she had settled Aileen and Siobhan in the spare room.

After a few hours in the fields, Patrick walked into the kitchen stopping dead in his tracks, he saw his Mammy with his aunt at the table, then his eyes turned to the girl standing over at the window, it was the girl in the cow shed! Patrick hadn't seen his aunt or his cousin for many years since he and they were incredibly young, he couldn't quite remember what they looked like, but he knew they lived in a village some miles away. Playing it cool, he pretended he didn't recognise her. Siobhan swung round when she heard footsteps come into the kitchen to meet his gaze. The look of surprise on her face dissipated quickly so as not to alarm her Mammy or Aunt.

Patrick gave an excuse of looking for one of the twins, turned right around and went out again. His mind went back to the cowshed; he hadn't noticed the bump as her clothes hid it well. He did, however, observe her breath-taking beauty, he sighed followed by a shiver as he went to cut more peat turves remembering how he had taken her months previously.

As they chatted, Mary heard the familiar footsteps of Paddy who was coming home from Doonhan's bar all the worse for drink, he stopped dead in his tracks when he saw Aileen and Siobhan.

"To what do we owe the pleasure?" his words were slurred but pleasant, something Mary didn't manage to experience much of when he had been drinking.

"Paddy, we're visiting with you and Mary as John is away at sea and thought it would be an ideal chance to catch up." Paddy's eyebrows raised, something in him stirred, he kept it hidden.

Mary told Paddy that Aileen and Siobhan were staying for a few weeks and that Siobhan will be staying on for a further few months to help, not mentioning the pregnancy just yet.

Paddy accepted this piece of information easily and with no question, though that evening in the bedroom it was different.

"Mary, we have enough mouths to feed! And you know money is tight!" He grabbed her arm and spun her around to face him.

Not only did he raise his voice but his hand, she shrunk back but thought fast, he calmed down after Mary responded with her carefully chosen answer, "Having help around the cottage, you don't pay for would benefit us all, Paddy."

Paddy thought for a moment, *I could be close to Aileen for a few weeks, but that was my little secret, and I wouldn't have to find money to pay for help, yes, I can do that.* He agreed that they could stay, and the extra help would be welcome. He had other designs but finding time alone with Aileen could be a challenge. That night Mary lay back and let Paddy be intimate, he was breathing foul-smelling beer breath on her… it was over in minutes, he turned over snoring straight away, Mary prayed that the good Lord would deliver her from her drunken and abusive husband, this was a prayer that was well-worn. Little did Paddy know he had his daughter and his unborn grandchild in the same house!

Chapter 5
Opportunity

Over the days, the cottage was full of cooking, girls, women and washing. The sisters enjoyed each other's company, they laughed together whilst playing with the twins. Siobhan was busy throwing up behind the cottage out of sight, desperately trying to keep the pregnancy quiet, making sure she wore loose-fitting clothes as much as possible. One Monday morning, Mary wanted to take the twins and her sister to the market in the next village for a few hours.

Paddy was working in a field near the cottage, Patrick had gone to a farm five miles away to help out with the harvest, it would be hours before he was home which left Paddy at the cottage alone. Aileen made an excuse to Mary that she was not feeling too grand and that staying put in the cottage was a better idea. There was no reason for Mary not to believe her sister. Aileen had seen how Paddy looked at her the night before, it said it all in his eyes; her stomach tied in knots at the thought of him.

That morning, at breakfast, Mary was busy cooking and Aileen lay the table with help from the twins, Paddy brushed against her, they both looked at each other, their eyes met, and Aileen's stomach flipped, the wanting was there and needed to be satisfied.

Within an hour of Mary leaving the cottage with Siobhan and the twins Aileen was watching out of the kitchen window searching for Paddy. Nowhere to be seen, she was shaking with anticipation, *where was he!* Then, almost at once, she felt strong arms around her waist and a man's body close to hers… he had crept up behind her!

"All these years Aileen, not hearing from you since that time you disappeared. No opportunity, but now…" she stood with her back to him; she was frightened to face him.

In his deep, manly voice, he whispered in her ear, "Aileen, I have spent years wanting you. You left, and I had no idea where you went, whom you were with, and why…?"

As he waited for her to speak, he gently held her bosom pressing himself against her, she could feel his excitement, he lifted her hair and kissed her neck as shivers ran down her spine. She spoke softly to him but with an urgency of wishing to be intimate.

"Paddy, I left home because…" She was frightened to tell him, and as her tears fell, she blurted out the truth.

"All these years, I have kept a secret from you Paddy… Siobhan is yours."

He staggered back a few feet, letting go of her, she turned and faced him. Paddy was visibly shaken with a single tear running down his cheek which he wiped away but said nothing. At first, he shook his head in disbelief then he cried inside at the thought of having a child already grown that he had no hand in bringing up.

"Jaysus, Paddy, I was so young; I didn't know what to do; I didn't want to end up at the Convent where I'd never see my family or keep my child. I wanted her as she was yours but could never tell anyone, please understand." He nodded gently and lifted her chin to meet his gaze.

She had aged but then so had he, her beauty still captivated him, he held his hand out and grabbed her to him finding her lips, kissing her hard and deep. He had not known passion like it for years and certainly not with Mary, he had to get drunk first and even then, could only do it after they had had a fight. There was no time to remove clothes as he needed Aileen right there and then.

They climbed the narrow wooden staircase to her room. Aileen could feel Paddy's urgency almost tangible, but she held him back slightly.

"Paddy, be slow with me; it's been a long time."

She thought back to John who had not touched her in years since the loss of their son. She was living like a nun but all that washed away as she lay back on the bed. Paddy gently lay beside her with his head on her bosom, he could smell her faint perfume as she caressed his head, he kissed her neck and finally, made love to her like it was their last day on earth. In the afterglow, she cried tears, tears of regret, tears for the life she could have had that would have been filled with love and let them fall away from her eyes down her cheeks.

"I will always love you, Aileen. However, we are in these lives, but I promise you, whenever you are near me, and if I can, I will make love to you as a way of ensuring our love never dies."

She cried against his chest as he took her with a rawness and yet with tenderness one more time.

Afterwards, they didn't speak of Siobhan or what had transpired that afternoon but the quiet understanding between them would always be there. They were indeed in other lives, she with John, and he with Mary, *it is what it is*, she thought… until a few months later.

―――――――

That afternoon, as Mary and the children arrived back at the cottage, she found Aileen sitting at the table with a cup of tea looking in a daydream.

"Aileen, you look flushed, are you feeling better?" Mary was concerned for her younger sister; she was almost like a mother as she had helped their own mother deliver Aileen some years ago when the baby came suddenly before a midwife could be called.

"I'm grand Mary, much better, thanks." Aileen ached in her heart with love from the intimacy she had had with Paddy that morning and coupled with the fact she may never have that experience again for a long time to come. She was happy with the knowledge but kept that feeling hidden. She felt tender below but with the warmth of knowing Paddy once again.

The weeks passed and, as Aileen prepared to leave and make her journey back home, she gave her daughter a hug.

"Don't you go getting into any trouble, Siobhan?" Aileen clucked with motherly love as they hugged each other.

Jaysus, I'm already in trouble and it's too late to be careful, Siobhan said to herself.

As Aileen gave her goodbyes that morning, she swore she could see a tear in Paddy's eye. The memory of their intimacy once more stayed with her as she started walking the eight miles back to the village where she lived.

Although Paddy agreed with Mary that Siobhan could stay, she was to have the old outbuilding near the Well. He wanted to hug his daughter but knew that keeping her at a distance would be best, *does she know I'm her Daddy?* he didn't want to mention his new-found knowledge for fear of further problems. He wanted to hide his knowledge of her from Mary and his other children to ensure the secret remained.

Mary hadn't told Paddy about Siobhan's baby, she wasn't sure how to, she knew the subject would have to be broached at some point as soon as it became apparent… *or can I hide it?* Her mind was in a whirl with planning what to do.

The cottage had a few outbuildings, one was used for goats, *it doesn't smell too much of animals,* Mary thought this was easy enough to sort out and cleaned it as best she could then make a little makeshift bed with a few spare blankets. This was to be Siobhan's home until the baby arrived.

Patrick couldn't get the picture of Siobhan out of his mind after seeing her in the kitchen. Discovering she was his cousin was bad enough but why was she staying with the family? He had an idea and so late that night, as Siobhan got ready for bed whilst the rest of the household were asleep, he wandered over from the cottage and stood outside of the outbuilding, peering through the cracks of the worn oak stable door. He quietly watched as she removed her clothes never having seen a completely naked girl before; he normally didn't bother to remove the girl's clothes he was about to deflower… or his for that matter, just enough for the purpose he had in mind.

He liked what he saw, her breasts were heavy and hips broad, then he noticed a large bump where her stomach was. He watched as she stroked her stomach, not making a sound, he just stood with his mouth open. Silently he turned away and went back to the cottage, he was to be a father! *I'm too young to be a Daddy, I'll say it's not mine.* He had a lot on his mind that night and tossed and turned until dawn.

Siobhan had no idea she had been observed, Patrick wasn't keen on letting anyone know what he had done a few months previously either. Whilst in the outbuilding, Siobhan had time to reflect. She had no idea she was closer to this family than she knew, the knowledge that Paddy was her father was not shared with her, and Patrick, not only her cousin but the father of her unborn baby, she fell asleep whilst the baby settled inside her.

As the weeks flew by, Aileen was about to go to the market and was suddenly sick one morning, she felt sure she was pregnant with Paddy's baby, her heart grew with love but then her mind raced, John was due home from sea and the mathematics wouldn't add up; so she began to form a plan, she would have to pass the baby off as Siobhan's!

Chapter 6
Prayers Need Answering

Indeed, by the time Patrick had reached eighteen, he had taken over five virginities from the local girls and his cousins.' He did this by putting the fear of God into them, threatening that if they told anyone then they would be sent away to a convent. With Beth it was easy, she wanted it as much as he did and there seemed to be no guilt attached to what she wanted or him for that matter.

Eventually, four of them 'disappeared' with one of them marrying quickly. Many young girls were sent to convents when they became pregnant, most through no fault of their own but just due to ignorance mostly or against their will; carnal knowledge was never discussed in families, that was for marriage. Beth never got pregnant.

Babies were born and sold making some convent nuns rich off the innocence of the girls in their charge, yes, they fed off childless couples alright. By ensuring the girls he had taken were too frightened to tell anyone about him, Patrick felt he had carte blanche with whomever he felt he wanted, whilst he was enjoying spilling his seed.

———

One Friday afternoon, Patrick was cutting peat for Mary who was waiting for Paddy to come home from the blacksmith at any moment. Cutting and stacking the turves in the drizzling rain, Patrick could see something in the distance; the shape of what seemed to be a man stumbling along the lane. The swaying character was indeed Paddy, much the worse for drink. He stumbled past Patrick and entered the house, tripping over the threshold on the way. He grabbed at Mary, which sent her sprawling against the wooden table near the fireplace. She tripped over the pile of freshly cut peat turves that had been stacked there previously by Patrick crying out when her cheek hit the table edge leaving a dark angry bruise. Paddy quickly went over to her, pulled her up by her hair, sat her at the table, kissed her forehead then promptly collapsed in a drunken heap passing right out in front of her whilst displaying a wet patch on his trousers where he had soiled himself.

Patrick ran into the kitchen to observe his mother at the table crying and holding her face whilst his father lay dishevelled, drunk, and snoring loudly at her feet. Witnessing these incidents on a regular basis, Patrick thought this was how all married life was and so took this to be, what he thought, was normal.

Paddy was lifted to his feet by his son who helped him to bed to sleep it off. As he struggled with him, there appeared on the wooden floor a little trickle of urine which formed a pool next to the bed. Patrick's sisters were too young to understand what they were witnessing, but after seeing this event many times in the past, they just accepted it as normal although it frightened them every time as they clung to each other sobbing. Mary just brushed it off and carried on as if nothing had happened. She scooped the girls up and took them around to a neighbour for the night as she was sure when her husband awoke, there would be the potential for a beating or the usual taking her against her will if he were able.

Holy Mary, Mother of God, I hate him! Mary made a vow to herself that when the time was right, she would leave him and take the girls. She said this every time he hurt her or abused her, but Catholic women didn't usually leave and so she put up with the abuse and marriage with little happiness. The first time Paddy hit her in a drunken rage, she was six months pregnant carrying Patrick, she managed to go full-term, and *God only knows how I managed to do that,* she wondered. She was bought up to believe in marriage and all that went with it. Paddy got her pregnant before their wedding and, when finding herself carrying a child conceived out of wedlock, she accepted her fate. With hatred in her heart for her husband and the love for her children, she kept going for their sakes whilst praying every day for salvation.

Chapter 7
Mary and Paddy

Rain is a feature of living in Ireland, it rains through all the seasons, although the lush green land has some respite in the summertime when it is said everyone *comes alive*. It was on a balmy, hot summer night that Paddy took Mary to a local dance. He had found the girl he really loved, Aileen, but she seemingly had gone off with another man, or so he thought. He decided to accept his misfortune and marry the next girl that he met who happened to be Mary, Aileen's older sister.

Mary's parents were heartbroken that their youngest daughter had left in the middle of the night. They suspected she may have been pregnant but couldn't prove it; they would never have turned her out on the street but didn't have the chance to let her know that.

Mary's parents agreed that Paddy could take Mary to the dance as there were many people there that night and *no chaperone would be necessary*, they thought. Alcohol was flowing (there was no age limit), Mary turned hers down when Paddy bought a glass over.

"No thanks Paddy, I have never had alcohol and don't intend to start now," was her answer, Mary had already witnessed its effects on her uncle when one night, many years ago, he entered her bedroom with no clothes on climbing into bed with her. Nothing happened. He lay snoring in her ear totally oblivious until he awoke the next morning finding himself in a strange bed. She had never seen a man naked and couldn't stop looking, then, silently, she crept out of the bed in the early hours, went to the kitchen and slept in the chair next to the hearth. She was sixteen years old.

Paddy went back to the bar and asked the barman for a glass of barley water, sprinkling Laudanum in the glass, which he had kept in his pocket in case he ever got lucky, he took it back to Mary. After about thirty minutes, she said she wasn't feeling her usual self and asked Paddy to take her home. He agreed, knowing that a couple of drops would give him the chance to make her more malleable, she would agree to his advances.

They went out into the night, looking at their breath as they breathed out in the cold air. Walking down the narrow lane towards her home, Mary appeared drunk and hung on to Paddy as she felt sure she would collapse at any minute.

"Paddy, I don't feel so grand, I didn't drink any alcohol."

Mary wasn't protesting but was trying to understand why she wasn't in charge of herself. As she leaned against him, he put his arm around her and slowly manipulated her along the lane and into a field. He took out all his frustrations on Mary that night, it was her first time and had not known a man in that way. With her head swimming and no fight in her, she let him take her, there was no love and tenderness, that was only for her sister, Aileen; Paddy kept that locked in his heart. Patrick was born nine months later and by that time Paddy agreed to marry Mary under the pressure of her parents.

Chapter 8

Margaret

A few years after Patrick was born, in the next village, Margaret, the eldest of three daughters, was born to John and Niamh O'Sullivan. Their marriage was one of love, after the initial accident of getting Niamh pregnant; they married with her bump slightly showing.

Margaret was the most stunningly beautiful of the three children. Her long, curly black hair and curvaceous figure, even at sixteen, turned heads and not the kind of heads a young girl at that age should be turning. Grown men would eye her and mutter to each other that they would if given a half chance.

Margaret noticed none of the attention she acquired and was innocent and chaste. Her Daddy spent most of his time at work but worried about his daughters becoming pregnant outside of wedlock 'how ironic,' he thought, and remembering back to the time, he got Niamh pregnant before they married. He tried to protect the girls as much as possible as unwanted pregnancies happened on a regular basis, he knew many young girls 'disappeared' from families, but everyone knew where they had gone—the Convent! Niamh always told the girls to 'stay away from men as they are the devil!'

This warning stuck with them and, for the most part, they went everywhere together, or their mother chaperoned them to and from the schoolhouse. Margaret's next youngest sister, Roisin, herself was a beauty and headstrong. One Summer afternoon on her way home from school with her sisters, she ran ahead with her need for independence high in her mind whilst her younger sister, Lizzie, was happy to walk side-by-side with Margaret. Roisin was always running ahead of her mother or sister to investigate up ahead; then, one day, she ran ahead and veered off into a field through a hedge, she saw a man. She recognised him as a widowed neighbour that her father had talked to on numerous occasions, never noticing how he looked at her or her sisters when he was walking past the farm, she was too young to understand the danger.

He looked up and saw her running along the inside edge of the field with her dress and hair flowing in the wind, he called out to her with a smile, having no fear of him, she ran over to speak. He made a grab for her, she struggled and wrenched herself free and screamed. Margaret came rushing over through the hedge; she held her sobbing sister in her arms, "What happened, Roisin?"

Between sobs, she told her a man had grabbed her and tried to kiss her, he was a neighbour she had recognised.

Grabbing Roisin and Lizzie, Margaret hurriedly made her way home. Upon entering the kitchen, Margaret told her father what had happened. Roisin was still crying with her face red and eyes bulging. John stood for a few moments looking out of the kitchen window with his fists clenched, he did no more than march round to the neighbour, who, when confronted, tried to protest his innocence. John beat him so badly that the neighbour moved away some days later never to be seen again just leaving the farm and everything in it.

From the moment the neighbour left, John kept a close eye on his daughters. They were called in before dark and not allowed outside the cottage without Margaret or their mother, this was stifling to Margaret, he insisted, and so, for quite some time, the girls were practically prisoners until a visitor happened by one afternoon…

Chapter 9

One out, One In

Goliath sat in his kitchen holding the keys that Patrick had delivered whilst smiling to himself.

Looks like I have a farm and a cottage to live in, his thoughts of having another woman in his life ran fleetingly through his mind. He was eager to investigate the property and didn't want hesitation or obstacles. He did no more than pull his boots on, unhooked his old moth-eaten coat from the rusty hook in the hall and made his way to *Shamrock Farm.* Jonathan lived three cottages away from Paddy and Mary on his own, his wife had left him for one of the farmworkers, she also left bitterness behind as she walked out the door.

Goliath walked the eight miles easily picking up the pace, he eventually found himself at the front door of his older brother's cottage.

There were no hugs or handshakes just straight to the point, "Jon, when will you be leaving for America?"

"Brother, I have a passage booked and will leave this island once and for all on Thursday. Come in and set yourself down whilst I tell you about the farm."

Goliath sat down, his real name being Andrew, listening intently at his brother's descriptions and information. He liked the sound of the tied cottage and wondered when he might move in.

"Andrew, there are tenants in there now, they work on the fields, there is no agreement between us just goodwill."

Andrew didn't want to hear that kind of information. Although he had his own place, he wanted to move to the farm and maybe let out his cottage.

"Brother, once you leave, I will have decisions to make which might not be favourable to the tenants, but I certainly will not cut my nose off to spite my face. I'll go and see them now and size up the situation before making my decisions."

Andrew wondered what and who he would find. He could do with a wife. Agnes had died some years previous and the thought of having a woman again in his home to look after him appealing.

He found himself walking past two cottages and finally to the last one where Paddy and Mary lived. As he walked up the path and into the kitchen, the only people in the cottage were Siobhan and the twins, she was looking after them whilst Mary shopped in the market and Patrick and Paddy were working in the fields.

The welcome sign touched his head as he bent to enter the kitchen, he didn't bother knocking. The scene before him was pleasant, Siobhan was at the sink and the girls were playing nearby around the hearth. He sucked in his breath, he had never seen such a beauty before, even his late wife was nothing compared to this creature he saw before him.

"Who are you?" she stammered.

Andrew pulled up a chair and sat himself down. "I am the new owner of this farm and the cottages tied to it as from Thursday."

One of the twins, Colleen, ran to Siobhan and grabbed her hand sensing the tense atmosphere. Andrew surveyed everything in the kitchen and even more so, Siobhan. The silence was deafening until she spoke.

"Paddy will be here in a few minutes and possibly Patrick too," she said in a defiant manner as if to frighten him, he just smiled then said he would wait for them to come to the cottage.

"Girl, I own this whole farm now and everything in it, I have all the time in the world to wait for what now is mine!"

Siobhan trembled and stood with Colleen gripping her little hand tight. Suddenly, the door swung open and there stood Paddy.

"Who the hell are you?" he shouted and puffed himself up against Andrew.

"I might ask the same question man," as Andrew stood up, Paddy could see he was no match for a giant of a man in his kitchen.

"I have been given this farm and cottages; my brother has handed it over to me as from Thursday."

Paddy couldn't believe what he was hearing, only yesterday he saw Jonathan, nothing was said about handing it all over. He just stood there with his mouth open, no words forthcoming.

Andrew was in no mood to bargain or back down, he stated his case, Paddy would have to agree and move his family out, but where to?

"You'll have to give me and my family time to find somewhere else to live, we are right in the middle of harvesting with the crops." Paddy could have done without this problem.

Whilst the two men discussed the situation, Siobhan took the girls outside and over to the little outbuilding where she was staying. She was nearing her time and gently stroked her stomach; she did not know what lay ahead of her whilst staying at the cottage but now there seemed a bigger problem.

"Paddy, I am not an unreasonable man, I also am not in a rush to move in but, we will agree that in four weeks' time you and your family will be gone from here for good as I will not want your labour and will hire my own."

Paddy nodded but slowly wondered how on earth he would find work; how would he tell Mary and Patrick they no longer had a home? Andrew stood up and moved towards the door.

"I'll be back here in four weeks' time, best you and your family are gone when I arrive." Andrew walked straight down the path and out of sight.

Paddy's mind was in turmoil, he did his best to hide it when Mary came home. He had a wife, two daughters, well three with Siobhan and a son to think about, he took his troubles to the local bar and proceeded to drink himself into a stupor.

Mary came back from the market and asked Siobhan about Paddy's whereabouts. She told Mary what had transpired a few hours earlier and how Paddy had gone to the local bar. Mary was silent but inside she screamed, with her mind turning to the possibility of another argument when Paddy returned but the one thing in her mind was the awful thought of having to move.

Just before midnight, Paddy rolled in and went straight up the stairs to bed, Mary was laying there pretending to be asleep, there was no beating, no argument, he just got into bed next to her tossing and turning through the night, then the pain arrived in his chest...

Chapter 10
Prayers Are Answered

Mary awoke the next morning, turning over to look at her husband, she thought he was noticeably quiet, more than normal. She got out of bed and looked at his face which appeared to have a greyish hue to it, she touched him, he was ice-cold; he'd had a massive heart attack in the night. She quietly went downstairs, started breakfast on autopilot, acting normal when the girls came down with Patrick, Mary told them all to sit down around the table. Siobhan walked over from the outbuilding and sat with them, Mary told them in a monotone manner.

"Your daddy's dead, and we are to be out of this farm within four weeks." It was all said so matter of fact by Mary who wasn't shedding a tear for her deceased husband as she turned over a piece of bread frying in lard.

The girls cried; Patrick went out into the fields; Siobhan just stroked her stomach. Mary's mind raced, different scenarios appeared before her, but none provided an answer to the problem of where to live or how to cope with no money coming in. After breakfast, she went to the Farmer's cottage and knocked on his door.

"Come in, Mary. What's the problem?"

"Paddy is dead." The words came out with no feeling in them. The farmer looked surprised as he offered her a seat at the kitchen table. With her predicament unfolding, he had an idea.

"Mary, as you know I am leaving for America on Thursday and my brother, Andrew, takes over the farm. He needs a woman to look after him, is it possible you could come to some arrangement?"

"I've just lost my husband and you're talking of me warming another man's bed before he's even in the ground!"

Jonathan was not always one to beat about the bush; he sat back and realised that his plan was blurted out before thinking about how Mary would feel, it was common knowledge Paddy gave her an awful life, *but maybe this was too soon?* he said to himself.

He apologised straight away; Mary listened as he talked over the plan he had in mind. Her mind went into overdrive, she could stay on the farm, Patrick would have work, the girls could carry on going to school and Siobhan could have her baby there. As she mulled these thoughts over in her head, she had forgotten that there might be more involved than she wanted to think about… *the Farmer's brother wanted looking after, how would I cope with that?*

She hadn't even buried Paddy and already was considering her future; her prayers were answered at last.

———

The funeral was a quiet affair, just Mary, Patrick, Siobhan, and the girls, plus the farmer in attendance with the Priest. She didn't shed a tear, Mary's tears had all been shed through her marriage, she stayed saddened for the sake of Patrick and the girls. However, her mind was darting to and fro regarding the farmer's brother, *how am I going to handle the situation?*

Chapter 11

A Marriage of Convenience

With the funeral over and the farmer gone to America, Mary was just waiting for the visit from Jonathan's brother, it came in the form of a horse carrying a huge man mountain, she had never seen Andrew but had heard about him from Patrick's visit.

Andrew dismounted tying his horse to the gate, he walked up the path not even knocking, the stable door was half-open. Mary could see him.

"Are you Andrew?" she said, a little shaken but stood her ground.

"Yes, Jonathan's brother, and now the owner of this farm and dwellings… you are?"

He knew who she was but wanted her to say it.

"Paddy's widow, Mary." Her voice was confident but curious. Her thoughts ran through her mind at a gallop, *would she keep his bed warm? What would he want from her? How long could she and her family stay?* All these questions she had for Andrew, but something in her wanted to know him better.

"Paddy's widow?" he was puzzled, only a few weeks before he had been speaking with Paddy in the kitchen regarding ownership of the farm.

She filled him in about Paddy's demise and awaited further questions. Andrew eyed Mary as though he was going to buy a horse wanting to know if she was a 'good runner.'

There were no further questions from Andrew at that point with his mind taking him into the bedroom and the realisation she could indeed keep his bed warm. Mary asked him to sit awhile, she made him tea and bought out bread and jam. All this time Andrew eyed her approvingly, she felt his eyes in her back… and other places!

"Mary, I have a proposition." Andrew was direct and didn't have time for the niceties of courtship in mind.

"Marry me and you can stay here with your family, I will of course expect my conjugal rights."

She turned around to see him with a smile on his face. *Could she agree to this contract? Was this a way out of her predicament?* All these things went through her mind, she thought about the life she had had with Paddy, anything was better than that and the life she was being offered would, indeed, help her and the children.

She made the tea, cut the bread, and offered it to Andrew, he didn't take it but just stood up. He was in her personal space; she didn't back away from him. As he put his arm around her, she could feel his breath on her neck. He hadn't had a woman since his wife died and seeing the opportunity in front of him was becoming quite exciting.

"Andrew, if I agree to your offer, I want you to wait until we are married, could you do that?" she sensed he wanted her there and then, it appeared there was to be no love in this marriage of convenience but at least some kind of moral high ground could be had, or so she thought.

"Mary, it's been a long time since I've lay with a woman, I've no doubt you would be agreeable. I'm not a romantic man, nor fancy. If I take you then I take you for comfort, marriage, and you to care for me." Mary mulled his proposition over. She had lain back many times for Paddy whilst he was drunk which was most of the time in their marriage. She asked Andrew one more question.

"Do you drink?" Mary waited for the sad and sorry answer, she knew most men did.

"I neither drink nor womanise." Andrew's answer was a breath of fresh air to her. He held her in a tight embrace almost taking her breath away, she felt his longing and was honest with herself, she had a way out and a way in, she gave herself to Andrew that afternoon never looking back. She agreed to his offer.

Chapter 12

Babies and Marriage

Ireland in the summertime, 'a fair stretch' was uttered amongst the population in July and August where the evenings could still be light until 11:00 p.m.

After the small, quiet wedding, Andrew went back to the cottage and farm with Mary. The girls were left playing at the neighbours and Siobhan was in her outbuilding, Patrick was working at a farm a few miles away… Andrew had Mary all to himself.

Once outside the stable door, he picked her up and carried her across the threshold, she gave herself to her new husband, she hardly knew him, but she had married in hopes of securing a home for her children, Mary was pleasantly surprised at his tenderness with her the second time, a feeling and experience she had never had with Paddy. He was rough around the edges sure, but she felt for certain she could accept all that came with the marriage and proceeded to make him happy.

She told him about Siobhan and the baby due any day, Andrew was nonchalant, in his mind women had babies out of wedlock, it happened, neither he nor Mary knew it was Patricks!

Preparing dinner a few nights later, she could hear shouts for help coming from the outbuilding nearby, the twins came running in looking scared and breathless pointing to the outbuilding where Siobhan was. Mary ran as fast as her legs would carry her to find the girl standing next to her bed with water on the floor.

"Don't be alarmed, Siobhan; it's only your waters breaking, they leave you before the baby arrives."

Siobhan was petrified and sobbing, Mary took her in her arms and promised her it would all be fine.

She made her comfortable on the little bed and went back into the cottage to fetch torn sheets with hot water to help Siobhan give birth. Just before she stepped inside, she wondered *what would happen when Siobhan went back to Aileen with a baby, did Aileen even guess her daughter was pregnant? Who is the father?* All these questions went through her mind and straight back out again. She was not in control of her niece's predicament, however, but they were blood. Siobhan was laying on the bed as her contractions were coming with a small amount of time between them, she cried as the next one arrived.

"When I say push Siobhan, just push and breath with little panting breaths between the contractions if you can."

Mary had helped her mother give birth to Aileen, being the eldest, many years ago and remembered what she was told. She helped Siobhan bring a baby girl into the world after a couple of hours not knowing it was Paddy's granddaughter.

"Aunt Mary, how will I take care of her?"

There was a pleading in Siobhan's eyes and tears rolling down her cheeks. Mary's niece was not quite seventeen years old, had no way of looking after a child and her mother maybe didn't know she was pregnant, Mary had no other course to take but offer to bring the baby up with her own children and let Siobhan go back to her mother.

After a while, and holding the baby to her breast, Siobhan began to feed her, whilst this was a beautiful sight, Mary still wondered who the father was. Siobhan was thinking of Patrick, the 'cow shed event' and how the news of the baby will be taken but she vowed she would not disclose him to anyone. Mary, after thinking up the solution of caring for the child, told Siobhan she would bring the baby up as hers, Siobhan agreed this would be the only way. Mary allowed her to stay for another few weeks as Siobhan was still breastfeeding then she should go back to her mother. The night the baby was born, Mary spoke with Andrew about her plan. He had no children of his own but listened whilst Mary told him of her proposal to bring the child up as theirs. After much discussion, he agreed and part of him melted, he would have a child although not his or Mary's it didn't matter to him. Unbeknown to them both, Mary was pregnant with their own child which she conceived that afternoon before they married.

Once Siobhan had recovered from the birth and weaned the baby from her breast, she made her way back to Aileen who was none the wiser.

She started the walk eight miles back to Aileen's cottage, it wore her out, she staggered through the kitchen door.

Looking at her mother, she noticed a large bump where her stomach was. Her surprise was met with Aileen's tears and the realisation of knowing she must have a serious talk with Siobhan.

"Sit down love, I have something to tell you and maybe it's news you might not want to hear. John is home soon, and I need you to agree that this is your baby." Siobhan had her own news as well as Paddy's passing which Aileen didn't know about.

Siobhan's shock was only masked by the information she had to give Aileen after that statement.

"Uncle Paddy's dead, Mammy, and I've just given birth to Patrick's baby." Aileen almost collapsed at the news and sat down at the tiny table in the Parlour. Siobhan told her about the cowshed and how Patrick had taken her against her will.

Aileen cried tears for Paddy. She sat quietly next to Siobhan and told her Paddy was her father. Siobhan looked shocked but both their situations were as bad as each other.

They cried together as their news to each other tore their hearts apart.

Aileen assured her there would be no retribution as a scandal would be the last thing they wanted.

"Where's the baby, Siobhan?"

"Aunt Mary is taking care of it and bringing it up as hers and Andrew's."

"Who is Andrew?" Siobhan proceeded to tell her who he was and what happened to the farm after Paddy's death.

"You can't ever bring it home here; John would know the child I'm carrying is not yours. Can you accept leaving your baby with Mary?"

Siobhan nodded and cried a bit more but gradually accepted her fate. Patrick's baby would be her sibling and not her child, a tangled web indeed.

For Siobhan, well, she was now a woman with knowledge, not just of having a child born out of wedlock but knowing what it was to lay with a man; she hated all men from that day. She cursed Patrick under her breath.

Mary held the tiny bundle with its shock of black hair and called her *Adele,* after her dear friend who died some years back. She would pass the child off as her own and Andrew's in the village, she hadn't spent too much time there lately, it would go unnoticed with no gossip ensuing. The child was to grow up thinking Mary was her mother and Andrew, her father.

Over the months, Mary's own baby started to show, she had no idea her sister was carrying Paddy's baby. One night in bed, Andrew wanted his conjugal rights as he called them. Mary turned to him, "Andrew, I'm carrying your child." He was more tender than usual, whispering in her ear that he was happy with the news, he had always wanted a son, maybe he will get one. The house was full of children; Colleen and Marie, Patrick, Adele and soon another baby to be born.

Chapter 13

Haystack Liaisons

Aileen made Siobhan promise she would say nothing to John upon his return home. She loved him, but not like Paddy. *His response I can't be sure of so it's best that the baby would be passed off as Siobhan's*, she assured herself.

One morning, Aileen awoke and went downstairs to make breakfast for them both. As she stood over the fire to put the water on to boil, she had terrible pain, water fell away between her legs, she knew it was time.

"Siobhan, the baby's coming!" she shouted; Siobhan came running down the stairs from her bedroom. She remembered what Mary did and proceeded to boil water and get some old sheets from the cupboard. Aileen's labour didn't take too long, she screamed but as she had had Siobhan already and John's little boy, she knew the next child would be delivered easier.

Gently, Siobhan dabbed her mother's forehead with a cold flannel and helped her deliver a baby boy after three hours of labour.

To Aileen the delivery was bittersweet, *Paddy was dead with the little baby boy looking just like him*! Aileen and Siobhan took turns in feeding the baby as both had milk-heavy breasts.

John came home from sea to a larger family than he had left. After hearing the made-up story about Siobhan, John accepted the baby into the family. Aileen never told John who the father was, *how could I?* she said to herself, and John never asked. Just before he returned to sea, they had the baby christened; they called him *James*, after John's late father. John doted on him, perhaps the love left over from losing little Andrew was still there.

Siobhan looked after James which helped her cope after leaving her own child with Mary.

Maybe one day I can bring my little girl home? she said to herself, all the while knowing it would be impossible, she cried a bucketful of tears and vowed never to allow a man near her again. She cast her mind back to the 'cowshed event;' she wanted revenge, but how would she get what she wanted? "I'm cursing you, Patrick; you will pay for your awful deed and the thing you did to me, one day…"

Chapter 14

Margaret

On a sunny Sunday afternoon some months later, Patrick walked with the twins to St. Ignatius where they were all baptised years ago, he caught sight of Margaret O'Sullivan. Paddy's old friend John's daughter was singularly the most beautiful girl in the village, one that Patrick hadn't had dealings with. He hadn't seen her for at least a couple of years or longer and couldn't stop staring at her; he watched as she came out of the church, laughing with her sisters and, in a short space of time, she became his obsession, so he made a promise to himself.

I'll have that Margaret O'Sullivan one day and soon, he said smirking, *surely she will not be able to resist me but, if I am to have her, for sure I must form a plan.*

It didn't take Patrick long to conjure up a story that might be believable, one that would fool her into trusting him. A week later he crossed the meadows from the cottage after he had finished his chores on the farm and walked along to Margaret's home. Feeling quite sure of himself he knocked on the bottom part of the stable door and waited patiently.

"Patrick?" the door was answered by Niamh, she asked him if something was wrong at home. Niamh always felt sorry for Patrick's mother in the past but since Paddy had gone, she felt more relaxed about the situation. He said he was there to ask if Margaret might like to cross the meadows with him to see his uncle in the next village as his uncle was ill and had asked for him. Niamh hesitated, and was about to make an excuse, "Patrick! My boy!"

A big booming voice over Niamh's shoulder exploded. John had always wanted a son after having three daughters, when he saw Patrick, it made his day. They shook hands and John, believing his daughter to be in good company, gave his consent without a thought. Niamh did not have a say in the matter having always warned her daughters, and particularly with what happened to Roisin a

49

while back, but she was overruled. The door opened; Margaret stepped into the small front garden.

Fresh air! she breathed it in through her nostrils and exhaled through her mouth, she was glad to get out and walk a bit; due to the overprotection of both her parents, it was difficult for her to have some independence and rarely had been on her own much, if at all. She had known Patrick since she was a little girl and had played with his sisters on various occasions over the years; she felt safe with him.

I can't believe I have her with me, Patricks' thoughts ensured he would have his wicked way with another innocent.

As they strolled along the dirt track towards the meadows, Margaret felt relaxed enough with Patrick at that point. He couldn't take his eyes off her, and all the time planning and hoping that he will get the prize he thought he deserved—her innocence.

She started a play-tag game with him and touched his shoulder. They ran around the haystacks as she started laughing, calling his name, begging him to chase her. Her long, black curly hair flowing in the wind excited him, they dodged behind the haystacks, trying to tag each other. But laughter soon turned to fear as Patrick caught her by the wrist, she looked at him questioningly, he then grabbed a handful of her hair, pulled her to him and kissed her hard. She tried pushing him away as he shoved her roughly against a haystack, she felt some jagged pieces of hay dig in her back. Margaret felt shocked, stunned, and frightened at first then, realising he was serious, tried to struggle free from his grip. Patrick pressed himself against her, the blood in his veins was pumping hard and his breath became short.

"Patrick, what are doing? Don't… please…!" she was crying out for him to stop; she knew that something was about to happen she wouldn't like.

He did no more than threw her to the ground behind the haystack, she winded herself as she hit the floor. Struggling to get up, he pushed her down and held her. She tried to scream but there was no one near, forcing himself upon her, she tried to fight him off… Margaret tried to bite his hand, with this, he slapped her and placed his hand over her mouth again with his fingers out of the way; no one came to her rescue.

His mind was on fire, his breath on her neck, but Margaret was miles away, she lay there without uttering a sound. She let him finish without her consciously being there, her clothes torn, her virginity had been taken.

50

They were in fields far away from any cottage, her struggle was in vain, he took what he wanted whilst her tears fell. Fuelled by her struggle exciting him even more, he then whispered in her ear, "If you tell anyone about what I've done they won't believe you, I will deny it!"

She cried in silence knowing this was wrong and unable to stop him, she only wanted to play and have fun never realising that this would fuel the blood of a young, immoral man who would soon be the father of her child just conceived.

Resistance was futile, she lay there, taking herself out of the situation thinking back to her friend, Alva, in a similar situation some years ago.

Chapter 15

Father Jonathan's Contemplations

Alva had herself, at the age of fifteen, become pregnant by a man from the village. The story of Alva went around like wildfire, it unfolded that it was a traveller, but Alva told Margaret what really happened to her… Father Jonathan was the baby's daddy!

Apparently, one Monday morning, the middle-aged priest went to visit Alva's parents knowing that they were away at the Market purchasing livestock for their farm and that Alva was on her own. At the previous Sunday service, they had innocently mentioned their intention to buy further livestock to him when shaking hands at the end of his sermon. Father Jonathan had already had a few 'home visits' under his belt. It was obvious in his congregation there were many widows who received his 'attentions' on a regularity that ensured he was always smiling and that the devil, who perched on his shoulder, had a satisfied grin.

Alva was different, she was a virgin he was sure, the widows he had were older women, *just one young one would be a prize*; he had designs.

When the morning arrived and he knew her parents were at the market, he made his way to the farm. Walking slowly to the door of the farmhouse, which had a half-open stable door, he stood there and knocked softly on the faded green paint; she opened the top part of the door, "How can I help you, father?" He smiled, seeing the top half of Alva he could only imagine what was behind the bottom half of the door. She was surprised to see him, but *nonetheless, when a Priest comes to your door you always make them welcome,* Alva didn't want to be rude so opened the door straight away.

"Father, what brings you to our humble home this Monday morning?" she was totally innocent and had no idea of his intentions.

He had made up an excuse asking if her parents were there, she told him where they were and not expected back for another couple of hours, however, he was welcome to wait. They had only been gone fifteen minutes, he knew already… watching from behind a nearby tree, his plan was coming to fruition. The excitement of knowing he may be on the verge of taking this young woman excited him so much he almost cried, *how easy this may be,* he said to himself.

She asked him in.

"Would you be liking tea, father?" Alva enquired politely and went into the tiny kitchen to put the pot on for hot water. He stood near the table looking around him, just trying to make sure he was totally alone with her and was convinced he could get away with his intended deed.

"Father, please sit at the table; I'll bring the tea with biscuits freshly baked by my Mammy this morning." Her voice was bright and innocent.

He was fighting inwardly with himself. Sitting on one shoulder was an angel saying, "*Father, you are a man of the cloth and what you have in mind will ruin this child forever, you will go to hell for all eternity.*"

He didn't listen but instead turned to the Devil on his right shoulder as he sounded more exciting, goading him to complete his wicked deed.

As he sat, his hand trembled on the table in excitement, he looked around and then at Alva as she leaned over to place the tea on the table, he could see the top of her breasts, he almost gasped with the stirring he felt making him frustrated even more.

She placed the cup and saucer down near his hand. It had been a while since he had been with one of the parish widows and being a Catholic priest, he was not allowed to marry or have relations with females, that never stopped him with the widow, Mrs McManus one afternoon. A small rotund woman who had lost her husband some years back, she had asked him to visit her for consolation. He consoled her alright, almost daily for weeks and one night, when he visited, he took her with such frustration she struggled to walk for a few days, she didn't leave her cottage for fear of what the village folk may say, the shoulder-devil smiled.

He thought back to the time when he went to visit another parishioner who had also lost her husband only a few months before, she came to him at the Manse one morning when the housemaid was shopping at the market. She cried and said she 'needed comforting.' He took this as an invitation; she was not wanting his advances just comforting or so he thought and as she entered the Manse, he asked her into the library.

Closing the door behind him and inviting her to sit down she moved over to where he was sitting. She sat close to him making him gasp at the sight of her ample charms, he put his arm around her, she let his hand slide down her blouse and cup her breast… after an hour of abandon he was left with a smile and satisfaction, it had been a few weeks since, and he needed more, it was like a drug!

Another female parishioner, Mrs McGuinness, a slim woman with a large bosom, ran into the church one evening and knelt at the altar, she wanted absolution from her sins and asked Father Jonathan to give her confession. Entering the Confessional box, she told him of her sins committed, he listened intently. She had slept with her next-door neighbours' son on more than one occasion. He was nineteen and handsome, she used to watch him work in the fields, and with her husband not paying any mind to her, she longed for male company.

One morning, she called out to him whilst her husband was away in the fields for a few hours. The young man came round to her front door, she answered it and asked him to help her with some chores which she made up. He had never been with a girl let alone a woman. She allowed him to see her breasts as she opened a couple of buttons on her dress. He looked surprised but his surprise turned to lust that morning. He visited many times more until her husband died. She told Father Jonathan that she had stopped for fear of being damned for all eternity. He wanted to add to her sins after hearing her confessional.

After she had spoken to him, he asked her to come into a small room where he would help to heal her bad thoughts and deeds, she followed him like a lamb to the slaughter.

He had no guilt, Father Jonathan knew he could easily take advantage of the woman, *surely, she was as willing as I was.* She entered the little anteroom where he was waiting. He asked her to sit on the wooden bench by the window where they could talk. Sitting next to him enabled him to look at her charms and try to assess whether he would have a chance with her. He didn't have to wait too long, the woman promptly stood up removed her skirt to display no undergarments to him! She took his hand and placed it on her breast, two hours later she left the Manse with a large smile and an incredibly grateful but tired Father Jonathan sitting slightly breathless at fifty-eight, the shoulder-devil smiled once more.

The very next morning after finishing his sermon, he changed out of his cassock and hurriedly made his way to Mrs. McGuinness's cottage two miles from the Manse. His excitement became apparent by the time he got to her front door and, with anticipation, he knew his luck would indeed be in. Knocking gently, he could see the door was already open, he pushed it, it appeared to be unlocked; she had just made a freshly brewed cup of tea which was the furthest thing from his mind.

"Come in, father; come in and sit yourself down; I've been expecting you," she seemed a different woman than the one that came to ask him for absolution and confession previously. She had barely covered her breasts and ensured she bent down in front of him on a few occasions whilst serving the tea. He didn't even touch the cup and saucer but rose and grabbed her arm. She struggled and slapped him, then laughed, he took this to be agreement that she was happy to allow him to have her. They made their way to a little room off the kitchen, there was a single bed with tattered bed sheets and a feather pillow that had seen better days. Quickly she slipped off her clothing and stood naked in front of him with no shame whatsoever. His eyes bulged.

"Father, forgive me, I am a sinner and am giving myself to you this moment," she looked down at her feet, her voice trailed off in his ears.

He didn't speak but took her hand, lay her on the bed and proceeded to carry on his intended deed, she was easy and now on his list. He could tell she had enjoyed the other day, but this was different, she wrapped her legs around him and held him tight to her, his urgency did not take long.

She cried a little when they were finished. "Father, I am ashamed, I never meant for this to happen."

He assured her it was normal but not to mention it to anyone, *she was the only one…* he told them all that.

Just the once? The devil questioned him as he put his trousers back on, the devil grinned and whispered in the Priest's ear, "This would be a regular visit, Father."

As the widows he 'comforted' had not seen periods for many years, he was as free as bird to take them as many times as they and he wished without the worry of babies, not so with Alva, she wasn't quite sixteen but had been 'showing' each month for two years.

His 'fun' finished a few months after it started, she was found dead after a stroke by an elderly neighbour, he didn't shed a tear for her, his sex life had ceased too abruptly with Mrs McGuinness, so he carried on with other widows of the parish until he saw Alva.

Placing the dainty blue and white biscuit plate on the table, Alva stepped away. The priest was suddenly back in the room from his thoughts and said quietly, "Don't be shy now, Alva," in a soft tone of voice he whispered to her "sure, you'll be going as red as the kettle that you will!" she blushed and giggled then went to sit next to him, her trust was complete, he patted the chair. As she went to sit, he grabbed her hand and placed it on his manhood. She quickly withdrew her hand and looked at him questioning, *why had he done that?* she had never touched a man in that way. Again, he grabbed her hand and placed it in the same position. She tried to get up and run away from him but, as she attempted escape, he grabbed her by the hair and pulled her back.

Through gritted teeth, he said, "Alva, no one can hear you and you'll be my little secret."

She screamed again as he put his hand over her mouth after slapping her; there was no one to hear her, the Priest had lain his trap and took no notice of her struggles, she hit him, but it was futile.

As he bared down on her she could feel his breath on her neck, he held her until he finished the evil deed, he had taken a prize he had not had since in his teens, a virgin!

He left the cottage with a smile and such satisfaction, the Devil on his shoulder smiled also, she collapsed in the kitchen with the sheer brutality, he had shown no mercy.

What transpired that morning changed her life forever. She was totally ashamed and couldn't tell her parents when they arrived home a few hours later and so hid in her room that night. After a few months of not seeing blood, but as weeks went by, she started to 'show.' Her parents insisted she tell them who the father was or be sent to the local convent. After much interrogation and a slap from her father, Alva said it was someone they knew, Father Jonathan.

She had been bought up not to tell lies but when these words came out of her mouth, her father went into a rage hitting her hard for lying; she fell to the floor holding her face shielding a large red hand mark. Grabbing her by the hair he spat the words in her face, "How could you say it was our Priest, you wicked girl!" he slapped her once more, threw her to the floor and left her crying in a heap.

All this time Alva's mother said nothing in her defence, little did Alva or her father know that the Priest had been paying his attentions to Alva's mother on more than one occasion, she couldn't have any more children after Alva as Alva's father never came near her for his conjugal rights once the baby was born, she kept her secret quiet but, still, *having a daughter disgracing your family is unforgivable* she assured herself.

Alva's father had known Father Jonathan all his life and would not hear one more word against the Priest. Father Jonathan knew he was safe after taking Alva, his reputation as a kindly Priest in the parish was not tarnished in any way, he did everything he could to ensure no harm would come to his standing in the village protecting himself from being found out.

Alva knew that telling the truth she would not be believed, not saying anything she would receive the same fate as many poor girls before her, she was sent to the convent sobbing and pregnant, never to be spoken of again.

Father Jonathan went to Mass the following Sunday and opened the door to the Confessional for Mrs O'Sullivan's declarations of sin, which she was about to commit the same with him.

Margaret missed her friend and felt that she would receive the same fate should she say anything. *Maybe I won't become pregnant?* she said to herself.

She had never 'known' a man but had spoken with her friend, Alva, before she was sent away and knew that what Patrick had done to her had happened to Alva and that was the way a woman got pregnant.

Once Patrick had finished, he looked down at Margaret with his desire abating; he left her lying there sobbing; she felt humiliated, violated, and frightened, too frightened to tell anyone what had happened and remembering his words, feared that her parents would never believe her anyway and the fate that Alva received was her reminder.

Chapter 16

Marriage

Patrick didn't go to his uncle's house that afternoon, it was a sham to get Margaret alone, he simply walked home with a smile on his face leaving her laying there in disbelief at what had happened.

Yes, I had her, just like the others, he said smirking to himself.

Margaret eventually staggered home with her dress in tatters, she made up a story of being trampled by a cow in a field as she felt so ashamed and couldn't tell them the truth for fear of not being believed as Patrick had said. Her tattered dress served as a reminder of the event, she cried inside. No more was said about it, but Niamh wondered where Patrick was in all this, he never came visiting again and the topic didn't arise until, over the course of the next few months, it became quite obvious that something else had transpired, with Margaret's tummy swelling!

John had never lost his temper in the past but when Margaret wouldn't tell him who the father was, he slapped her hard across the face, she reeled against the kitchen table.

"Patrick's the father!" she blurted out whilst holding her cheek, she confirmed she hadn't agreed to his advances, this fell on deaf ears. John did no more than grabbing her by the hair, marched her to the Ryan cottage to confront Patrick. Patrick answered the door going slightly pale but acted nonchalantly. He said, when questioned, he loved Margaret, she had given consent and had agreed to his advances. He also stated that he desperately wanted to marry her but was worried that her parents would say no. He used this as a deflection from a potential beating, being the coward that he was.

Margaret could not believe what she was hearing, he had tricked her five months earlier and had never bothered contacting her since, even though she tried to see him and tell him about the pregnancy, and now he wants to marry her to avoid a beating from her father! John, upon hearing this, agreed as there was to be no shame on the families, hurriedly a marriage was conducted in the local church. It wasn't what Patrick wanted but he agreed. Margaret had no say in the matter, John warned her a few days before the wedding that if she didn't marry Patrick the family would completely disown her and throw her and her baby in a convent. Knowing Alva's doom and that she may never see her family if she didn't marry, she went through with the ceremony and accepted her fate.

At the little church in Margaret's village, there were not many guests as neither family wanted the villagers to see Margaret in her condition. However, there was a young girl holding a black-haired baby sitting at the back of the church, it was Beth, she was praying. The shame on the families would have been immense and so it was literally family members, the Priest, and his clergy... the priest was Father Jonathan!

Niamh hugged her daughter and told her to be a good wife to Patrick, wifely duties she should carry out without question... just like Niamh had done with John; Margaret prayed her life wouldn't be hard with Patrick, ...she had no idea.

Chapter 17

Married Life

After the church service, John's horse and cart took the newly married couple to a little Inn on the outskirts of Dublin to a village called *Sandymount*. As she sat in the back, Margaret held her nose most of the journey due to the stench of animals that had been transported in the back of the cart previously whilst Patrick was upfront driving the horses, *this was the way it would always be in the marriage*, she thought and silently cried inside.

They turned the corner of the lane, seeing the Inn, it looked a bit tired and worn out, its dirty curtains hanging at the windows with mud stuck to the boot scrapers outside the large weather-beaten oak door.

The cart stopped, Patrick stepped down from the driver's seat and just watched laughing as Margaret struggled to get down from the filthy hay. They found themselves on the doorstep waiting for someone to answer their knocks. The door creaked opened, there stood an Inn Keeper with a shock of grey hair, , black eyebrows and with hands as big as shovels; he beckoned them in.

Over in the fireplace, Margaret saw peat burning which produced a dense smoke and a sweet smell as it drifted up a single chimney. Most of Ireland used peat as it was cheap and burned well. Even though it was late Summer it was normal for fires to be lit as it rained most of the time and everything was damp; nearby an old, grey-muzzled Irish Setter lay quietly snoring on a threadbare rug not even raising its head in acknowledgement of their presence.

Margaret waited for Patrick to have a couple of whiskies at the bar, she then followed him to the room. Her heart beating fast, she wanted to run, to flee *but, how could I?* She felt completely trapped and in fear of what Patrick would do to her if she tried to escape and now, she couldn't go home either, carrying his baby gave her no way of escape.

Their wedding night was just as bad as the day Patrick had run around the haystacks after her. She walked over to the little fireplace to get some warmth, hitched up her skirts and saw it was a smaller version of the peat fire downstairs, the sweet smell drifted through her nostrils. Removing her wrap and shoes with some of her clothing, she rubbed and patted her arms blowing into her cupped hands. Suddenly, Patrick was behind her! As he got close to her, she could smell the whiskey on his breath. He grabbed her and threw her onto the bed which squeaked and groaned as he took her against her will once more even though she was pregnant. She had no choice but to endure his attentions, she cried into the pillow once he had finished.

"You're mine now, I married you and didn't want to but here we are, you will attend to your wifely duties!"

His words burned into her soul and as they did, she said inside, *Please God, hear my prayer, release me from this awful nightmare I'm living in!—I'm not even Twenty yet for pity's sake!*

Her prayer was sent, she awaited an answer.

Chapter 18
Alfie

Patrick made his way downstairs to the little bar next to the reception desk the next morning to speak with the Landlord, Margaret stayed in their room just looking out of the window. She vowed to herself that escape would come at an opportune moment, she prayed more than she ever had done in her life, *maybe, just maybe release will come soon?*

"I'm looking for a room, it must be cheap and allow me to have enough money for myself."

Patrick was married but fully intended to carry on the life he enjoyed before Margaret, drink, and women, easy or not. The Landlord said he had one left in an old tenement building in Dublin near the river.

"It's not the best place but the room is cheap and at one shilling a week, I think it's a bargain," he said in a monotone answer.

Patrick took the key and handed over two weeks rent that Mary and Andrew had given him as a wedding present.

With the keys to the room, they walked the three miles from the Inn, it was raining cats and dogs with the odd rumble of thunder thrown in for good measure. John picked up the horse and cart from the Inn a few days later but never bothered to ask where his daughter and her new husband went, it wasn't his problem anymore. It seemed the longest three miles of Margaret's life, she couldn't wait to rest when they got there; after a while, the tenement building came into view. A filthy hovel where families lived cheek-by-jowl, sharing one toilet located in the back yard, Margaret cried inside. Once through the front door, which appeared in need of some painting, they climbed the stairs to the 4th floor whilst passing all the other family's rooms then they walked down the small, dimly lit corridor towards their room. It contained an open fire in one corner for cooking and rusty nails crudely banged into the back of the door for clothes. The bed had a moth-eaten mattress with bits of straw sticking out of it and an earthenware bowl with a jug for washing yourself was resting on an upturned wooden box. A small wooden table stood with two rickety chairs set near the fireplace.

Living in the tenement, Margaret made the best of it by keeping herself to herself, however, just down the corridor she did befriend an elderly lady who appeared to have no husband or children. Bridget had lived in the tenement for over thirty-five years, she always said good morning to Margaret and asked how she was, this went a long way with Margaret and, little did she know, she would need Bridget's help on more than one occasion.

The days turned into months as Margaret's tummy grew, there was no let-up from Patrick, he treated her like a piece of meat, there for his pleasure no matter how uncomfortable it all was. She only got his attention when she managed to cook something he liked after he had been drinking on his way home from the bar after work.

Winter climbed into the room as it became draughty with high, albeit ornate, ceilings and windows almost impossible to see out of due to the filth that was encrusted outside… and in. Margaret kept them shut to keep out the cold. Being heavily pregnant, she thought she would collapse at any minute when trying to fetch water from the single tap they all shared in the back yard, the smell emanating from the single toilet near the tap made her heave.

Most mornings, Margaret threw up which was a by-product of the pregnancy or the smell from the toilet or maybe both, she was tired most of the time through lack of good nourishment plus being kept awake by Patrick's drunken snoring. When he did come home rather than go to the bar, it was usually after he had worked at the Docks labouring until late in the evening. He got the job from the labour exchange once they married as his days cutting peat turves had ceased upon their moving to the tenement. He took to calling in to the local public house for a few which sometimes turned into many. Falling asleep in the chair, Patrick usually passed out after a good time at the bar filling himself with beer.

One night, as he climbed the stairs, Margaret could hear him huffing and puffing, she wished him to fall down the stairs, but he never did. As he flung open the door one night, he found her laying on the single bed they shared, she was tired and nearing the end of the pregnancy.

Shouting at her with a slurred speech she attempted to get off the bed, but he was on her in a flash, pulling at her clothes, and as she struggled to get him off her one night, he slapped her so hard she bit through her lip with a single drop of blood running down her chin. The only thing that kept her going was the baby growing inside her. She neither voiced an opinion nor gave him any affection, she hated the sight of him and lay there waiting for it all to be over quickly.

She managed to stand, after he had had his way one night and proceeded to cook his meal whilst going on autopilot as he sat at the crudely made table not uttering a word. He watched her as she struggled with her chores, Margaret being heavily pregnant was beginning to repulse him, his mind wandered to Beth.

She prayed every night, and sometimes during the day, that something or someone would save her from this life, even if it were death, it had to be better than what she was going through with Patrick but feeling her unborn child start to kick kept her from ending it all.

Early, one night, he arrived home literally just before the baby was due and beat her for not having food on the table in time, she crawled to the bed staying awake all night praying whilst Patrick slept off his hangover. In the morning once he awoke, he got himself ready and went to work not saying a word to her. Margaret fetched water, but found it heavier than usual, the stairs and her impending motherhood saw the pains around her stomach once she reached the room with two full buckets. She lay down but the pains didn't stop, they got worse, she stood and cried knowing that the baby was coming, suddenly water spilt out from between her legs on the floor which frightened her as she didn't know what it meant. Some months previous, Bridget assured her she would help deliver the child and to knock a couple of times when the time was close. Margaret staggered her way down the hall to Bridget's front door.

She held her stomach and, sobbing, stood outside a door with its green paint peeling off and a small dirty brass knocker. Knocking softly twice, the tiny elderly, grey-haired woman answered with a smile.

"Please help me, Bridget; I think my baby is coming," Margaret was pleading, crying and desperate.

She was ushered into an almost identical room to hers and Patricks.'

"My dear, you just lay down here on the bed, I will help you deliver your baby," Bridget spoke softly to Margaret.

In her time, Bridget had delivered several babies, many knew her as 'the Midwife' in Dublin, although she had never had professional training because there was none back then… women took care of women when their time came.

Hot water and grey-looking but clean towels ready, Margaret began to push at Bridget's insistence, she screamed at the same time, Bridget ushered her to "shallow breath and pant, it would make it easier if you did."

Margaret looked at her and said, with tears in her eyes, "It wasn't conceived out of love."

"My dear, many are not but it doesn't mean that we will not love them any the less." Bridget's mind drifted back in time.

She remembered from her own experience, going back through her own events, to the time when she bore a son, many years before, by a man who had taken her against her will, her cousin, George. She was fifteen and was visiting her aunt and uncle with the family. George seemed friendly enough when they spent time walking around the fields during the visit. They always got on well when they were younger but since she started to grow into a young girl George had other ideas. He couldn't see anything wrong with the feelings he had, *they were normal after all* he thought to himself.

George took her innocence that afternoon; they found themselves struggling in a small outbuilding he had said he wanted to investigate. The floor was hard on her head and back and that's all she can remember as he took her innocence that cloudy Autumn day. Bridgit had no idea what it meant, she almost enjoyed it, but soon found out months later she was with child and fled to County Cork to have the baby where no one knew her except an old family friend of her mothers who took pity on her.

She made lace handkerchiefs which she sold to keep body and souls together; she called her son *Christopher,* he was the image of her cousin which was bittersweet, but she loved him just the same.

Never returning to her family, she struggled to bring him up, often going without food herself so he could eat. She returned to Dublin eventually and rented a room in the tenement. She had told people her husband died and left her with the child to bring up. One afternoon, when he was twelve, Christopher was playing in the street and got trampled by a horse and cart, her heart broke, she never recovered from his loss but helped women in trouble as a way of coping with her feelings and remembering the help she had received from other women.

Suddenly, she was back in the room wiping Margaret's sweat from her face and after three hours of labour a final push, a baby boy came screaming into the world and was born to Patrick and Margaret Burke. Holding her tiny son against her breast, Margaret began to cry… she blessed her little son with tears.

"I have no money Bridgit," Margaret was penniless but promised the old lady she would find a way to repay her one day, but Bridgit just shook her head and said it was alright, no money was expected.

She lay there for a while as the woman cleaned her up and made her comfortable. Falling asleep, Margaret drifted in and out of consciousness.

When she awoke, Bridgit asked, "What will you call him?"

She was trying to be pleasant and take Margaret's mind off things.

"I'll call him *Alfie* after my father's brother Alfred whom I loved dearly but he died incredibly young," and so *Alfie* it was.

After resting a few hours, she gathered Alfie up in a little tattered blanket Bridgit had given her then swaying and struggling she made her way down the passageway carrying her new-born bundle as she knew Patrick would be home soon.

The future? Margaret had no idea what that would look like for her and Alfie, but she knew she wanted something better than what fate had given her and, nursing her son in her arms, felt this wasn't the end of her story.

Patrick didn't come home that night. She slept soundly on the bed with her baby by her side and when dawn broke, the sun shone through some of the holes in the curtains which woke her. Alfie carried on sleeping.

Margaret studied every crevice and every part of her new son. She cried but silently so as not to wake him.

Patrick finally arrived home and, as he walked into the room, he took one look at the baby and smiled. Margaret had never seen Patrick smile since the day they married, but by God, his grin was as wide as he lay eyes on his new-born son. He turned and glanced at Margaret; she shrank back away from him slightly for fear of a clout. He eyed her breasts heavily laden with milk these past months and just kissed her on the cheek, eating the crude stew she managed to make earlier that morning; he left for the bar to celebrate the birth of his son as he had finished at the docks unloading a ship that day, he never even asked if the baby had a name.

All the men in the Old Strand bar celebrated with Patrick. They slapped him on the back, gave him as many beers as he could drink, and all Patrick could think about was what woman he would have that night whilst his wife had only just given birth a few hours before, they drank, cheered, and congratulated him.

Whilst the bar was busy and the drink was flowing, Patrick had eyes for one of the barmaids, a raven-haired beauty with a large bosom, he winked at her. She turned away from him and made herself busy, many of the men she had served winked at her thinking her 'easy' and that she would be available for their pleasures once the bar had closed but she only had eyes for her husband, Eammon. Eammon didn't drink, an unusual thing in Dublin or anywhere else for that matter, it made him sick for some reason. Often in the winter months, once her bar duties finished, he would wait for her outside and escort her home in the dark, he loved her and felt bad that to subsidise his low income as a gravedigger, she had to work but she was happy to do it.

As Patrick made his way home to Margaret and his new-born son that night, he felt he was being followed, he quickly spun around to look but there was no one there, so he just carried on swaying down the road to the tenement building. Once he arrived, he stumbled and passed out on the stairs leading to their room, Margaret heard a noise and went to investigate. She saw him lying there stinking of beer and tobacco and, even worse, he was laying in his own urine, rather than help him up, she turned her back on him and just let him lie there.

Time went by quickly in the small room, little Alfie grew into a sweet-natured little toddler, with his loving and calm character taken from his mother's side. Late one night Patrick was so drunk he had to be taken home by one of his drinking partners, they threw him on the back of a horse, lead him along, pushed him off and left him outside the tenement building where he was found by a neighbour in the early hours loudly snoring and dishevelled. The neighbour helped him to the room, knocked and returned to their own room for fear of getting involved. Margaret heard the knock, opened the door, Patrick fell forward promptly throwing up on the floor and relieved himself where he lay; she cleared the mess up and whilst mopping the floor, Patrick had crawled to their tiny bed where he passed out again.

This life is not mine, please hear my prayer oh Father, release me from it soon in whatever way you see fit, Margaret prayed once more as little Alfie and Patrick slept.

Chapter 19

Escape

Margaret held Alfie to her breast and nursed him one afternoon, looking at him suckling her and feeling the rush of a mother's love in her heart for this little boy; she listened hearing troubled footsteps and a child sobbing from the corridor. Suddenly, a loud knock with a whispered cry for help coming from a woman's lips. As Margaret opened the door, there stood an old friend she hadn't seen for some time… it was Alva, she had a little girl with her.

"Sweet Jaysus, Alva, come in, come in!"

Alva entered the room, stick thin and holding onto a little girl who seemed tired and sleepy, Alva lay her on the bed next to Alfie, she fell asleep almost immediately.

"Margaret, I've run away from the convent after finding little Sinead living nearby with a couple who had adopted her, she's mine and I'm needing help to leave Dublin and find somewhere safe."

Margaret was in no fit state to give Alva any financial help but could give her and Sinead some of the leftovers from breakfast at least.

Alva told Margaret the story of her planned escape.

"When I had the baby, the Nuns took it away from me, Margaret," her tears fell as she relayed the story.

Alva went on to tell her how she found out where the baby was and then formed her plan to escape and find a new life somewhere where no one knows her. The Nuns must have been furious as they received money for the baby and every girl that had given birth had helped to fill their coffers even more. The couple that took Alva's baby lived just down the road from the Convent, and it was whilst Alva was near the gates, she saw little Sinead with her new parents. She knew the baby was hers, there was a small brown birthmark on the baby's right hand, she spotted it from across the road. Father Jonathan had one similar on his right thigh, but Alva didn't disclose this to Margaret. It was some months later that she managed to escape at night and break into the house where her child was.

"God, it was so easy, Margaret," she said, "I can't go back. I would end up in prison or worse."

Alva had pleading and sadness in her eyes but a strength to carry on.

After Alva's escape unfolded, Margaret felt sorry for her promising to help as much as she could.

"I've got nowhere to go, Margaret; please help me," Alva said begging. Margaret asked how Alva found her. Apparently, Margaret and Patrick's wedding was attended by a family friend that knew Alva, they used to visit her at the Convent, Margaret told her she had married Patrick and they were living in the tenement.

Then Margaret remembered Bridgit down the corridor and wondered if she could help.

"Alva, give me a few minutes and I'll be back; I have someone that may be able to help you."

She quickly made her way down the corridor to that green door again, knocking quietly. The old lady opened the door, Margaret told her the story.

"Yes, I can help your friend, Margaret. Bring her here in a few minutes, I'll see what I can do."

"I'm in your debt Bridgit," but Bridgit wouldn't hear of it and told Margaret just the pleasure of being able to help was enough, she returned to the room.

"You're a good friend Margaret, thank you so much, I'll never forget your kindness."

Whilst thanking Margaret, Alva picked up little Sinead, who was still asleep, then went down the corridor to see the old lady. Alva tried to tell Bridget her story, but the old lady said there was no need, she had heard many stories over the years and Alva's was probably on the end of a long list of girls' misfortunes.

That was the last time Margaret saw Alva, they hugged and cried saying goodbye. Bridgit had managed to get her a ticket on a steamship leaving Dublin for Liverpool the next day and onwards to America. She took her and her baby to the docks in the early hours, *A woman in distress* she told herself, the old lady had done another good deed.

Chapter 20
Planning

Every day was a struggle for Margaret, food, and clothing yourself as well as a toddler and a husband that provided next to no money who would, instead, drink it as soon as earned made life unbearable.

Alfie was growing fast, his hair was as black as Patrick's with piercing blue eyes, his smile could charm the birds from the trees. Patrick didn't argue with the baby's name choice, he said he couldn't care less after Alfie woke him most nights crying for his mother's milk and comfort. Margaret, whilst queuing with little Alfie for poor relief one morning, would hear the other women say, "He will break hearts one day, that he will!" She didn't want him to break hearts but knew she loved him above all else and hugged him to her as they shivered in the queue.

The slums of Dublin were worse than those in London, Glasgow, or Birmingham, with mortality rates higher than those in London, Margaret feared for her son. She would sit with him after finishing all her chores and sing to him old Irish songs that her mother sang to her when she was small. She always kept him warm during the winter months and had allowed him to breastfeed right up until he was three!

In her mind, whilst singing to Alfie, she was planning an escape, getting away from a husband who was drunk and abusive, took your body when he wanted, breathed stale tobacco and beer breath over you and didn't care if you had enough to eat; this was hell for Margaret. Her education was minimal, but she was brave inside with a strong heart and endured her lot until such time as she felt it right to leave this awful situation and take her beloved son with her... whenever that may be.

One night, a few years later, after the Old Strand emptied of its customers, the barmaid, Mary, was finishing cleaning the glasses then, gathering up her moth-eaten shawl, she looked for her husband through the window. He was nowhere to be seen. Later, it was told he had had a heart attack on his way to meet her and dropped down dead in the street. No sign of Eammon, she hung back after the place was emptied of its customers but still no husband. She was worried about walking home on her own as it was getting dark but consoled herself that it was only a short distance away and, maybe, Eammon had fallen asleep in front of the fire.

Patrick saw Mary looking for Eammon, he felt he might have a chance with her if Eammon didn't turn up, leaving early, and to cover himself he told his drinking friends he was going home to his darling wife; this was to provide himself with an alibi. As he left the bar, he waited around the corner in an alley for Mary to finish her work hoping that he could get to her before her husband arrived. It was pitch dark as she turned the corner, Patrick was waiting in the shadows. Jumping out on her, and to stop her screaming, he clamped his hand over her mouth, she tried to bite him, she struggled to free herself, this got Patrick even more excited.

He then dragged her into the alley behind the bar, she continued to fight him off, but he was too strong for her and, after slapping Mary hard in the face they fell to the ground. He slapped her hard again, she saw blackness. He pulled up her skirts and, finally, took her against her will whilst she was semi-conscious leaving her lying on the ground dishevelled. Finishing his evil deed, he got up, straightened his clothes, and whispered to her that no one would believe her as he said he was going home to his wife, she never heard him. Patrick knew if he threatened Margaret, she would vouch for him which would provide him with an alibi and allow him to have his filthy way with more poor helpless women when he saw fit.

Smiling, he said to himself, "*I had the barmaid, it was grand, and I'll have her again another time when the opportunity presents itself.*" He smiled and walked home leaving her laying there half-conscious.

As she came round, Mary staggered the few streets to her front door; the fire was still burning in the hearth with no sign of Eammon. She sat wondering who her assailant was, it was too dark, and no words were spoken but she had a feeling she might know… there was a knock at the door; three men stood there with the news about Eammon…

Chapter 21
The Shame

One night, as Margaret lay under Patrick, all she could think of was the day when maybe he wouldn't come home, she didn't want more mouths to feed at a time when food was scarce and no money to pay for it. She was always begging at the St. Francis Charity Hall for shoes, clothes, and food, they knew her well there.

"See that young woman," the other women queuing would say, "she is only young and already seeming so old as to be looking like her husband's Mammy, so she does!"

Margaret sometimes heard the hurting words, she thought they didn't know what real hardship was, they didn't have a husband that drank all the money and didn't have a care for her or their son.

I must get away from him, she said to herself, *God help me, there must be more to this life!*

Over time, as little Alfie grew, he knew well not to upset his father for fear of a clout. One night he was sitting up with Margaret and Patrick walked in from the bar. He was drunk and staggering around, threatening Margaret, he slapped her. Alfie flew at him but was not grown enough to defend himself or his mother, Patrick hit him to the floor, "If you ever hit my mother again, I will kill you!" Alfie spat the words out after witnessing his mother's anguish too many times, at seven years old this just made Patrick laugh.

———

Many years later, as Alfie matured, he kept witnessing his mother living in fear of his father; Alfie vowed it would change soon and so it did but without his intervention.

One night, after Patrick left the Strand to make his way home, all the worse for a drink, someone grabbed him around the throat and dragged him into the same alley where he had taken Mary against her will a few years previously. He was beaten so badly he died from his injuries that night. All who knew him had said it would happen one day and that he had it coming to him. Patrick had been with another man's wife too many times and was caught in the act by a husband who followed him; revenge was meted out, no one came forward as a witness. Patrick's body was never found.

Wondering why her husband hadn't come home that night, Margaret sat awaiting news. She went the few yards to Bridgit's door and knocked gently.

"Bridgit, Patrick's not home yet, and I don't know what to do?"

She waited for an answer, Bridgit just looked at her, "Just pray Margaret, just pray…"

Margaret didn't expect this response, *does Bridgit know something I don't?*

––––––––––

She fell asleep in her clothes with Alfie lying next to her totally oblivious. The next morning she awoke, no Patrick in sight.

Karma had indeed bitten Patrick.

She plucked up the courage to go into the Old Strand and ask about his whereabouts; no one had seen him. She could only think he had run off with another woman and, sitting in the filthy, damp room with Alfie, she knew her chance of escape had finally arrived.

Where will we go? How will I support us? She had next to no money, she sat on the bed just staring at the floor.

I must do something; I have been given an opportunity to leave this place with my son, my prayers have been answered.

Her mind was wild with thoughts on how she would go forward, with no friends and only a few shillings she had hidden from Patrick over the years she was at a loss as to the course of action she needed to take. Alfie came in a few minutes later from playing outside.

"Mam, I heard there is a big ship in the docks and lots of people are coming off it, come and look with me!"

Alfie had always been fascinated by ships and boats and had spent most of his time down at the docks looking at them. Margaret suddenly had the idea that they could try to get on the boat under darkness but all she had were the clothes she stood up in, nine shillings in her skirt pocket and a few things for Alfie, this didn't deter her. Grabbing little Alfie's hand, they went down to the dockside, sneaking onboard the ship whilst no one was looking as darkness fell. They hid in one of the lifeboats with no food or water with only hope in their hearts that they may find a better life than the one they had just left. It seemed like eternity, just lying there, and keeping quiet for fear of being found out.

Margaret didn't have time to say goodbye to Bridgit who had helped her when Alfie was born but she knew in her heart that the old lady would understand.

Alfie was getting hungry, he started to get anxious, she tried to placate him but didn't know where their next meal would come from. The funnels booming as the ship was setting sail, she prayed once more. The boat moved and swayed as Alfie fell asleep, Margaret gave a huge sigh as if a weight had lifted off her shoulders, the boat went further out to sea.

She had no idea where the boat was going but thought she heard someone say London and then onto Gravesend, wherever that was. After the ship had set sail and left the dock, the decks were patrolled with the crew checking the lifeboats for stowaways. Margaret held her breath and Alfie's little hand tightly as voices got nearer; one of the sailors found them hiding. She gasped as the tarpaulin was pulled back, and daylight poured in.

Victor had found many stowaways hiding over the years but this one was different, there was a child involved. Victor's weather-beaten face had a huge smile, Margaret noticed everything about him. He was ready to blow the whistle on them but listened as Margaret explained what they were doing and what had happened to put them on the boat.

"Mister, I've got no money and only the clothes I stand up in, this is an escape from an awful life I found myself in and am seeking to find a better one for myself and my little boy." Margaret proceeded to tell him the rest of her sorry tale.

Victor said he would not alert anyone, he bought food and water for them both over the days, his kindness saved her and little Alfie, she thanked God for it. Victor took pity on them, he ensured they had food and water through the voyage.

Chapter 22

Safe Passage

He came every night to see them, his kindness moved Margaret and as the days passed, he got close to her and little Alfie.

"You're so kind, Victor," Margaret said one night, "we would have perished without you."

Victor held her hand, "I have been widowed many a year and feel that maybe we can help each other," he said with a slight tear in his eye. "What will you do when we dock at Gravesend?"

Margaret hadn't thought any further than just leaving Dublin, she constructed her answer carefully.

"We will manage, thank you." Her independence took Victor aback, but he understood this to be confirmation that she had nowhere to go.

"I own a small, terraced house near the docks, it's not much but you and Alfie would be welcome to stay there. I am away quite a lot; it would be home for you until you find something else." Margaret squeezed Alfie's hand, "Are you sure, Victor? We wouldn't be any bother, I would clean, cook, and help to look after the house whilst you're away and when you come home, well…"

Victor's smile told her it was something he wanted. It seemed like an eternity staying hidden whilst the ship sailed, first to London and then to Gravesend. Margaret held Alfie tight to her as the ship swayed and bobbed on the water. They had no idea that some of the food they were given was Victor's, he never told them.

After leaving London and the short trip down the Thames, it was time for the ship to dock again, they alighted together, standing on the dockside Margaret looked at Victor.

"I can't thank you enough for all you've done for us," she said with a little tear of gratitude.

He took them to his home in nearby Albion Road and as they walked through the door, she knew she was safe at last, little Alfie would have a better life. That night, after washing herself and Alfie she put him to bed and came back downstairs to the tiny sitting room with a roaring fire Victor had made up. He beckoned her to sit next to him; he hadn't held a woman in his arms for an eternity, well since his wife and child died in childbirth.

He slowly held Margaret's hand kissing it gently. She flushed as she had never had a man be so tender and kind. She turned to him, their lips met, he kissed her with a tenderness which, again, she had never known. Lovingly, he held her against his chest where she felt safe and for the first time in her life Margaret knew what safe felt like. Victor knew he had found someone special, someone that he could home to, that would provide a life for him away from the sea.

He took her to the little kitchen with its oak table and sat her on it. She looked at him questioningly. He removed her dress and kissed her breasts, she sighed and closed her eyes, never had she been shown such tenderness. Gently, he lay her back and after a short while he made love to her as she had never been made love to before. They then moved to the little bedroom upstairs where they went to heaven together again, soon after they slept in each other's arms until morning. Margaret awoke to the sun streaming in through the tiny bedroom window, and as she lay in Victor's arms, he awoke explaining that he had to go to the ship in two days' time and back to sea for the next part of his voyage. They made love once more with such tenderness she cried on his shoulder tears of happiness, sadness, love, and gratitude.

She sobbed silently with her tears falling to his chest, having found so wonderful a man she had to say goodbye to so soon.

Victor whispered to Margaret just before he left, "Margaret, when I'm back from my trip I would like it if we could become a family, I'd take care of you and Alfie and make you my wife," her heart leapt.

She kissed him and waved him off an hour later, she felt complete. A man who treated her gently, passionately and with kindness was her saviour; she would give him her heart.

Chapter 23

Gravesend

Margaret and Alfie settled in their new home. She found a little job sewing for some wealthy ladies along the Darnley Road and knitted shawls for a lady who owned a shop in Perry Street. Waiting patiently, Margaret kept herself busy and was counting the days and months to Victor's return to Gravesend, to the little two-up, two-down and a future for them all.

As she went through the house and its contents, she came across a drawer in a little table, inside she found a note. It read *should anything happen to me Margaret, this house is your home, Victor*. She stood open-mouthed with a tear in her eye. Folding the note, she placed it back in the drawer.

Months passed and one morning Margaret held and stroked her stomach as she looked out of the bedroom window thinking of Victor, it was that same feeling when she was pregnant with Alfie only this time the baby would be born out of love.

As the time for the baby's arrival got closer, Alfie was watching ships coming in at the docks when he overheard men talking about a ship going down near Australia and no survivors, he ran home to tell his mother.

Margaret collapsed at the news knowing she was carrying Victor's baby and he was sailing down to Australia, a million tears were cried that afternoon. There had been no word from Victor, *maybe it wasn't his ship? Maybe there is confusion, and his ship is already heading back?* these questions she asked herself over the next few days and refused to acknowledge that she would not see Victor again.

Alfie went back down to the docks a few days later and enquired as to the name of the ship that went down, he heard Margaret talk of the *Vennachar*. Alfie found a couple of sailors on the docks and stopped them.

"Excuse me, do you know the name of the ship that sunk recently near Australia?"

His eyes were pleading with them for information, they could see his concern.

"Son, the *Loch Vennachar* sank just off Kangaroo Island, Australia some weeks back, all her crew lost."

Alfie was devastated, not for him but for his mother.

How will I tell her? he asked himself and, on his way home resigned himself to be direct and await the fallout.

As he walked up to the house, Margaret was hanging washing out in the small yard, she turned to see his face, it spoke volumes and volumes she didn't want to hear but had to.

"It's Victor... isn't it?" she sobbed the words out. "Mam, the ship sank, and all the crew were lost, I'm sorry."

She cried and stroked her stomach with the agony of knowing Victor will never see his child and a child growing up without its father.

My release from a terrible life came, and I paid the price.

The words fell from her mouth keeping the thoughts she harboured to herself.

Margaret sobbed when she thought how Victor had saved her and then to lose him so suddenly and within a short space of time was too much to bear. She carried on for Alfie's sake and gave birth to a little girl whom she named, *Victoria* after the late Queen. Alfie loved his sister and eventually, once he was able, started working in the docks to support them all, he subsidised his mother's earnings.

As Victoria grew into a beautiful, lively little girl she became the image of her mother but had Victor's eyes. Alfie ensured there was enough money to keep them all, he worked hard and put them first. Late one afternoon a few years later he came home to find Victoria playing in the backyard with no sign of his mother. He went back into the front parlour, he found Margaret in the sitting room slumped in a chair, she had had a heart attack. Knowing what his mother had gone through before they arrived in Gravesend it didn't surprise him she had died at such a young age. Margaret often went without food so Alfie could eat when he was young and the lack of nourishment over those early years had weakened her with further childbirth taking more from her body than she could ill-afford.

Alfie scooped Victoria up in his arms and held her, he couldn't explain that their Mam had died as a little girl would not understand the event, so he told her Mam had gone on a long journey, and that he didn't know when she would be back. Victoria's face crinkled, she started crying, Alfie just held her and rocked her whilst wiping away her tears.

Once the funeral was over, he walked little Victoria back to the house, *how will I take care of her and go to work to support us both?* His questions were answered by a kindly neighbour woman who attended the funeral and knew Victor and his late wife. Mabel, said she would see to her until Alfie came home from work each day. Bereaved of his mother and Victor he was now head of the household, he felt alone in the world save for little Victoria.

Chapter 24

Emma

In post-Victorian England, Gravesend, Kent, a beautiful young girl, Emma Stedman, arose early one morning, as she did every day, to tend to her invalid mother, Ethel; helping Ethel out of bed and into the bath chair was hard work but she did it with love. She washed and dressed her with the utmost compassion and care; she made a breakfast of eggs from the hens in the garden and, before leaving the cottage for her position as a maid in the Brockington household, she ensured Ethel had everything she needed before Emma could return home. She took the twenty-minute walk through the narrow streets towards the churchyard and out the other side, always her pace quickening, she knew why.

The little white weather-boarded cottage, where Emma lived, Library Cottage, had belonged to Emma's Grandparents; when they died in a tragic carriage accident, her mother carried on living there. Emma loved the cottage with its fragrant garden and peaceful surroundings near the Docks at Gravesend.

After her father had died very young, Emma's mother was having difficulty finding money to keep them both. She came home one night to tell Emma that she was marrying a man she knew, Albert. He had lost his wife some years back and would care for them. Emma was genuinely surprised as it seemed quite soon after her father had passed, she was also aware that money was needed to survive and her money from being in service wasn't enough to cover the outgoings.

Ethel's new husband joined the household with just a few personal effects, he had designs on making life sweeter for himself and not having to pay much out, as his ready-made household will do as he bid.

Albert lacked compassion; he was a selfish bully and an unkempt man whom alcohol had taken over. He had sweet-talked Ethel after getting her drunk in the Three Daws Public House one night and made sure she was agreeable to his advances. Short, stocky with brown hair and a handlebar moustache he walked with a swagger like he owned all he saw. His brusque, to the point conversation, missed words like 'please' and 'thank you.' He would ensure Ethel stayed at home and could not leave him as his other wives had done! Spinning the yarn to Ethel that he had a wife previously who had died of consumption was his way of getting her to agree to the marriage. Committing Bigamy, he was still married to a previous wife that had escaped him!

The night of the accident was etched in Ethel's mind, Albert had come home from the public house that was a stone's throw from the cottage, he came straight to the bedroom where Ethel was preparing for bed, it was late. He grabbed her by the hair and forced her to the bedside, his hand over her mouth, she was already half-undressed. She refused him his conjugal rights, he was drunk and reeked of tobacco and stale beer which made her feel sick.

He slapped her, she fell backwards, trying to pull away from him, they fought further, he slapped her again. His anger welled up but so did his excitement as he ripped what undergarments she had on and forced himself on her, she tried to scream but there was no one in the house to hear her. Once he had finished, they struggled as she tried to get away from him. She was near the door of the bedroom; he took this as his opportunity to have total control over her, so he gave her a hard push and watched as she tumbled down the small narrow staircase in the nude. Ethel lay motionless at the bottom. He thought he had killed her which wasn't really his intention, and, at that moment, Emma walked in through the kitchen door from the garden, she had been visiting a friend and came back late.

Seeing Ethel on the floor, motionless, Albert told Emma her mother had misplaced her footing at the top of the stairs; Emma ran out the door quickly for the doctor a few streets away saying her mother had had an accident. Regaining consciousness, Ethel came around with just a few bruises but the inability to walk. Alas, nothing could be done, the Doctor confirmed Ethel had injured her back and so Emma's mother stayed in her bath chair from that moment onwards.

Her legs seemingly useless gave Albert carte blanche down at the docks with any woman that would allow him his desires being as Ethel was unable to provide his conjugal rights, however, he still had a roof over his head and conducted his own affairs from that moment on.

Emma had her doubts about the accident, but her mother kept the story of her misplaced footing, *it was easier*, Ethel said to herself.

Chapter 25

Albert

Albert did nothing to help his invalid wife, always thinking of ways to get Emma on her own and vent his frustrations on her, he was just waiting, always watching for the right time. Once, when she was growing into maturity, he pressed himself against her whilst she was making her way through the garden gate, she could feel his excitement which made her feel afraid, she was only young and did not know how to handle the situation but was too frightened to tell her mother as she didn't want to cause trouble. Emma pushed him away, he laughed and slapped her bottom as she ran into the kitchen where her mother was sitting in her bath chair...... looking out of the window; Ethel saw this exchange and held her tears. Emma clung to her mother and just hugged her not knowing what else to do.

One morning, before Emma went to work, she looked out of the leaded-light window in her tiny attic bedroom, she loved that little room, she felt safe, and it was comfortable, although sparsely furnished it was hers. Her little bedstead was brass once belonging to her grandmother. She studied the flowers in the small cottage garden that spring had produced; it was 1910 with King George and Queen Mary ascending the throne after King Edward VII had died, she didn't realise it then, but she was a royalist.

Anything relating to the Monarchy, and all things royal, she eagerly took in. Opening the window, she breathed in the fresh air smiling to herself saying *I wonder what today will bring?* she then proceeded to remove her nightclothes washing herself in water from the China basin that was sitting on the oak dresser nearby as she prepared for work.

Whilst Emma's bedroom door was ajar, she couldn't close it properly due to the wood having expanded in the winter, slow footsteps ascended the narrow wooden stairs. Unbeknown to her, a pair of red-rimmed eyes were now peering in between the crack of the door, she was being watched!

Emma bathed herself. She hesitated at the parts of her body that were maturing and noticed the changes her body was producing. The curves of her breasts and the hair sprouting down below gave her assurance her womanhood was well on its way. The red-rimmed eyes were watching her with wide pupils now and a single tear fell from one of them as they slowly looked her up and down which forced the onlooker to gasp in frustration quietly. Beads of sweat gathered on the voyeur's forehead, he backed away and tip-toed down the narrow stairs; entering the shed at the bottom of the garden and, after a few minutes, finally leaving the cottage for work. The red-rimmed eyes muttered to themselves, "I will have her soon, damn it; I can't wait much longer!"

As Albert walked to work, he noticed a passenger ship had arrived, the people were disembarking with many of them having children tagging along, he huffed and carried on to his place of work down at the docks in Gravesend near the Three Daws Public House.

At just fifteen, Emma had gained employment as a maid for Lord Brockington of Higham. The cleaning work was long hours and back-breaking, but she did it out of love for her mother and to help pay bills that her stepfather wouldn't contribute to. As Emma walked to work, she noticed people around the same ship her stepfather had seen that morning, one young man stood out to her. With black curly hair, blue eyes and a smile that captivated her she couldn't help staring, Alfie caught her eye… she smiled and blushed back at him; their fate sealed.

Once past the docks and on her way to work through the graveyard, Emma thought about the young Indian woman, Pocahontas who had died at the tender age of 22 in 1617. Remembering the story about the Virginian Indian woman and how the 'George' ship stopped at Gravesend for food and water but before it left for its way back to America, Pocahontas died and was buried in the Chancel. She just thought about how young Pocahontas was and what her life must have been like.

As Emma neared her place of work, she suddenly shuddered with the thought of running into Lord Brockington's son, George. George had jumped out on Emma a few times startling her, running after her, and trying to kiss her whilst lifting her dress with his chubby hands, she changed her route often but somehow, he still found her.

George was born out of duty, his mother had lain in the marital bed for her husband, the whole experience was completely mechanical with no tenderness or love involved. George was spoilt growing up, indulged, and with no friends had his every whim pandered to, he was the epitome of a snobbish gentry child. Having ginger hair and freckles, with a rotund physique, made him winey and always wanting his own way, he never left his mother's breast until he was four!

Lady Brockington tried to love her son but because it was expected that she produces an heir, and with her husband's inability to be kind and gentle she had nothing but disdain for this little boy whom she couldn't really stand the sight of. He was devoid of a mother's love which left him with hatred in his heart and was cruel to anyone who tried to show him affection.

One morning when he was sixteen, his Nanny found him on her bed with no clothes on waiting to give her a shock, she didn't scream but walked out of the room and never mentioned it to anyone for fear she may lose her job. George thought this was a good game and every now and again would do this, though as he got older, he wanted more than to shock.

Once in the house, Emma's work was an endless polishing of brass, cleaning of fire grates and their dogs[2] plus washing dishes as well as pots and pans. It was well-known in the house that Lord Brockington had had his wicked way with several of the maids, having heard about this, Emma tried to avoid him wherever possible. In Victorian times, and then early Edwardian, this kind of behaviour was all too common with the young girls in service with many of them having children out of wedlock. They were there for the lord of the house to vent his frustrations on it seemed or just take them when he had a yearning to do so.

The Housekeeper, Mrs Dawson was more like a mother to many of the staff below stairs. She ensured the Butler, Mr Sefton, was fed first followed by the maids, then other lowlier ranking staff. Everyone knew she had her eye on the Butler; he was widowed with no children, but his caring attitude made everyone feel that he would have loved having them had he have had the chance.

Mrs Dawson went into the pantry one morning whilst Sefton was there, she made the excuse to rub past him closely as she needed to get to a cooking pot, the feel of him made her shudder and gasp quietly.

Maybe he will want me someday, she lived in hopes.

---

[2] An andiron or firedog, firedog or fire dog is a **bracket support**, normally found in pairs, on which logs are laid for burning in an open fireplace, so that air may circulate under the firewood, allowing better burning and less smoke. They generally consist of a tall vertical element at the front, with at least two legs.

Sefton was a tall, slim man and impeccably dressed. He ran the household with Mrs Dawson but also kept the lecherous secrets of Lord Brockington. Those secrets had to be kept as he needed his job and times were difficult enough.

One afternoon the bell rang downstairs for the Butler to go to Lord Brockington's Library. He made his way quickly and quietly passing a young maid on the stairs in tears, holding her face. He knew at once what had transpired and knocked quietly before entering the library. There he found Lord Brockington with a red face, puffing, and smiling, he had just had the maid or at least had dalliances with her.

"Sefton, no word of this to anyone, you know the drill."

The words he had heard quite often. He did not condone the behaviour of his employer but merely nodded in agreement.

"Shall Sir be wanting anything else?" Lord Brockington smiled and said, "Yes, a large Brandy."

With that, he winked and sat in his usual chair with the daily paper for a read. Sefton took this as dismissal so turned and left.

Some months later, the young maid that was seen on the stairs was asked to leave, she was pregnant it was clear to see. She was given a sum of money and told if she were to say who the father was, she would be in trouble with the Police for stealing, it was the only way Lord Brockington could keep the silence of his vicious deeds, it worked… for a while.

Chapter 26
Second Sighting

After six hours of back-breaking work, Emma would head home to comfort her mother and take her for a walk in her bath chair. They walked in the park above the docks before going home and cooking a meal. As she walked, Emma's flowing auburn hair blew in the early spring breeze. She possessed a figure most would envy and very quickly blossomed into a woman at sixteen.

Emma covered her mother's knees with an old blanket to keep her warm until the summer months came in. They noticed the sounds of the birds; Sparrows, Blackbirds, Thrushes, and Magpies, on their way home, as they passed the little sweet shop near their cottage, they could hear the tinkle of loose sweets hitting the metal dish on the weighing scales as children were queuing up for their favourites.

One morning, as she walked to work, Emma could hear the sound of barrels being unloaded from the drays and sent down the Shute into the cellar of The Three Daws public house with the shouts of the Draymen to 'watch out below!'

She could hear her own footsteps sometimes as she neared the churchyard which made her quicken her pace, she hurried along as dead people wouldn't hurt her, but she knew the living could! The aroma of freshly baked bread wafting out of the old bakery in Perry Street and the pungent smell of tobacco from the tobacconist shop in nearby Selby Street made her quite heady.

Alfie had grown to just over 6ft looking every inch a man. He never missed a day at work and the men he worked with had respect for him at such a young age.

Over the first two years of Margaret's passing, Victoria grew into a little girl who had hair just like her mother and a smile like Victor's. Alfie cared for her; he was her world.

He would sit Victoria on his knee like she was on a horse and bobbed her up and down, she loved it and giggled helplessly.

Suddenly Emma looked up stopping in her tracks, Alfie was watching her. As she got closer, he smiled, she watched him as he worked, his muscles rippled and sweat beads formed which ran down his face onto his chest. She found herself blushing and turning away but not before Alfie had winked at her. Her tummy flipped!

Each day, Emma found herself longing for this young man at the docks, she didn't know his name, she had never spoken to him but the attraction to him was like a magnet pulling her. Soon she would pluck up the courage to speak with him somehow. She wasn't quite sure how to act but she felt in her heart that he was the 'one.'

Ethel was sitting in her bath chair looking out of the kitchen window one evening patiently waiting for Emma to get home from work.

Chapter 27
Goodnight, Albert

Emma arrived home after dodging George yet again! She needed her weekly ablutions to freshen up after cooking tea and putting Ethel to bed. The old tin bath that hung in the small kitchen was only used once a week in front of the fire when they took turns on a Wednesday night. The water was heated over the fireplace and eventually the bath had enough to wash in. Albert would be first then Emma would help to wash her mother in it, drying her and putting her to bed. When it came to Emma's turn one night, she was heating more water and removed her clothes ready to step into the bath.

Firstly, she bent over to test the water, her back was facing the kitchen door and, as she stepped in, she let the warmth of the water surround her then lay down. She closed her eyes and let the day wash over her. Once she had relaxed for a little while she stood up as she preferred to stand and wash herself. Unbeknown to her, Albert was watching! He was standing in the doorway with the door just slightly ajar so she couldn't see him. His eyes widened as he watched her move her hands over her breasts with the washcloth and other private areas all the time not knowing he was watching, waiting…

Her back was facing him, he crept in, and upon entering the kitchen quietly, he stood motionless as she stepped out of the bath, then, before she could wrap a towel around her, he grabbed her from behind like a flash! His hand over her mouth to stop her screaming and gaining the attention of Ethel, he said in a low quiet voice in her ear, "If you scream and wake your mother, I will hurt her."

Emma immediately stopped struggling, she was crying silently inside, and terrified, she let him touch her. His hands were all over her breasts and thighs. He bit her neck and pressed himself against her buttocks, she could feel the sick rising inside her throat. When Albert came into the kitchen, he had already divested himself of his trousers and with his manhood rising he was ready to take her but, in his haste, he hadn't noticed that Emma had been peeling potatoes earlier for supper. There was a sharp vegetable knife next to the sink, she saw it, moved quickly, and held it to his throat! They wrestled as he tried to take the knife from her but in the struggle, she stabbed him in the neck.

She then found herself repeatedly stabbing him and carried on until he dropped to the floor with blood spurting out everywhere. She stood over him, naked, covered in blood watching him take his last breath as it slowly gurgled out of him, his eyes bulged, his body twitched once or twice then lay motionless next to the bath with blood covering the kitchen, him, and Emma. She looked at him for a while, there he was with no trousers on and a look of disbelief on his face in his death throe. She gave a little laugh and thought how funny he looked but then dread filled her.

I didn't mean to do it, she said in a quiet voice, but she remained calm.

Oh my God, she cried in her head, *What to do with his body? I didn't mean to kill him.*

As if she was on automatic pilot, and very calm, Emma worked through the night, quietly digging a shallow grave under the allotment at the end of the garden. The cottage had a 100-foot garden with a vegetable plot, coal cellar, shed and area where they burned their rubbish, Emma calmly wrapped him in an old sheet then dragged him into the hole she had dug, the sweat dripped off her, it took her four hours to complete the task. All this time her mind was racing, how would she explain his disappearance? Thinking on her toes she worked out a plan, cleaning the kitchen from all the blood as best she could she emptied the tin bath and fell into bed for just a few hours until morning.

She awoke with a start upon hearing her mother call from her bed. As she made tea and took it to Ethel, she was about to leave Ethel's bedroom and return to the kitchen.

"Where is Albert," her mother questioned.

"Mother, I don't think he came home last night, my guess is he is with another woman or drunk somewhere down at the docks."

Emma's heart was beating so fast, she thought back to what happened in the kitchen only hours ago and felt no remorse whatsoever. She settled Ethel in her bath chair after breakfast and began to get ready for work. A sudden relief poured over her, she remembered her stepfather touching her, about to take her against her will. The times he had grabbed her in the garden and held her against him. She had taken a man's life, *but it was self-defence, wasn't it?* she went to work and didn't look back.

Chapter 28

In Service

In the Brockington household, Mr Sefton, the Butler, liked Emma and acted as her unofficial protector. No children of his own, he felt protective of all the youngsters working in the household. Lord Brockington, on the other hand, had had his way with a couple of the parlour maids from what Emma had heard. Apparently, he would make an excuse to keep the Parlour maids busy in his drawing room and threaten them that, if they screamed, they would lose their job. Many of the young girls were no more than sixteen and the result of his lust would ensure they lost their jobs anyway as they quickly became pregnant and had to leave; everyone was too frightened to do anything about him; the secret was always kept by Sefton.

Emma helped Mrs Withington, the Housekeeper, in the kitchen most days. A stout, kind lady who must have been a beauty in her day, she baked, cooked, and kept the house running having been there for over 20 years and, after losing her husband, felt there was nowhere else for her to be useful, so she endured and stayed.

She always had a special yearning for Sefton, but he could never see it. He was too busy attending to Lord Brockington and keeping his nasty secrets.

Lord Brockington, a five-foot four-inch tubby bald man, was always looking for a new maid to dabble with. Mrs Withington warned all-female staff to be 'aware' they must not loiter above stairs under any circumstances, Emma found out first-hand why not.

Lord Brockington was given to mood swings, possibly suffering with 'Little Man Syndrome'. One day he slapped a Maid for not bringing his paper quick enough and another he pushed against the wall when the paper wasn't ironed. Always expecting the morning paper to be ironed before reading it, it was the perfect excuse to get a maid on her own for his delights, he thought.

Lady Brockington was a tall and elegant slender woman with long blonde hair who had endured her husband's lust on the maids for many a year, she knew all about his behaviour and why. He was a man with no kindness, care, and consideration for a woman, particularly in the bedroom. He took her many times against her will, but it was her duty as a wife to be available for her husband at any time. Eventually, she found herself in the arms of a lover who looked after their horses and carriage as well as doing odd jobs around the estate.

Robert looked after the horses and had been in the Brockington's employ for many years. He took up the post just as he came out of the Boer war, losing a hand and struggling to find employment, Lord Brockington had lost a brother in the same war and took pity on him. He managed perfectly well whilst having a grace-and-favour cottage in the backfield woods.

A rugged, tall man with a shock of blond hair and very slightly muscle-bound, Robert cut a handsome figure but never was above himself in the Brockington household.

He felt lonely on occasions never venturing near the house, he was quite happy in his cottage until the day when he heard a woman crying nearby one morning. He looked out of his kitchen window and saw Lady Brockington sitting on a log holding her face with tears running down her cheek. He ran over to her.

"Ma'am what is the matter?"

She was embarrassed and didn't realise she was being watched, she thought it was private with no one seeing the injury she had sustained at the hands of her husband.

"I'm fine, really…" she was still holding her face and trying not to let Robert see the red weal on her left cheek.

"Ma'am, please let me help you, I have some balm in the cottage which may help calm the injury down."

He didn't ask how she came to get the weal on her face, but he could guess it was by a man's hand.

His words were kind, she tried to deny his help, with her face was very sore, she followed him to the cottage.

As he opened the door letting her enter first, she couldn't help noticing that the cottage lacked a woman's touch then remembered it was probably due to his injury. She looked around, there was a small wooden table with two chairs, an old butler sink, a large black pot over the hearth and a small single bed over in the corner. One mug, one plate and cutlery lay next to the table on a small shelf.

As he took the lid off the balm with one hand, she watched intently as he gathered up a small piece of lint, placed some balm on it and proceeded to dab her face, his touch melted her. She found herself wanting more of his touch, this was not right, she felt frightened, her heart racing but something in her awakening.

She thanked him for his care and proceeded to the door… stopping as he held out his hand to her, for he too felt something awakening in him.

Turning towards him, he kissed her gently, she returned his kiss and passion engulfed them. She went to the cottage every day for many weeks for she could not deny herself the pleasure of laying with Robert, but eventually, when common sense prevailed, she wondered how she would handle this going forward?

Experiencing the tenderness and warmth with Robert she eventually fell in love with him. As they had lain many times in the little cottage on the grounds of the house, she remembered the first time they met, how their eyes locked with each other, the touch of his hand on her face and the eventual intimacy they both enjoyed on many occasions. She laughed when she remembered Lord Brockington looking for her one day, she had shed her clothes in the cottage with Robert, he was behind her whilst she was looking out of the window as they stood making love. She could see her husband getting irritated with the staff for not finding her, she could not care less and let her lover take her to heaven.

One day Robert asked her to leave with him. He didn't want to carry on as they had been doing. He wanted a proper union and felt the same love she felt. Lady Brockington was torn between the love for Robert and the duty of rearing her young son by her husband as he would succeed the title of Lord Brockington one day; she decided to stay eventually regretting that decision. Robert left to find love elsewhere, her heart was broken. She vowed her husband would never touch her again.

Some months later, Lady Brockington's stomach started to swell, she was pregnant with Robert's child, how would she explain this to Lord Brockington when he hadn't touched her since the time he took her against her will as she tried to fight him off then ending up with Robert in the cottage many months ago?

Chapter 29

Separation

Lady Brockington felt she had no alternative, she would leave that night with a few clothes and enough money to find Robert, if she could.

Earlier that morning, Lord Brockington, was in a lustful mood knowing he would have his wicked way with a maid that day. He was indeed on a mission, Emma was on duty to bring papers and tea to him. With the knowledge she had she was nervous about going 'above stairs.' She climbed the huge wooden staircase to his drawing room. She knocked lightly.

"Enter!" was Lord Brockington's sharp answer. As she bought the tray over to the table, she handed him his ironed newspaper and moved away as quickly as possible.

"Girl, you will stay here until I have finished my tea and have read my paper!" His tone frightened Emma so she stood very still.

"Sit on the chair next to me whilst you are waiting," he said, gesturing to the nursing chair on the other side of the table that had the tea tray.

The chair was only a foot away from him and in easy reach of his hands, she was ready.

As he opened his newspaper the thought of her near him got him quite excited in a sexual way and opening the buttons on his trousers, he exposed himself to her. Emma almost fell off the chair in shock, she had never seen a naked man except for Albert's private parts in the kitchen after she had killed him.

"You will sit there and not move my dear!" Lord Brockington took his manhood and showed her his erection laughing at the shock on her face. Then, as quickly as he had shown her, he buttoned his fly and carried on reading his paper. Emma was disgusted by his behaviour but was too frightened to move for fear of losing her job. Eventually, he put the paper down, drank his tea and allowed her to leave. Emma was flushed, embarrassed, frightened, and shaking as she was leaving the room, he was laughing at her embarrassment.

"Girl, tell me your name, now!" she replied in a small voice, "Emma, your Lordship."

He stood up and walked towards her, "How old are you?"

As she backed away, she said, "I am sixteen, my Lord."

He replied, "Old enough, my dear, old enough; do not breath a word of what has happened in this room, or you will lose your job, and I know you need it, now go!"

As Emma descended the stairs with the tray, she vowed he would not make her go through another episode of his disgusting behaviour again.

Later that morning, Sefton climbed the stairs to break the news of Lady Brockington's departure after the chambermaid found her bedroom empty of clothes and Lady Brockington, she had departed in the middle of the night.

On hearing the news, he just lit his pipe and carried on reading his paper, he couldn't have cared less.

On Emma's way home, Lord Brockington's son, George, was waiting behind a post box nearby. He gave Emma the creeps and, as she turned the corner into Perry Street, he jumped out on her trying to grab her, she slapped his face in defence and ran, he just laughed and walked back to the house, his father's son.

When Emma returned home, she found her mother in her usual chair by the window.

"Emma, I have some bad news."

Emma felt panic rising inside as she remembered what had happened a few nights before.

"A man from the dockyard has been to advise me that Albert and some other men were crushed against the hull of a ship last night as it docked but they were not able to identify the bodies properly. He told me, as Albert hadn't been seen at work, that he must have been one of the men in the accident."

Emma cried inside with relief. She knew Albert wasn't one of the men and couldn't have cared less about him. Inside Emma was thanking God for his mercy and relief. Her mother never shed a tear and never talked about Albert again.

Ethel's widowed sister lived nearby in Northfleet and could never visit whilst Albert was alive, she too was an object of his desire, so she felt it best not to be there. Upon learning Albert's 'fate' she went on to visit her sister every day.

Chapter 30

Flowering Love

At the docks, Alfie was working hard, the beads of sweat fell from his face and down his chest. Emma was making her way to work one morning, he looked up and saw her, their eyes locked. Emma was already studying him and thinking of ways to speak to him. She need not have worried as he spoke just a few words, she melted.

"Top of the mornin', lovely girl," he said in an Irish brogue and threw her a wonderful smile. Emma's heart thought it would burst!

"G… good morning," she said stuttering the words as she spoke.

They exchanged names, he said if she came to the docks after work perhaps, they could talk further but if she is busy then… Emma immediately agreed she would make her way to see him around 5 o'clock. Her heart and pulse were racing, she had never felt like this before wondering if it was normal? She would go home first after work letting her mother know she will be out for an hour or so walking in the park, this was her plan, so she could see Alfie, her heart beat fast at the thought about their first kiss.

When she arrived at work the next morning, she noticed there was a young girl crying with a large red welt on her face in the scullery. Mrs Withington was trying to calm her down, "What's the matter?" Emma asked the housekeeper.

"Lord Brockington has been up to his old antics again," Mrs Withington explained.

The girl cried even louder. "Shush your noise, Alice, or the whole house will know." Mrs Withington was drying the young girl's eyes and wiping her face with a cold cloth.

After a few minutes, she told Alice to go home and not to mention any of this to anyone or she would lose her job. Emma could only guess what had happened as she had been 'compromised' herself a few weeks before. Mrs Withington told Emma that Alice had taken Lord Brockington's tea and paper to him, and he slapped her for spilling the tea on the floor, whilst she was cleaning it up, he forced himself on her pulling her down onto the floor as she tried to stop him. The young Alice never came back. Emma was left to take tea and papers to Lord Brockington in the short-term until another maid could be employed.

She was watching the grandfather clock in the large hallway and, as it got closer to 4:45 p.m., her heart quickened, she knew she would meet and talk with Alfie at the docks. This was all alien to her; she felt the pull of him already as heat arose around her neck.

Making her way out of the gate she was shocked when Lord Brockington's son jumped out on her again. "Hello, Emma." George said sneeringly.

Emma ran out of the gate and away from him, he ran after her laughing and only a few feet away started puffing as his excess weight slowed him down. He walked back to the house and vowed Emma would be his, *Well, my father can have any young girl, why shouldn't I?*

George was on a mission!

Alfie was waiting for Emma by the gate. She stopped to look at him, his black curly hair, blue eyes, and wonderful smile, she thought to herself, *I must be in love? I don't want anything to change this feeling, I hope he feels the same.*

As she neared, Alfie took her hand, she felt it was large and slightly rough but strong. They walked to a little bench in the park, he shuffled a bit closer to her. They sat and chatted about backgrounds and dreams, they held hands for a long time, that night Emma felt as light as a feather, she had fallen in love with Alfie a long time ago when she had first laid eyes on him.

Their meetings were frequent and always on the park bench. Alfie had fallen in love with her. Emma could hear her mother's words, "Let the man tell you first."

Emma told her mother about Alfie, Ethel smiled and remembered Emma's father in the early days of their courtship, an age long ago when Queen Victoria was on the throne. How he had held her tenderly, kissing her, and she him. Ethel longed for him after his death only to have chosen a bad replacement, Albert, but that was all history, and her heart was light with love for her daughter.

One morning when Emma was walking her usual route to work, Alfie waited at the gate of the park for her, she was surprised to see him.

"What's wrong, Alfie? You're usually at work?"

He stumbled over his words but wanted Emma to come to his house that night. He hadn't told her about Victoria but thought maybe she could be looked after by a neighbour just for a few hours. Alfie had never had a woman and, like Emma, was a virgin. His intent was gentlemanly though and, after a few moments thinking, Emma agreed she would see him that evening after work. He walked back to his work with the biggest smile, she floated to Lord Brockington's house without a care in the world.

Chapter 31

George

"Emma, can you take the paper and tea to Lord Brockington please?"

Mrs Withington knew she could rely on Emma not to get in trouble with his lordship. As Emma climbed them, the stairs seemed to go on for an eternity, her legs were like lead.

She opened the door to see him sitting quietly with one of his books, Lord Brockington ignored her at first.

"Put my tea and papers down on the table, girl!"

"My name is Emma your lordship."

Emma said this through gritted teeth ready for the aftershock. She stood firm and waited for a reprimand; it never came. Lord Brockington walked towards her, grabbed her hand, and kissed it. She shrank away from him. He tried to grab her hand again and the tussle ensured her back was against the door as he swiftly moved his hand onto her breasts and with the other over her mouth, he felt pleasure at that moment which was enough for him… *for the time being*, he thought.

She struggled and felt him getting excited as she remembered her stepfather had done the same to her when she was younger. She jerked herself away from him. Wanting to scream, she fought and tussled all the time making him excited.

This is what he wants she thought. She stopped struggling. He thought she was giving in and let go of her for a moment, when he pulled away, she quickly left the room and bid him good morning.

Her heart was beating fast as she headed along the landing, *I must keep my job at the household, I'll get even one day!*

Chapter 32

Confirmation

Emma looked at the clock in the hallway when it chimed its three-quarter hour, she then left for Alfie's home in Perry Street. Walking through the park, she couldn't see George anywhere, Emma didn't bet on George hiding behind a tree and, as she went past a particularly large pine, he suddenly jumped out! He didn't run after her this time but asked if he could talk to her. *He is trying a different ploy* she thought but was on her guard.

"Can I walk with you through the park, Emma?" he asked in a type of whiney voice, she agreed with hesitation and carefulness.

"I know my mother has left, it's no surprise to me as they haven't got on for a long time." Emma just listened and nodded. They were coming to the part of the park where piles of leaves were overshadowed with shrubs and not many people around, Autumn was almost upon the garden of England, the daylight was fading.

As they approached an old bench, he sat on it and patted it for her to sit down. Emma wasn't used to this kind of George, normally he was making fun of her and trying to lift her skirt or kiss her but as she gently sat down, she could see he had shed a single tear and almost crying said he would miss his mother, all this time seeking sympathy and trying to get Emma's defence low.

"Please sit with me for a while," he asked again, and, in his mind, he knew he may have a chance with her if he tried a different way to get her alone.

He recovered sufficiently and, no sooner had she sat, he was on her, tearing at her clothes, he slapped her face and grabbed her hair as she tried to restrain him. Emma wanted to scream but his hand was over her mouth in a second before a sound could come out, she bit his finger, he slapped her again. They struggled and fell off the bench to the ground. He was on top of her and as they thrashed around a figure nearby was observing, then the figure started getting closer. In moments, George was grabbed by the collar and punched in the face several times, it was Alfie! Alfie had decided to meet Emma from work a little early and walked through the park to ensure her safety.

"Alfie!" Emma screamed and pleaded with him not to keep hitting George, George's face got bloody, his lips split and finally gurgling as Alfie broke his jaw, a red mist had descended over Alfie as he remembered his mother being beaten and abused by his father years ago back in Dublin. Finally, when he stopped, it seemed like George wasn't breathing.

"Oh my God! Alfie, you've killed him!" Emma was beside herself, what would they do and all the questions in her head that wouldn't come out of her mouth. There were some dense bushes nearby where Alfie dragged George's lifeless body. Just before he let go, he kicked George in the groin and let him drop.

"Alfie, why didn't you stop?" Emma sobbed and held onto his arm.

"I didn't want him to touch you ever again, Emma."

All Alfie could do was think about those awful days when his mother would try to hide the bruises she wore for weeks, these were etched in his mind's eye. The constant abuse, her blood, bruises, and tears were all he could remember.

They started to walk back to Alfie's house with both their minds racing, Emma went back to the night she killed her stepfather, Albert, she didn't stop and finally when she did, he was dead.

What will happen when George's body is found? We don't have any alibis; we will both surely hang; she was turning all this over in her mind.

No witnesses in the park, nobody seeing George with Emma and certainly no-one saw Alfie hitting George; *our secret would be safe*, she thought.

"Emma, you have to go back to work tomorrow morning, so it looks like you had nothing to do with it," Alfie said in a low voice. Indeed, it was the right thing to do, and she knew it.

Emma's mind was scrambled, all the time thinking of what happened to George and what to do when they got back to Alfie's house.

In moments, they were at his front door where she just fell into his arms and cried. For a few moments he held her, she went to speak, he put his finger on her lips then kissed her. His tongue sought hers, she felt his excitement. Emma felt the horror of their actions melt away; she was in love with him. As they entered the tiny, terraced cottage, he picked her up and carried her to his small bedroom and, as she lay down, he smiled at her, she was his first and only love and nothing else mattered. Alfie's heart was beating fast, he could almost hear it in his head and with his blood coursing through his veins he wanted to make love to her there and then, he stopped.

"Emma, I love you, and I want to keep you forever," she told him she loved him too and had done for a long time. As she lay back on the tiny bed, watching her breast heaving with her shortness of breath and excitement made Alfie warm inside.

Slowly they shed their clothing, and as he held her tightly, he kissed her mouth so tenderly she thought she would cry. Alfie had never made love to a woman, and certainly, Emma had never been with a man, they melted into each other… their love was true and pure.

She lost count of the times they made love in those next hours, it was tender and then fierce, she held him tight to her and loved every inch of him, his touch made her lose her mind.

She made her way back home to Ethel's who was waiting at the kitchen window.

"You know love, Emma." Ethel knew that look from her own memory of a long time ago.

Chapter 33

Searching

Lady Brockington didn't know where to start looking for Robert, but he did mention a sister in Stratford-Upon-Avon, some time ago.

She decided to use just her full name, Sarah Falstaff and not the title that belonged to her husband. Her journey began by horse and carriage then by train until finally arriving on a sunny Sunday morning.

She had no idea of the address of Robert's sister just that she lived near the local church.

"This will be a hard task for me, knocking on all doors and hoping one will help me," she wondered.

As she walked along the lane toward the tiny church, she could see a few rows of houses, some of them being Alms right next to the church and others just ordinary cottages with some terraced rows. The first cottage in sight had a cosy look about it, she paused at the wooden gate.

What shall I say? She pondered and stood motionless for a moment. Then the thought of Robert and the baby she is carrying pulled her back into the real world. She walked up the path and, using the old knocker on the oak door, she prepared her questions.

An elderly lady with red cheeks opens the wooden door.

"Hello, my dear," the woman looked her up and down then stopped at her stomach which was quite prominent.

"How can I help you?" Sarah proceeded to tell the woman about Robert, who she was and how she found herself there.

"I don't know a Robert, but I do have a neighbour who has a brother that has worked in the south, I haven't seen him in a while. She lives in the cottage with a painted green door, you can't miss it just another 100 yards down the lane." The woman smiled as Sarah nodded. She was overjoyed, her heart raced at the thought she was getting nearer! Stroking her stomach, a warm love enveloped her.

Her steps became lighter with the knowledge Robert maybe just feet away, she may be in his arms in a heartbeat!

Hesitating, she stood at a wooden gate with a '*Failte*' sign hanging above the door, she had no idea what it meant though. Gathering all her bravery, Sarah walked gently to the door and knocked. It opened slowly, there stood a beautiful girl, long black hair and with a slightly bulging stomach just like hers.

"Good morning… how can I help you?" Hiding behind the girl was a small boy looking shy and hanging onto her skirts.

"This is Robert," the girl said, "he is my brother's child."

Sarah's mind was in a whirl, doing maths in her head, there was no conceivable way it could be Robert's child, he never mentioned he had children. The little boy appeared to be around 7 years old with hair the same colour as Robert's. She had all sorts of different stories and reasons going around and around in her head.

"I am looking for a man called Robert." Sarah went numb, the words came out slightly robotic.

"My brother is called Robert, he is working in the fields near the church, 'little Robert,' as I call him, lives with me since his mother died in childbirth." The story was unfolding, it was about seven years ago when Robert joined the Brockington household. His wife died; he needed work and came south where there was more opportunity.

"Thank you for your help." Sarah was so grateful and started the walk to the fields in hopes that she will find Robert, her heart lifted, her stomach fluttered at the thought of him.

As Sarah walked toward the church with the fields surrounding it, she saw a shadow of a man sitting on a small stone wall, she got closer, and from the back, it looked like Robert. She called out to him.

He turned around and, indeed, it was Robert, bronzed from his time in the fields. She thought she would faint and strode over to him.

"How did you find me, Sarah?" His voice quivered, she noticed his eyes watered.

"Why are you here now when you wouldn't come away with me?" His question cut her to the quick, she stood motionless.

"I stayed out of a sense of duty, stupidly thinking that's what I should be doing. He beat me to the floor one night because I was refusing his advances. It was then I realised I loved you and only you and to hell with duty! God help me, Robert… I'm carrying your child!"

His face changed as he took in her news. He loved Sarah as he had his late wife.

"Sarah, I can't give you the life you left, all I have is the ability to work the land and, with one hand, I am slower than most. Is this a life you can take on and one with a man who already has a child?" He needed to know she was there for the long haul, that no matter what she would be by his side.

"Robert, I love only you and forsaking all others only want to be with you. Our child is being born out of love, I can't think of anything I want more than being here with you." Sarah was crying by this time as she pleaded with him.

He stood up from the stone fence, turned around and took her in his arms. He held her as tightly and kissed her full and deep, she was his.

They went back to Robert's sister's cottage and his son. After a few weeks, a cottage became free for rent nearby, they moved in together, Sarah gave birth to a little girl some months later, her new life was complete.

Chapter 34

Investigation

As she walked back through the park for work the next morning, Emma looked over and winced as she passed the leaves around the shrub where George's body had been dumped; they were disturbed.

How could this be? she said to herself. George was as good as dead, she witnessed Alfie's handling of the incident and thought for sure George wasn't breathing when they left.

After George had taken the beating from Alfie, he lay unconscious for a few hours as darkness fell and then, gradually looking around, he wasn't quite sure where he was for a moment remembering he had been sitting with Emma.

He brushed the leaves off his clothes and, with fuzzy light-headedness, made his way back home under the light of the gas lamps.

The brass door knocker in his hand he softly knocked it on the gleaming red door for effect and sympathy when what he wanted to do was smash the knocker as hard as he could but hesitated in doing so.

Sefton opened the door with George falling onto the hall carpet, blood running down his face. Sefton helped him into the library and shouted for Mrs Dawson to come quickly to attend to his injuries.

"What happened, Master George?" Sefton was concerned and called for Lord Brockington, as he stood in the doorway and saw his son, he started to show concern where before he would have left it to his wife to sort out; he called the police, they couldn't attend until the morning.

Unable to speak properly, his jaw badly bruised but not broken, George waited with interest, he was certain Emma was involved.

Two policemen arrived at 8:00 a.m. the next day with notebooks in hand. Sefton led them into the Drawing Room to wait for Lord Brockington.

When Emma arrived for work, she saw the Police in the Drawing Room through the window and tried not to panic staying just outside the Drawing Room door eavesdropping as best she could; she could hear some of the conversations.

"His face was a mess," one of the policemen said.

"Took a right good beating, and he doesn't know why," said the other.

Lord Brockington had his head in hands, his wife had left him and now his son was beaten within an inch of his life but luckily surviving, he feigned shock and concern but all the time wondering *who did this to my son?*

Silence fell in the room. The Police asked Sefton to find Emma for a statement; she was listening outside and, as the door opened, she pretended she had just arrived. She stood at the door, one of the officers motioned for Emma to come in, she gulped and tried to stay calm. She was questioned at length about her relationship in the household, about her and George and their movements in the park. She gave an account of meeting him which was true, there was no mention of Alfie.

Emma kept as calm as she could.

"Yes, I was with George yesterday. We chatted as we sat on one of the benches." George nodded. She never mentioned he made a grab for her.

"Was there anyone else with you, miss?"

Emma said she didn't see anyone else and had left George to go home to her invalid mother.

The Police took her statement, their faces showing no signs of emotion. George couldn't remember the events but, not wanting to lose face, decided he would stay with the story that he had been drunk and fallen on the way home after seeing Emma. This was more credible than telling the Police that a woman had hit him or so he thought, thus no damage to his ego.

Emma panicked inside, when she got home to Alfie that night, she told him about the Police and George. Alfie went quiet and sat with his thoughts for a while.

"This is our secret, Emma; no one else knows and doesn't need to."

Alfie held her in a tight embrace, he was her hero and her love, she felt safe.

The case was dropped due to lack of evidence.

Chapter 35

Can't Wait

Quite a few months after Lady Brockington had left to find Robert, Lord Brockington got restless, he was tired of trying to take advantage of a maid and wanted his physical needs assuaged as and when he wanted them.

He interviewed several young women as a personal assistant to him, one in particular he took a shine to, *she's the one I will have in my bed, no doubt about that!* He eyed her and her breasts, *she is unmarried and seeking employment, an easy target and promises made will ensure her willingness!* He had a smile like a Cheshire cat when she agreed to his terms.

The woman moved in almost immediately and joined him in his bed that night after supper with many glasses of his Lordship's best Claret! now Emma knew she would not be bothered by him or any of the staff downstairs.

Sefton felt that he need not keep any further secrets with the arrival of the personal assistant except one that occurred a few nights later. He was sitting in the kitchen below stairs after all the other staff had gone to their homes, as he did this most nights. All was quiet, then, he looked up as the bell rang from Master George's bedroom, not a common occurrence and one that Sefton felt was a tad unusual. Making his way through the hallway, he climbed the large staircase, then, gently tapping on George's door, he waited to be invited in. He was not prepared for what he was about to witness. Lord Brockington's new 'personal assistant' was in bed with George! George had rung the bell for amusement, to shock and to show off. Sefton closed the door quietly and returned downstairs. In his mind, he was disgusted but, in a strange way, excited by what he had witnessed. He kept that secret incredibly quiet, particularly from Lord Brockington, however, as he thought back over the event, he thought *this may give me leverage over George in the future at some point, that's one for the back pocket,* he smiled to himself.

When Emma finished work one afternoon, she went back to Library Cottage and told her mother she and Alfie wanted to be together but could not afford to marry. After a few sentences, she then told Ethel she was pregnant. Ethel looked shocked but then smiled when she thought back at a similar event she had had in her own life with Emma's father and the time she had to go home and admit, she too, was pregnant to her own mother.

"I don't mind Emma, as long as you are happy that's all that matters to me." Ethel knew that her daughter had not had it easy what with Albert and his disgusting behaviour but felt love for her daughter *and soon I will be a grandmother!* She smiled to herself feeling a warmth of happiness.

Packing her things in a tiny case that belonged to her grandmother, Emma was moving in with Alfie as they had agreed. She hadn't said what day but said to him it would be soon. She wanted to surprise him, so she made her way to his house with her belongings and the yearning for intimacy with him once again. When she knocked on the door a little blond-haired girl answered.

"Hello, my brother is not back from work yet, who are you?"

The surprised look on Emma's face when she was confronted by a little girl in Alfie's house, she thought maybe she had the wrong house and asked the little girl if Alfie lived there, this was verified.

The girl let her in and proceeded to play with the doll that Alfie had bought her the previous Christmas. Whilst she waited, Emma couldn't remember him mentioning the child and waited for him to come home from work with some questions on her mind. There was a knock at the door, Victoria answered it, she threw herself at her brother as he was her world, she loved him.

"Alfie, there is a lady in the parlour, she is beautiful!" Instantly, he stepped into the room and Emma stood to greet him.

"Please let me explain," he said to Emma as he looked at Victoria and hugged her. He revealed everything about his mother, Victor, and little Victoria. He was worried that Emma would not like the fact that he had a child to look after but she was his blood and had no one else.

"Alfie, I don't mind in the slightest, I will help look after her with you." Alfie's smile was priceless, he had the two girls he loved with him, and all would be well.

That night, after Alfie put Victoria to bed, they sat in the front parlour. Emma had built a small fire, the glow of it was against her face. It lit her up and put her in his glance. He took her hand holding it for what seemed like an eternity, but it was fleeting. He then guided her up the small narrow staircase to his room.

As they entered the bedroom she took in a deep breath, he was behind her and held her to him. She could feel his breath on her neck, he kissed it which sent a shudder down her spine.

He started to take her clothes off slowly and then hurriedly as his wanting her overtook him.

He turned her to face him and then, with the lightest of touches, his lips concentrated on her breasts, she gave a gasp as he finally lifted her up and placed her on the bed. His lips sought other parts of her body where no one person had ever been. She cried in ecstasy and held his hair whilst his mouth was on her. Finally, he took them both to heaven, they lost themselves in their love for each other the second time being even more intense than the first.

Emma honestly believed she had never been so happy as she was at that moment. She lay in his arms and put her head against his chest of black curly hair. Breathing his manly odour, she let a single tear fall and soon found herself asleep in Alfie's arms.

She carried on working for Lord Brockington, although the wages were a pittance really, it did help with bills as Alfie earned even less than she did on the Docks.

A few months later, Emma was bathing in the kitchen and noticed she had no blood showing as she normally did each month, she cried as she realised, she was carrying Alfie's baby.

That night when Alfie came in from the docks, she wanted to surprise him with her news.

"Alfie, I have something special to tell you… I'm having your child."

Emma was waiting for a response and what she heard next made her heart leap.

"Emma, the thought of having a child with you has filled me to the top of my head with joy. This means that there will be three people in my world I adore and love. I cannot think of anything else I would rather have. Just one thing though…"

Emma held her breath.

"Can we call the child Margaret if it's a girl and Victor if it's a boy?" Alfie was beyond overjoyed and lay his hand on her stomach stroking it.

"Alfie, we can call the child whatever you wish." Upon this agreement, they had tears of joy and proceeded to tell little Victoria she will have a nephew or niece; they spent a while trying to explain what that meant to her.

Over the months and into the new year of 1912, Emma began to bloom, and her stomach expanded. She struggled at work when it became too much, and with her pregnancy advancing, she felt she must carry on for as long as possible as they will need the money.

At night, when they wanted each other, Alfie was so gentle and respectful it made Emma want to cry for the beautiful man she had conceived a child by. One morning he gave her a ring that his mother had worn, it was all he had left of her, Emma wore it on her ring finger never thinking about marriage but in her heart, they were already a couple and soon-to-be parents.

Alfie looked after her working all the hours God sent. He loved the fact that he would be a father, *a better father than mine had been to me,* he thought.

One morning, before he went to work, Alfie looked in Emma's eyes, "I want to provide for you, our baby and Victoria," he said, "but I just don't earn enough here on the docks."

With only months to go before the baby was due, Alfie heard of a ship leaving Southampton for America in April, it was called the '*Titanic*' a ship that '*would never sink*' it was said. He raced home after work that day and told Emma his plan for going to America.

"I'll get a better-paying job and send money for you, the child and Victoria to join me for a better life there; please say you'll join me in the new world?"

He had heard it was the land of opportunity, of plenty, and if you worked hard, a good life could be had. Many people with '*backgrounds*' moved to other countries, he felt he could wipe the slate clean for them both.

Emma's heart sank, she would not see him until the baby was born. "*What would happen if he doesn't come back? if he meets someone else, if...*"

Her head went into a tailspin and as it did, she cried inside… his ticket was booked.

Chapter 36

New Horizons

As the day arrived for Alfie to travel to Southampton, he held Emma in his arms and stroked her tummy.

"As soon as I have enough money, I will send for you, Victoria, and our child," he said with his eyes wet and Emma crying into his shoulder.

"It will not be long; we have our new life before us, Emma." He left that morning for Southampton.

On 10 April 1912, after the ship arrived on the 3 April, the *Titanic* set sail at noon stopping off at Cherbourg before heading for America with Alfie aboard in Steerage and, as she sped across the cold Atlantic, Alfie could only have hope in his heart and the love from Emma lifting him.

He stood on the prow of the ship when steerage passengers were allowed on deck, his eyes searching in the distance, his heart full of love for his little family.

Darkness, shouting and screaming, water, and at 2:20 a.m. on 15 April 1912, The RMS *Titanic* sank into the North Atlantic Ocean about 400 miles south of Newfoundland, Canada. The huge ship, which carried over 2,000 passengers and crew, had struck an iceberg two and half hours before. Only 705 individuals survived.

Emma went about her days as normal whilst getting ever closer to having Alfie's child. Not hearing any news and no way of knowing about the *Titanic* she went down to the docks. One of the men that worked with Alfie spoke with her.

"Emma, I am so sorry to tell you we just heard late last night that the *Titanic* sank just off the coast of Newfoundland, many didn't survive." She fainted.

As she came to, the man that had broken the sad news helped her up, she then started to rationalise what she was being told.

"*No one knows for sure who has died and who has survived, perhaps Alfie got off the ship and is in America somewhere?*" her mind was a mess.

"I'm sure he survived and will send for you soon."

The man smiled at her.

One month went by followed by another, no news.

Part Two
The Search

Chapter 1

Journey

Emma's time was nearing delivery of the baby, she started contractions whilst at the Brockington household. Sefton knew he had to act quickly for Lord Brockington would not approve of a child being born in his household and to a parlour maid either. He enlisted the help of Mrs Dawson, the housekeeper, she helped Emma back to her mother's house to have the baby whilst Victoria was being looked after by a neighbour.

"Thank you, Mrs Dawson, you've been so kind." Emma looked into the old lady's eyes. Mrs Dawson smiled, turned, and walked back to the Brockington household. She couldn't help but wonder if the child was Lord Brockington's as Emma had never mentioned a husband or any other man in her life.

"This is a secret to be kept until another time, there will be no mention of this to anyone above stairs." Mrs Dawson said to herself.

Mrs Dawson was not the squeaky-clean lady Emma thought she was. It turned out that the babies fathered by Lord Brockington over the years were sold on by Mrs Dawson, she pretended to help the poor maids that endured his behaviour, but her heart was black… All told, she had sold on sixteen babies.

Ethel did the best she could as, still confined to a bath chair, it was a struggle for her to help deliver her own grandchild. In the dimly lit kitchen, she managed to help Emma deliver her baby.

"Emma, it's a boy!" Ethel was beside herself and cried along with Emma. She helped clean him up whilst Emma rested.

"Emma, the baby needs to be fed." These words came slowly into Emma's ears as she awoke from a very deep sleep.

Ethel gave the baby to Emma's breast, he latched on for all he was worth.

"His name will be Victor Alfie Ryan." Emma looked down at the tiny bundle and smiled, his hair was as black as Alfie's. She felt weary and lay down for a while after feeding the baby. After a few days, Emma returned to Alfie's house on the terrace and little Victoria joined them from the neighbour's care. All that was missing was Alfie, her heart ached, and sadness stepped in.

Emma visited her mother regularly and explained to her why the baby's names as well as her hopes and dreams for her and Alfie with their little family. The sacrifices Alfie had made for them all and how, in time to come, she will join him with Victoria and Victor. Ethel was sad that her daughter and grandchild would leave England but felt happy for Emma. She looked out of the kitchen window as if wishing for her old life when she first met Emma's father, *God, I miss him and always will...*

Chapter 2

Introduction

As Emma sat with little Victor feeding him in the parlour, she looked out to see Victoria playing in the front garden.

We will have a new life and, hopefully a better one she said to herself.

Victoria looked up waving at the window, she came running in straight to Emma and Victor, "Can I hold him, please?" Victoria was so excited she couldn't stand still, Emma asked her to sit and have the baby on her lap.

Victoria slowly looked into the baby's eyes, then looked up and smiled at Emma. Emma realised that their bond was blood, "He's my brother?" she didn't understand the relationships, "No Vicky, he is your nephew," Emma tried to explain that relationship which Victoria tried to take on board. Emma sat and watched as Victor gurgled and held Victoria's hand with his tiny fingers. *I had no idea my heart could hold so much love*, Emma felt her heart would burst.

"Emma, have you heard from Alfie?" suddenly Emma's thoughts were back in the room. She took a sharp intake of breath, and before she spoke, she thought long and hard about her answer.

"Victoria, I haven't but I'm sure he is busy and will contact us soon." Emma held back the tears so as not to upset her.

Victoria went back outside to play in the autumn sunshine, the leaves were falling from the trees, there was a slight cool breeze coming in from the river. Emma's thoughts went to Alfie, she ached for him every day.

Was he alive? Will I ever see him again? Her questions to God remained unanswered. For now, she will have to be content.

Chapter 3
John

He walked away from the docks in just what he stood up in after the crew from the *Carpathia* had dried and fed him; newspapermen wanted his story; one he couldn't give as he had no idea who he was… or how he came to be on the ship. Officials were asking for names of the survivors and pieces of information from him, but he still couldn't help them.

Many survivors were being sent to the American Seaman's Friend Society Sailors' Home and Institute on Jane Street, New York. Everyone called it 'The Jane.' He made his way to the large boarding house down by the Hudson Park. Looking at all the huge buildings, the people dressed differently from him, horses, and cars going at speed which he wasn't used to, with no memory it was as if he had been transplanted to another planet!

He walked up to the large imposing building hesitating before opening the doors and going in.

"Can I have your name please, Sir?" A rather large well-built woman with long blonde hair was staring straight at him and was awaiting an answer.

"My name, errr… my name is John, yes, John." Alfie looked around for something to help him with a surname.

"John Park, that's my name." Looking across the road from where he was standing, it was right by the Hudson Park that was good enough for him. Staring right back at the blonde woman for approval, he felt sure that he had provided her with enough information.

"You're one of those that survived, aren't you?" the woman was attempting to strike up a conversation, she wasn't wrong, however, Alfie felt uneasy as she leaned over the counter and displayed her breasts for him to enjoy.

"You can stay here whilst the investigation goes on, John Park, but you will have to find work soon as you will need to pay for your keep here or find somewhere else, you will need money."

Alfie heard the words but didn't want to think further than something to eat, he couldn't remember the last time he ate. He couldn't even remember what he liked but it didn't matter at this point.

Maybe my memory will come back soon? He assured himself. *I need work and money, what do I do for work?*

All these questions he had gone around and around in his head with no answers. He heard there was a dining room of sorts and survivors, as well as seamen who were encouraged to go there for something to eat, Alfie found himself with over 37 men in a huge room queuing up to fill their plates.

He agreed in his mind what he would say and as he went out into the daylight of Jane Street after he had eaten, he could sense he was near a body of water, the Hudson.

He walked a couple of blocks until he saw a Merchant Seaman's office. He started walking up the wooden stairs to an office, there was a bald, fat man in his 60s sitting behind a desk.

"Yes Son, what can I do for you?" The man was busy with a small glass of whisky whilst his buttons on his shirt screamed the words *too tight* across his large bulbous stomach. He had also forgotten to button his flies, so Alfie was witness to some off-white underpants.

"I need a job," Alfie was prepared to take anything at that point, but he still didn't know what he could do onboard a ship.

"Hmmm… OK son, the next ship in needs a cook, can you cook?" The man awaited an answer. Thinking on his feet, Alfie confirmed he could although knew this to be untrue, he would learn fast.

"Alright son, be here at 7:30 a.m. on Wednesday, and we'll get you all squared up ready to join the ship."

Alfie hastily agreed, they said their goodbyes then he walked back to The Jane.

Walking through the door, the well-endowed receptionist spotted him. He tried to walk past her, she looked up and was on his case straight away.

"Hi, John… do you have some spare time maybe for a drink, keep me company on my break?" Alfie, with his memory shot, had no idea if he was married, in love or had another woman, but there was no doubt in his mind that this woman wanted his attentions and not just for a drink.

"Oh, go on honey," she whispered in a demure tone displaying her breasts once more across the counter.

"I have whisky and drinks in my room on the 6th floor, room 617, and you're welcome to share."

Alfie was trying his best to get out of the sticky situation. Part of him didn't really need this kind of diversion as he struggled with his mind, but he was young, virile and had the same urges as any normal man, the opportunity had presented itself. She was insistent and no sooner had he turned around she had him by the arm and led him to the elevator.

Chapter 4

First Heaven

Every experience Alfie was having he only knew to be his first as without his memory he was as vulnerable as a child.

"John, my name is Marilyn and I'm gonna take real good care of you, yes I am."

Alfie had an idea that what may take place was something he would be agreeable to. *I want to taste the Whisky and damn it, anything else she has to offer*, his mind centred on her ample charms.

Marilyn opened her door ushering Alfie in. He sat in one of her chairs near the window, she poured him a large whisky and water, not too much so he stayed sober but just enough to take the edge off.

"Marilyn, do you live here alone?" he asked her whilst sipping the whisky and letting it slide down his throat which in turn gave him a warmth inside.

"Yes, John I do, and no other man has set foot in this room before, so you are honoured, honey." Marilyn wasn't entirely truthful, Alfie didn't buy it either.

Hmmm, let me see, she said to herself. *Black or white*. She was hell-bent on getting Alfie into bed by hook or by crook. His physique did something to her, she had to have him stay… just for a while.

Suddenly, after two more whiskeys, Alfie started to feel the strain and stresses of what he had been through since being saved from the ship wash away from him. He relaxed enough for Marilyn to sit across from him in another chair, he didn't remember her wearing next to nothing when they came in the room earlier, her clothes were gone and, instead, she was wearing frilly black undergarments which he could see right through!

"John, I want you and I to be awfully close friends if you get my meaning?" Marilyn walked over to Alfie slowly, he looked up at her and smiled.

She held her hand out to him and as they walked over to her bed, she divested herself of her undergarments and let him touch her.

I've never had an experience like this, or have I? With no memory, Alfie was like a virgin, Marilyn felt it too, but with her experience, she was sure she could make him a man; that afternoon she took him to heaven; it *won't be the last time.* She smiled to herself.

Chapter 5

Sailing

"Hi, friend."

A black man in his late 50s with a well-worn face and clothes to match beckoned Alfie to sit with him in the dining hall and get on the subject that was on everyone's lips.

"How did you come to be on the *Titanic,* friend?" Waiting patiently for a response, the man offered his name and personal details.

"I'm Owen, I've been a sailor all my life and this here place looks after me when I'm back from my voyages."

Owen held out his hand to Alfie, they shook each other's.

"My name's John Park pleased to meet you, Owen."

It still sounded strange, Alfie heard the words and didn't recognise the name, but for now, it will have to do.

"John, tell me how you came to be on the *Titanic*."

Owen waited patiently for an answer. Alfie had no idea how he came to be on the ship but there must be a reason he just can't remember it. Alfie made something up to keep Owen happy.

"I was looking to work as crew on the Great Lakes."

Alfie thought this would appease his dinner partner, but it didn't seem to work, and more questions followed.

"So, John, what ship will you be joining?"

Alfie had no idea and was getting deeper into telling lies and more than he wanted to. He fidgeted in his seat as he waited for inspiration.

"I thought I was a goner as they dragged me out of the water."

Alfie remembered that night spluttering and coughing up seawater and feeling frozen to the bones.

"So what is your reason behind being on the ship that wouldn't sink?"

Owen said this tongue in cheek, everyone had this on their minds, the newspapers were full of it.

"To be honest Owen, I don't know."

Alfie was still without his memory and nothing from his past came to light to help him provide a kind of compass to navigate his way through his predicament.

"That's tough John, surely there must be something you can tell me about your time before arriving here?"

Again, Alfie shook his head and looked at Owen for inspiration. He wracked his brain, nothing would surface.

"Well, your accent says you are from Ireland or England so that must be a start?"

"Of course," Alfie said to himself, *"that narrows it down,"* but still nothing sprung forth.

"Owen, I've enlisted to join a ship going into the Great Lakes, I need to work and there is a ship docking in a couple of days, so I'll be ready for it."

Upon hearing this, Owen's mind took him back to his last voyage on the *Ocean Spray*. A voyage that almost took his life making him shudder. She almost floundered in Lake Superior taking all the crew with her but a handful, it wasn't his time, mother nature was kind that night.

Finally, that seemed to help Owen with his questioning with both men finished their meal. It was getting late, but still light, Alfie enjoyed their discussion as much as he could and felt the warmth of knowing Owen.

Room 629, 6th floor, was etched on his key fob, and so rather than taking the elevator, he used the stairs to strengthen his legs which seemed to be dragging since the ship went down.

As Alfie approached his door, he hesitated for a split-second remembering Marilyn and her ample charms, how she made it so easy for him that afternoon. He felt a twinge and wondered if he was being too presumptuous and forward, but he had a hankering for tasting her wares once more. He turned around and slowly walked down the hallway. He noticed the carpet was threadbare near her door, he stood for a moment. Just about to knock, he heard noises that he recognised; she wasn't alone.

Chapter 6
Lake Bound

That night, Alfie couldn't sleep, he tossed and turned as day broke. He awoke aroused at the thought of Marilyn then suddenly all that dissipated as he remembered her bed was not even cold and another occupant was enjoying her wares, literally straight after him.

So, I wasn't exclusive, never the mind, but I will indeed have her before I set sail! Alfie's lust for the large-busted blonde could only be assuaged by his physical touch of her, his mind wouldn't rest until he had savoured her once more.

Washed and dressed, he remembered that he had a free day before going to the shipping office to meet the ship and its crew on Friday. He was hungry and went down to the dining hall, he thought about Owen and the possibility that he may bump into him again.

As Alfie closed his door, he heard a familiar voice, it was Marilyn, standing in her doorway with next to nothing on. Alfie couldn't take his eyes off her, she had nothing on but her thin dressing gown… revealing all her womanly attributes!

"Well, good morning, John." Marilyn was batting her eyelids and playing with a lock of her blonde hair which seemed to cascade down to her breasts. He stood with his mouth open and felt another twinge.

"Marilyn, good morning. I didn't see you there." She knew damn well he had seen her and had prepared herself for his eyes. She beckoned him to her room with her finger and a smile painted with red lipstick.

"You weren't shy yesterday, John." She whispered in his ear as she touched his hand and held it to her breast.

"Are you in a hurry… John?" Alfie slightly pulled away from her, but his instinct was too strong, his physical being needed tending to and that morning she was his. He pushed her back on her bed and took her many times that morning, his youth allowed him all the recovery time a young man in his early 20s needed.

When he left her room, and her, Alfie had his breakfast, a quick chat with Owen and then found himself out on the street walking in the spring sunshine to investigate his surroundings further. He had the biggest smile on his face and satisfaction but no feelings of love, just lust.

Unbeknown to Alfie, Owen was in the reception area just minutes after he had left The Jane, Marilyn wanted Owen, she wasn't stopping at anything to get him. It didn't take much to catch his attention, he had been looking at her the night before and had it in his mind to 'visit' with her at some point that day.

Owen 'paid' for his keep at The Jane via Marilyn's visits, she couldn't get enough of this huge black, quiet man and he knew it.

When he started visiting her, she had no idea that the man-mountain she had let in her room was insatiable, she didn't have anyone else that first day as Owen was enough…until Alfie came along.

Chapter 7
Media Attention

As Alfie walked down the road across Jane Street and into Greenwich, he found he was being followed.

"There's one of them!" he heard a voice shout and before he knew it two newspaper reporters from the recently founded New York Herald surrounded him.

"So what was it like almost going down on the ship?"

One of them with a brown hat and a large notepad was insistent on getting a story.

"Why were you on the ship? Was there anyone else you knew on the ship?"

The questions were like being shot out of a gun towards Alfie; he hurried to get away from them, but they were not giving up easily.

Suddenly he spun around to them and said, "Look, I have no memory, my mind is a blank, I won't help you even if I could!"

They both looked at each other and then almost said the same question, "So, what's your name?"

Alfie was getting near the end of his tether at this point as this wasn't the first time he had been asked.

"It's John Park, but that's not my real name, I had to make it up because I don't know who I am. Now, will you both leave me alone!"

The men could see he was getting upset and decided to leave him alone... for the time being.

Alfie walked at a quicker pace. It seemed like ages that he had been walking, it was further away from Jane Street, but he didn't care. He didn't have a plan and just wanted to be alone with his own thoughts, well only recent ones, but he was wondering what the ship would be like, how was he going to cook when he didn't have clue and what the voyage would be like.

A few hours later, Alfie turned around and made his way back to The Jane. Marilyn was behind the counter and smiled at him knowingly. Alfie wondered how many others she *smiled* at that day.

"Hey, John!"

Owen was just going down to the dining room for dinner and beckoned Alfie to join him.

"Oh John, I had the best time this afternoon, that blonde behind the front desk gave me all her loving and more, it was almost like she engulfed me and had never had a man before, I made sure she didn't have anyone for the rest of the day!"

Alfie kept quiet.

My God, she even had Owen in her bed, he said to himself and shook his head, *that's the last time I'll enjoy her charms*.

Chapter 8

Bon Voyage

Alfie took the slow walk to the shipping office and saw the same man with the same clothes waiting for him looking at his watch.

"John, you're just in time, the ship has docked, here is your ticket for boarding."

Alfie held out his hand and studied the ticket, '*Assistant Cook*' it said in large black letters. He thought he was the only cook on the ship but after speaking with the clerk, he was told that a cook from another ship checked in the day before and signed up. Alfie breathed a small sigh of relief.

I hope he can teach me to cook and doesn't mind, Alfie's thoughts were all over the place as he knew he had to learn quickly ensuring him the ability to earn money for his keep and to buy some new clothes.

As he walked aboard the *Sea Spray*, the other men turned and looked at him, then carried on with their own conversations. He was accompanied to his quarters and told to be in the galley for 12:30 p.m. Alfie's voyage was for 5 weeks then a turnaround and 6 weeks further. The funds from these voyages would ensure his pockets felt money in them.

The ship carried Iron Ore, she was a *Laker* and was making her way to Silver Bay. Alfie had only heard the men mention this information and took it all in; as the ship set sail, he looked forward to learning new skills and earning money, little did he know what was ahead of him.

Chapter 9

Restraint

Down in the galley, Alfie found himself alone for a few minutes until a black man mountain, with muscles in all the right places plus tattoos and scars came through the door greeting him.

"You must be John." Alfie looked up at this six-foot six-inch man and stared straight into his eyes.

"Yes, I'm John and pleased to meet you," Alfie held out his hand, the mountain did the same.

"The name's Matthew; call me Matt."

Straight away Alfie was at ease. He told Matt that he hadn't had a lot of experience cooking but can follow orders. Matt smiled; this wasn't the first time someone had joined the ships' company not knowing what they were doing. Matt told Alfie he would be fine and just to follow what he asks, all will be well. Alfie nodded and smiled; Matt smiled back.

Then the questions started, Alfie told Matt only what he could remember and that wasn't much. He did tell him about Marilyn and Matt laughed.

"What's so funny, Matt?"

Alfie wasn't annoyed but thought maybe Matt was laughing at his experience or inexperience. Matt assured him this wasn't true but what he did say left an aftertaste in Alfie's mouth.

"John, I'm not laughing at you son, I'm thinking back to a few weeks ago when I was staying at The Jane myself. Marilyn came onto me so hot I thought I'd melt, and eventually, I did… along with many others. You're not exclusive and neither am I! She called it 'giving comfort to those that need it.' I called it something else."

Matt laughed until tears rolled down his face. Alfie and Matt were going to get along real fine.

As the *Sea Spray* made her way through the canals and locks towards an open lake, Alfie could feel the sick rising in his throat. The calmness of the canals and then eventual rough water soon shook him to the reality that he was sailing on a huge ship that wouldn't save him from getting seasickness. Matt saw the look on Alfie's face.

"John, keep looking at the horizon and you'll be fine. It takes a time to get used to, but you can do it."

Every time Alfie felt the sick rising, he looked out the porthole in the galley, and it all calmed down. Under Matt's instructions, Alfie learned about peeling vegetables, baking bread, and making gravy and biscuits. He had no memory of eating any of the food but strangely he knew what he was eating and whether he liked it or not.

One morning, Matt was baking bread, he asked Alfie to fetch more flour from the larder. As Alfie went into the adjoining room to the galley, he saw something familiar to him but had no idea why. It was suet. A flashback to when he was a child flew across his mind, he could see a woman making dumplings in a dimly lit room to put in a pot with a small child at her feet... it was him!

He ran into the Galley to tell Matt but there were two of the crew in there talking with him so he decided he would keep quiet for now and share what had happened later.

It was getting dark outside, the night was falling, crew were heading for their bunks and Alfie was yawning his head off. Matt looked at him gesturing towards the galley door, "Hit the hay, John, and tie yourself into your bunk, it could get rough. But, before you do, I have something for you."

Matt gave Alfie a peeling knife.

"But this is yours, Matt." Alfie looked at the man-mountain.

"Take it, John, you may need it to earn your living one day, or it may save you from an attack, I have plenty, it's yours."

"Thanks, Matt. I'll never forget your kindness and friendship." Alfie put the knife in his pocket.

Alfie knew when Matt said something it was with previous knowledge and experience. That night the ship was tossed around like a matchstick. Alfie couldn't see the horizon, but he did see the bottom of a bowl a few times in the night, he lay on his side with it next to his bunk.

The next morning, he got ready for work and just about to leave his cabin, then he heard a noise outside the door. It was someone shouting like a maniac, he listened, "I'm coming for you and when I find you, you're dead!"

Alfie stayed in his cabin and carried on listening. The shouts were getting closer and suddenly there was a knock at his door.

"Just open up man and let me in."

Alfie knew it was the same man that was shouting earlier and decided to keep the door firmly shut. Matt had mentioned to him a few days into the voyage that men lost their minds and went crazy at sea sometimes. It seemed this was a time when the very same was happening. He listened for what seemed like an eternity and stayed put for a while longer. He carried on listening and heard two other voices getting closer to his cabin, they were wrestling with the first voice and as the fracas ensued, he understood they were trying to restrain him.

"John are you OK in there?" Alfie didn't recognise the voice and asked who it was.

"It's OK, John; it's Henry, one of the engineers; we've got him now."

Alfie slowly opened the door seeing the two men with another man who was on his knees with handcuffs behind his back and a wild look in his eyes.

"It happens, some lose their minds at sea and at the next port we will have to get him hospitalised."

Henry looked knowingly at Alfie and then helped the hand-cuffed man to get up steering him towards the cabin used as a cell for this type of event occurring.

Alfie made his way to the galley to help Matt with breakfast, no Matt to be found. He called out but nothing, there was nothing cooking, no bread baked and nothing ready in the Mess for the crew.

Where could Matt be? I'll check his cabin, maybe he's sick.

Alfie was worried and took a particular scene away from his mind.

As he went off in search for Matt, he found himself outside Matt's cabin, the door was ajar. He looked in and what he saw made him throw up immediately. Matt was lain across his bed but had been chopped to pieces, there was blood on every surface and pieces of Matt laying on the floor alongside a huge knife.

"Oh, my God!"

Alfie put his hand to his head trying to take in the sight that was in front of him. He ran along the corridor looking for someone, anyone. Finally, he came back to the Galley and the Mess where men were gathering.

"Where's Matt?" they were asking one another. Alfie flew into the Mess and stood there as white as a ghost.

"Matt's dead," he stuttered the words out, "I've just been to his cabin, someone has killed him!"

The crew members looked at each other, and then when realisation dawned on them, they knew it had been Stu who did it. Stu was the one with a Machete running around the ship in the night finally stopping outside Alfie's cabin. He must have knocked on Matt's door then Matt wondered what the commotion was opened it and was butchered.

Alfie felt sick to his stomach, poor Matt. The Captain came down to the mess and spoke to the men.

"Men, we need to dock at the next port, Stu, as you know, went on the rampage and now Matt is dead. I need you to be sensible and calm. Can a few of you go to Matt's cabin and clean it up. Matt will be buried at sea tomorrow." The men dispersed then the Captain turned around to Alfie.

"John, can you cook for the men until we get to dock where we will need another cook to come on board?" Alfie nodded his head in agreement, he had learned a lot from Matt during the short time onboard but felt he could cope for a few more days. His head was spinning, and his heart was sad at the thought of Matt losing his life.

The next morning, Matt was lain on a wooden board used for sea burials. Over him was draped the flag belonging to the ship, they slid his body into the dark blue water as the Captain read a prayer.

Chapter 10
Short-Order

As the ship neared the docking bay at Duluth, Alfie felt he couldn't go on with the voyage. What had happened on board a few days before had changed his mind about seafaring, this was the opportunity he needed to get off and find something else to help him earn money. What belongings he had he tied up in a bundle including Matt's knife, he left the ship. This was considered 'desertion' until the Seamen's Act of 1915 which meant Alfie had no claim on wages for the time he had been at sea but at least he had been fed and had a bed.

Duluth was bustling. People coming and going, ships docking and sailing. Alfie had some skills now, thanks to Matt, he briefly thought about Matt and smiled for him as he headed into town.

Ahead of Alfie, he could see a little diner called the *Old Red Lion* just past the City Hall and Police station, huge brownstone buildings the like he had only seen recently in New York. He stopped and wondered if the Diner needed a cook. Well, he had his own knife and was ready to work feeling sure he could earn. His luck was in, there was a sign in the window asking for a 'Short-Order Cook' he had no idea what that meant but it had the word *cook*, and he could do that.

He opened the screen door slowly then suddenly the handle slipped from his fingers, it slammed shut behind him.

A tall slim woman with blonde hair and ruby-red lips was behind the counter and shouted out to him.

"Hey, you, yeah, you!" Wilma was looking at Alfie and beckoned him over to the counter.

"Hi, handsome, what can I getcha?" with that she winked.

"I'm looking for work and saw you had a sign in the window." Alfie tried to sound not too desperate but couldn't take his eyes off the beautiful woman in front of him.

The blonde stood back, looked him up and down, then with a soft drawl she said, "Hey, you have an accent there, where ya from?"

Alfie didn't like all these questions, he had to make so much stuff up he was having trouble remembering it all.

"I've come in from New York on the *Sea Spray*."

He raised his eyebrows and smiled at her, she melted. Alfie's good looks may get him into trouble again. He couldn't see it as many men can't, but she had the hots for him alright. After he told her his name, she said his name softly two or three times to herself.

"Well just come round the back of the counter and show me what you can do… John." She was itching to get to grips with the new cook and Alfie knew it.

Customers started to come in, she took their orders. Alfie cooked as best he could for over an hour then asked her if he got the job.

"Yes, you do honey, you got the job alright."

Alfie hadn't even asked what the pay was, she leaned over and whispered in his ear, "You'll get 30 cents an hour too."

The heat from cooking and his tiredness kicked in after about eight hours with a few breaks, he hadn't even found somewhere to stay that night.

"Honey, you got somewhere to put your head down tonight?" Wilma was standing so close to Alfie; he could smell her perfume and felt the heat from her body.

"I haven't thought about it… what's your name?" she turned to him and said in a soft drawl, "why, it's Wilma, honey."

Alfie felt that familiar feeling again he had with Marilyn a few weeks ago at The Jane. He tried to suppress it, but it wouldn't go away.

"Well, I've got a spare room at my house just down the street a bit if you want to rent a room for a while until you get settled."

He accepted the offer, they both walked to her house after the Diner shut at 8:00 p.m.

They turned the corner, her house came into sight, green weather-boarded with a white picket fence. As she unlocked the door, he could see it was a woman living alone, there was no hint of a man in the house. *A good-looking woman like her*, he thought.

I wonder why she lives alone.

Alfie's thoughts were answered with Wilma's voice bringing him back into the room.

"John, I'm widowed, the sea took my Jim six years ago one night, he walked out the door, I never saw him again… he left me with twin daughters, they live with my mother at the weekends and with me in the week. It's Saturday so they're not here."

He felt a moment of excitement course through his veins and following this was a physical reaction he tried to keep from view.

She led Alfie to a little room off the kitchen, it had a small bed and side table, a wardrobe and chair with a white China bowl and jug. It looked like heaven to Alfie after sleeping in a bunk and being thrown around on the open lakes.

"This is your room John; you can stay as long you need somewhere to live. Just one dollar and thirty cents a week are all I ask."

Alfie nodded his agreement.

Setting his belongings down on the chair, he looked around for a moment, Wilma had her eyes on him all the time.

She walked back through to the kitchen and poured them a scotch and water, she didn't ask Alfie what he drank, there was nothing else in the house except water or lemonade. She poured him a large one, his mind wandered back to Marilyn as Wilma held the glass out for his hand.

"Come, sit next to me on the sofa."

Marilyn patted the seat and beckoned him.

"You've got a lovely home here, Wilma," Alfie was looking for conversation, anything other than what he knew she wanted, well, what he wanted too. He wanted comfort, physical release and a bed and thought that was the same for her?

She looked into his eyes, in all her thirty years she had never seen such a handsome man, even Jim didn't come close. She shuddered and put her arm around his neck leaning in to kiss him. He stood up, picked her up and carried her to her bed.

There was no tenderness in their coupling that night, it was hard, almost brutal and with no love. The release for both assuaged their wanting and both fell asleep in each other's arms.

Wilma and Alfie were not an item but the lust for each other ticked the box and so he was content… for a while.

Chapter 11
Moving On

Weeks went by with them sharing work and sharing a bed with no expectations except one morning, when the Diner was opened, a dark, six-foot black guy walked in ordering coffee and pancakes. Wilma gave him the eye straight away. Alfie's back was facing the man, Wilma winked. He returned her wink, and her knees went weak with her blushing profusely. She knew she had the looks that could melt a man but also knew she had the experience to make them want to come back for more, she loved the attention.

"John, pancakes, and coffee for the gentleman."

Wilma spoke to Alfie all business-like, he turned to face her and saw the man sitting there up at the counter checking her over.

Alfie's mind wandered to Marilyn again, *what is it that makes a woman give herself to men one after the other? What are they looking for?*

Then Alfie thought that really, he had no hold over Wilma, she wasn't his to own or keep, indeed not his to love but he felt the jealousy rise in him all the same.

Summer was almost over. The sun shone through the windows of the Diner and bathed everything in its warmth. Wilma loosened her blouse to show her charms a bit more to the man eating his pancakes, he gave another wink to Wilma and tossed the money for his breakfast onto the counter leaving with a smile. After about fifteen minutes, Wilma spoke to Alfie.

"John, I've got to go shopping as we are getting low on flour and milk, I won't be long, and you'll be ok minding the Diner, won't you? We're not that busy right now."

Alfie thought nothing of it and carried on as he nodded his agreement.

Wilma was out the door and hastily walked up the little path towards her house, she saw the car in its driveway, it belonged to a six-foot man who had been in the Diner earlier. She walked round to the stoop behind the house, he was waiting for her on the swing chair, his excitement evident. The girls were at school.

"Didn't think you were gonna make it honey?" he said in a drawl.

"You know it's you and me on a Tuesday and Friday morning, Jeez, I've been aching for you."

Wilma quickly opened the kitchen door and beckoned him in, he started to undress her even before they got to her bedroom, soon he was on her with urgency, Wilma gasped as his weight held her.

She made her way back an hour and thirty minutes later with a bag showing she had been shopping, Alfie wouldn't know until that night what she had been up to that morning. Her mind was on Friday already!

———————

It was getting dusk, and Alfie was ready to go, everything had been washed down and put away. Wilma was just cashing up and walking toward the door. She had been out later in the morning 'on business' leaving him coping with a busy Diner.

They walked together without much conversation towards the house, Alfie had forgotten the girls would have been dropped off as it was Friday night, he wanted Wilma and soon. The girls were already in the house, they had been dropped off and were waiting for their dinner which Wilma had made up at the Diner.

Alfie went to his room but, as he passed Wilma's bedroom he glanced in, the bed was dishevelled and a pair of her panties were on the floor at the bottom of the bed, *Hmm, when we left this morning, her bed was made and nothing on the floor*, he thought to himself.

Once the girls had had their dinner they were bathed and put to bed. Their room contained two identical beds with soft furnishings and was in an adjoining extension to the kitchen so Wilma could have *company* and not worry the girls.

Wilma turned to Alfie, "Scotch?"

She was just ready to pour but Alfie stopped her with his question.

"Guess the six-foot stranger kept you busy lunchtime? When were you going to mention your liaison with the guy at the Diner?"

She spun around with a look of thunder.

140

"How dare you question me in my own house, what I do is none of your business!"

Alfie was getting quite uptight by this time, he blurted out, "You've taken me to your bed on regular occasions and that's not enough? What the hell is this all about Wilma?"

She looked Alfie in the eye and, in a nonchalant voice said, "Listen, honey, if you don't like it, you can find somewhere else that suits you better, don't be fixing to stay with me much longer and don't outstay your welcome!"

He stood and grabbed her arm swinging her round he saw her right breast with a small bite mark. Upon seeing that he walked to his room and gathered his belongings. Echoing in his ears was Wilma cursing him as he walked out the door. The girls heard nothing, Wilma sat with her scotch and thoughts of next Tuesday again…

Chapter 12
Jenny

The Summer of 1913 arrived around the lakes with the usual humidity and heat. Alfie had walked miles from Duluth until he came to another town, *Forest Lake*. A small town but one that he was grateful for, it had quite a few diners and a couple of restaurants. The second one Alfie tried took him on, he took his experience working in Wilma's diner with him then left the thoughts of her behind.

Not having a lot of money but Alfie saved what he could in case something else happened, in the event he had to move on. He managed to get a small room in a guest house owned by a black family that needed the money. Segregation wasn't quite apparent in the town at that time but there weren't that many blacks. Alfie drew his mind back to Matt, Matt was black and really the first black man Alfie had ever talked to or had a friendship with, he smiled at the memories of his friendship and the sadness of Matt's death.

The little room at the top of the house was his for next to nothing as he bought home left overs for the family who were really grateful. The extra gratefulness came in the form of the eldest daughter, she visited his room one night bringing with her everything he wanted and more and on a nightly basis, there was no resistance from him, she was of age and knew what she was doing alright.

Alfie worked hard in the restaurant, he made friends with the others that were working there equally as hard as him. Earning a small wage was better than nothing, he spent a bit and saved a bit.

As the months rolled on Alfie wondered if this would be his life forever, no recollection of the past before New York but his accent gave away the fact that England was in there somewhere, he just needed to unlock it. The reason he was on the *Titanic* wouldn't return to his memory and so he resigned himself to his fate as it was.

Lately, there was news of unrest back in Europe, talk of a potential war between two countries trickled into the newspapers with discussions on people's lips.

The whispers in the restaurant were comments from seated customers nearby, "Doesn't look good," said one guy with a huge moustache.

"Never any peace it seems," answered a large rotund man in a brown suit. Alfie didn't show any interest.

What had Europe got to do with me anyway, he thought.

At that moment, there was a fracas outside the restaurant, Alfie looked out the window. A horse had bolted and trampled a man to death on the street, it was common and not a lot of fuss ensued. Alfie had never seen anything like it and the horror in his eyes was there for one of the customers to see.

"Look Son, don't get yourself upset, happens a lot and ain't no surprise." Alfie heard the words, but the experience stayed with him.

Finishing up one Friday night, he was aware there were two women sitting at a table talking and not making a move to leave the restaurant anytime soon.

One of the waiters went over to them, "Excuse me, ladies; please finish up in the next twenty minutes as we will be closing."

They nodded, one of them swung a look over at Alfie and smiled. He returned the smile; it had been a while since Wilma but he still had the daughter back at his digs.

————

As the two women left the restaurant, one hung back and waited outside. It was clear she was waiting for Alfie to finish work. As he opened the door and took a couple of steps, the one with bright red lipstick and a low-cut blouse was on him.

"Excuse me, I couldn't help noticing you look familiar, almost a double for my ex-boyfriend."

He hadn't heard that one before but let her carry on.

"Is your name Fred?" she asked innocently.

Alfie shook his head and was prepared to carry on walking, but something stopped him.

"I'm going for a drink in that little bar near the police station, would you two ladies like to join me?"

They nodded, put their arms in his and off they went. Alfie smelt their perfume and drowned in red lipstick and deep blue eyes, almost as blue as his.

"I'll have a Scotch and water; the ladies will have…?" He looked at them for an answer.

"Yeah, we'll have beer please."

They found a table, red lipstick told him all about her ex-boyfriend, her early life caring for her mother and younger sisters, a father who deserted and a promise of marriage that didn't happen. The other woman was brunette with brown eyes and was quieter but gave Alfie the eye, he knew he would be taken to heaven at some point.

Alfie told them roughly what he knew as well as his new name, also what happened since the *Titanic* but made the rest up, he figured they wouldn't be checking up on him so not to worry.

"John, are you married? Do you have a girlfriend?" they went on with further questions and only stopped when he held his hand up.

Listen, I just want to have a drink and relax, you haven't told me your names?

"It's Jenny, after my mother, and this here's Rosie."

Red lipstick looked at Alfie's face for approval, there wasn't any, he just nodded instead.

They stayed a couple of hours, and the effects of the drinks on all of them were apparent as they let their guard down.

"John, Rosie has her own apartment, maybe we could go back and get comfortable?" Alfie knew this as an invitation, there was that old familiar feeling again, almost like a devil on one should and an angel on the other… the Devil won and said, "Two ladies; you've hit the jackpot!"

They walked a few blocks to an apartment block with a large green door. Alfie went to heaven with lipstick and Rosie that afternoon.

A few weeks after the double-date, Alfie couldn't stop thinking about Jenny, the one with the red lipstick. He wanted to see her without her friend and, whilst he was working, looked out for her every day. Finally, Friday came one week, she walked in; smiling warmly at Alfie; his stomach lurched at the thought of her next to him only weeks ago.

She sat directly opposite where he was preparing the food and looked over again, he winked, and she smiled; he was in.

She waited for him to finish work, nothing was said, it didn't need to be. As Alfie left work, Jenny walked out with him.

Jenny took Alfie to her home a few blocks away, the crept through the bedroom window at the back of her home. The pull was immediate, she took her clothes off and stood before him, his body ached and that afternoon he didn't leave her for a couple of hours, Jenny was in his mind. As the evening drew to a close, Alfie had to get back to the guest house for some food and rest. He was trying to be the gentleman that only a few hours ago took advantage of Jenny but it's what she wanted too. They slipped out of the bedroom and went to the front of the house, Jenny opened the door to make it look like they had just arrived. Her mother greeted her, then looked surprised.

"Who is this young man Jenny?" slight alarm in her voice, Jenny's mother rocked in her chair just that bit faster than normal.

"Ma, he is someone I met in the restaurant when I was with Rosie. He said he would walk me home to make sure I'm safe." Alfie nodded.

Jenny's mother asked Alfie to sit a while, but he said he would go and, as Jenny said, just seeing her home. Jenny opened the front door, tugged Alfie's sleeve for a kiss.

She had never had a man like Alfie before; her friend Rosie had made fun of her virginity. Rosie saw Alfie and a dare had been put to Jenny in the restaurant.

As Alfie held her, she trembled. He left Jenny with a smile on her face... the devil smiled once more on Alfie's shoulder.

As he made his way to his room in the guest house, he quietly opened his door, the daughter was in bed naked, patting the bed she said, "John, you're one helluva man, come and make me happy." Alfie obliged.

Chapter 13

Gravesend

Emma took Victoria to school and nursed Victor to her breast that morning. Her mind swung to Alfie, her heart heaved and ached for him. Was he still alive and, if he was, why didn't he contact her?

In her mind, she was wanting to move on but the thought of it made her cry, she hugged Victor to her for quite a while and rocked him. The Summer of 1913 and all this time had elapsed with no word from Alfie, there was no way of Emma finding out the list of survivors for quite a while, but she knew there would come a time when she should know but wasn't there just yet wanting that knowledge set in stone.

Ethel looked after Victoria and Victor as best she could under her circumstances whilst Emma worked at the Brockington household. One morning as Emma opened the door to the kitchen below stairs, George was waiting for her. He was growing into a man now, his voice had broken.

"Emma, good morning, tell me something?" She held her breath, he was standing just inside the kitchen as the door opened. He had not spoken to her since the night after Alfie had beaten him and left him for dead, but for some strange reason, he struck up a conversation.

"Have you a husband or man in your life?" She remained calm and came back with her answer.

"George, I have someone, but he is a sailor on a voyage at present."

Emma thought this would be enough to keep George happy, but it didn't seem to work.

"I've never seen him, I thought you were single and would have need of a man to father any children, do you have children, Emma?" Her mind darted to Victor and Victoria.

"Yes, I have two; my mother helps me with them."

She found this line of questioning quite invasive but was being truthful.

"George, I'm going to be late for reporting to Sefton, please let me pass."

He stepped aside but left the smallest of space for her to squeeze past him hoping their bodies might brush against each other. He was that close to her he could smell her perfume and as she brushed against him quickly, he felt the excitement of wanting her.

Emma ran along the small passageway and bumped straight into Sefton. She said her apologies and got busy with the brass and cleaning the fire surrounds in each room.

The library reminded her of the times Lord Brockington tried to molest her, and she shuddered, but with his new mistress, she felt safe in the knowledge that those horrible experiences were history.

As she went upstairs, she knocked on the door, holding his paper and tea tray in the other hand. No answer. She knocked again, still no answer. Emma put the tray down on the hall table, then opened the door to find Lord Brockington dead in his chair!

She shouted out for help, Sefton came up immediately from the kitchen.

"Oh, my God!" Sefton was beside himself and ran over to Lord Brockington, shaking him but there was no life.

"Emma, please go down to Mrs Dawson and tell her, she knows what to do."

With that request, Emma ran down the stairs and then returned with Mrs Dawson who closed Lord Brockington's eyes whilst saying a small prayer.

Lord Brockington's mistress was in her bedroom when the news broke…with George. Without any emotion whatsoever he went into his father's study and just stood there, *looks like I'm Lord Brockington now*, he smiled to himself. She didn't shed a tear, as far as she was concerned, he was an old man that gave her money and looked after her to look after him in a way that repulsed her but her and George had been more than close since she joined the household, and she was twelve years his senior!

Her mind went into overdrive, *Would I still be able to stay here?* She thought to herself. This question was answered in no uncertain terms when George closed the door to her bedroom and proceeded to enjoy himself with her and his father not even cold!

At the funeral, there were several people Emma didn't know but all the household were there, George and his father's current wife as well as Sefton. It was a small affair and over within an hour. The wake was held at the Brockington home.

That evening, after the funeral, George gathered all the household staff, including Emma and gave them notice to quit. He wanted none of his father's retainers and had thoughts of starting anew. The only person he didn't fire was Sefton. He knew he could rely on this Butler but also Sefton had many secrets that may come in handy in the future.

Emma went to Library Cottage; Victoria was playing in the garden with Victor fast asleep in his cot.

"I have no job now," Emma told Ethel what had happened after the funeral of Lord Brockington.

"Don't worry Emma, you and the children can move in with me for a while until things get better and money starts to come in then you can go back to your house."

Emma smiled at Ethel and so stayed there at Library Cottage taking in washing and ironing.

Chapter 14
1913

Emma made more money looking after an elderly gentleman in a cottage the next street away in Clarendon Road than she did at the Brockington's. His wife had died some years previously and his stroke had caused some loss of movement in his right arm. He was glad of the help, Emma was glad of the money.

As Spring turned into summer, Emma saw Victor take his first steps whilst Victoria was growing up into quite the little lady. She sat quietly in the kitchen with her thoughts that always went back to Alfie.

God, I miss him so much, my heart tells me he is still alive, but my head is saying move on, she looked over at Ethel.

"Emma, you would have heard something by now, have you not enquired as to the list of passengers from the ship?"

Ethel wanted her daughter to find a new love and help her bring up the children, but Alfie was firmly locked in her heart.

"Mother I can't help myself; I don't feel ready to move on without absolutely knowing whether Alfie is dead or alive and no, I haven't seen the passenger list yet… it's too final for me, I can't do it."

With those words, she burst into tears.

One morning, a few months later, after Emma fed the children, she helped to wash Ethel and finally sit down to eat breakfast, there was a knock at the door. She opened it, there stood a man no older than her, he had curly brown hair and a happy smile, he had a bundle of clothing in his arms.

"Good morning, you're the lady that takes in washing, aren't you?" Emma nodded and asked for the name so she doesn't get the laundry mixed up.

"It's Gregson, Mrs Gregson from Perry Street. I'm her son, Arthur." Emma smiled; it had been a long time since she had.

She took the bundle telling Arthur to come back in two days' time, time enough for the washing to dry and her to iron it.

Emma liked the look of Arthur, she tried to suppress her thoughts which were taking her somewhere she had not been since Alfie was with her. As the day wore on, she found herself with Arthur stuck in her head, he just wouldn't leave.

The next morning, she still had Arthur in her head. Emma made herself busy and checked the washing, some had dried overnight but other things needed a bit longer. Ironing as she went, her thoughts turned to Alfie, her heart ached.

Chapter 15

Arthur

Wednesday morning came, Emma got herself ready after feeding the children and seeing to Ethel. She knew she would see Arthur and busied herself with him stuck firmly in the front of her mind.

Suddenly the knock at the door shook her from her daydream.

"Good morning, Emma." Arthur's voice made her weak at the knees, a feeling she hadn't experienced in such a long time.

She opened the door feeling the physical pull to him.

"You had better come in, Arthur; I have just a couple of pieces left to iron, please sit down."

Emma felt herself blush slightly.

"Emma, my mother is struggling to keep on top of the housework, do you know anyone that would be willing to help her? It's just a bit of cleaning and dusting really."

Emma felt herself wanting to say yes but she hesitated and thoughts of being near Arthur she tried to suppress.

"It would only be for a few hours a week and would give someone extra money."

Arthur had a small ulterior motive but wanted to make sure his mother had assistance as his work took him away for days at a time, he was a smuggler on the Kent coast, no one knew about his 'work.'

Emma took on the cleaning for Arthur's mother just on a Tuesday and Friday afternoon, coupled with seeing to the children and Ethel, she had enough on her plate to keep money coming in to support them.

One Tuesday afternoon, she was cleaning one of the bedrooms at Mrs Gregson's and heard the front door open. She went to the top of the narrow staircase peering down. It was Arthur. She could hear him call out to his mother and the faint answer of her from the kitchen.

Arthur had a large bag in his hands and took it into the kitchen. Emma came downstairs once she had finished, she couldn't believe her eyes! On the kitchen table, there was butter, milk, bread, meat, eggs, fruit and two bottles of brandy, her mouth dropped open!

"Emma, I've bought extra for you and the children, it doesn't look much, but you are more than welcome to it."

Arthur looked at her smiling, something inside her melted.

"Arthur that's so kind, I just couldn't really… I…"

He scooped up half a dozen eggs, a pound of butter and some fruit for her.

"Please take it but, before you do, I have something to ask of you, can you come into the parlour so we can chat?"

She felt herself walking on air into the Parlour with Arthur behind her, he closed the door as they entered.

"Emma, I've had nothing but you on my mind night and day. You have consumed my every waking thought, I want you."

They were standing a few feet apart; she felt a hot blush of her cheeks and her stomach flipped for just a minute. She hadn't known a physical event since Alfie left all that time ago.

"Arthur, I don't know… I haven't thought…" her words trailed off as he held his hand out and took hers. Tenderly he held her in his arms, his mouth sought hers with her kiss returned to him.

Suddenly she backed away from him but then went limp as he pursued her mouth more eagerly. When they stopped kissing, he spoke in her ear.

"Emma, I want you to be my wife, I will love and cherish you and your children and treat them as my own, your mother will want for nothing, we can have a happy family life, please say yes."

Emma's heartbeat quickened, she wanted to say yes but Alfie was in the back of her mind, as always.

Arthur put his finger on Emma's lips, "Don't say yes just now, think about my offer and let me know soonest, my heart is yours."

Arthur was serious and, with his words uttered, he turned and walked out of the room leaving Emma with her mouth open and a heavy breath that heaved her chest.

That night, after she had left Mrs Gregson's and Arthur she walked back to Library Cottage, the children and Ethel.

"You know love again Emma, I can see it in your eyes." Ethel knew that look; the look Emma had when she had fallen for Alfie.

Chapter 16
Decision

Emma tossed and turned that night. It was the Autumn of 1913, getting cooler as she lay and thought of nothing but Arthur.

What if Alfie is still alive? How can I marry someone if Alfie comes back? but then I'm not married to Alfie, Gradually, she fell asleep until the sun arose, it shined through her little bedroom window.

"Mother, I'm going to the shipping office to see if I can find further information about Alfie."

Ethel turned around from her bath chair and nodded in agreement.

"I do hope you find peace Emma, has Arthur asked you to marry him?"

Ethel knew the answer but wanted to hear it from Emma.

"Yes, he has, I want to say yes… but Alfie."

Emma was close to tears again but turned and walked down to the shipping office in search of the truth.

———————

As she walked up the rickety wooden steps that peeled their paint, Emma knocked on a door that had a pane of glass missing with a brass door handle.

"Come in!"

The words were shouted from inside the office, there was a desk, chair, and a man with overflowing paperwork strewn about.

"What can I do for you?" he was officious and looked Emma up and down, admiring her.

"I'm enquiring about the sinking of the *Titanic* and the passenger list."

Emma felt as though she almost didn't want to know *but it's different this time, Arthur has asked me to marry him,* her mind and body want to say *yes.*

"Well, let me look, it's been a while since that event, I just need to move a few things to get to the list, can you give me his name please?"

Emma speaking Alfie's name bought a lump to her throat, but she forced it out.

"Alfie Ryan."

The name was out which sent the man searching through a lot of paperwork. She was still standing almost half an hour later when he spoke.

"Ah-ha!" he made her jump, but it got her attention.

"His surname, Ryan?"

"Yes, Alfie Ryan."

Emma confirmed again and waited.

"It appears he went down with the ship; I'm sorry."

Upon hearing this news, she sobbed and hurriedly left the office.

On her way back to the cottage, she stopped off first at the docks watching as ships docked with men unloading the cargo, she thought back to when she first saw Alfie, her heart melted and then she realised that the love she had for Alfie would have to be just a beautiful memory with the child and sister he left with her being constant reminders of their love.

The next morning, after a sleepless night of crying, it was her usual trip to Mrs Gregson's to do the few hours of cleaning. She had cried that night for Alfie but when she awoke, Arthur was in her mind and almost in her heart where Alfie had been for a long time.

Emma knocked on the door, Arthur answered it. He had tears in his eyes and blurted out that his mother had had a stroke, she was admitted into Gravesend hospital very poorly.

"When did this happen?"

Emma walked behind Arthur into the Parlour.

"It was late last night, she was in the kitchen and collapsed, the right side of her face was sagging."

Arthur had tears again, Emma wiped one away with her finger, he reached out and held her close. Part of Arthur wanted her, but this wasn't the time.

"When will you visit her Arthur?" Emma wasn't sure what else to say, Arthur seemed slightly distant but was still holding her. Gently he kissed her again and suddenly with an urgency that told her that he needed her that moment.

"Arthur, I... shouldn't we... wait?" Her words fell on deaf ears, he did not more than sweep her up in his arms, took her to the sofa and lay her down, her eyes filled, his attentions made her scream out in ecstasy. She held his hair whilst his mouth sought her lips then her bosom. But he did not rush, he took her hand, they went upstairs to his bedroom where he lay her down and that morning, they became one.

"Will you marry me, Emma?" He whispered in her ear, she found herself saying 'yes' and then abandoned herself to him.

Chapter 17
Conflict

As time went by Arthur's mother passed within a few months of her stroke, World War I had started at the end of July 1914.

Arthur was sent to France and Emma found herself alone with the children and Ethel. She pleaded with him to come home safely crying a lake as he left to join up. Briefly, she turned her thoughts to Alfie, but it only lasted a few moments.

The war raged on, with many men killed. More than two million soldiers from the United States fought on battlefields in France from 1917, one of them was Alfie Ryan.

For Alfie, he felt an affinity with the Americans, he was saved by Americans, he worked with Americans, and had spent some special times with Americans. But when the time came for him to join up, he didn't hesitate. World War I was the first time in American history that the United States sent soldiers abroad to defend foreign soil. The Americans didn't join World War I until 1917 however, the British and French were fatigued after such a long and arduous time of fighting and dying. Arthur Gregson went to the Front at the start of the war and died just a few months later.

Alfie found himself on the battlefields of France, experiencing death first-hand, seeing more than his fair share of the atrocities of war. His comrades only knew him as John, there was still no memory of the life Alfie had known before that fateful night, just a hint of his accent mixed with an American twang.

One night, asleep in a field with others, Alfie awoke to the sound of shells exploding. Nearby, there were some farm outbuildings where Alfie and his comrades ran for shelter not realising that it could be fateful. Alfie found himself in a small shed with the others finding shelter in adjacent buildings. Suddenly, shells were falling all around them. Alfie's building took a direct hit. He woke up in a field hospital with a large shrapnel wound to his leg, his comrades were not so lucky, they all died of appalling injuries when a shell hit two barns close together.

———

Emma found herself looking out of the tiny bedroom window of Library Cottage once more, thoughts of Arthur interspersed with Alfie drove through her mind. One big question was *would Arthur come back to her when the war was over*. She put herself in situations like *how life would be when Arthur returned* and *how will I live life in the event he didn't*. They didn't have time to get married, she would not be classed as a widow, she wrote to him every few months expecting an acknowledgement; no replies and so she resigned herself to the fact that maybe he wasn't receiving them or *was he dead already?*

Chapter 18
1918

It was called the 'Spanish flu' as the first reported cases were in Spain. During World War I, newspapers were censored (Germany, the United States, Great Britain, and France all had media blackouts on news that might lower morale) so although there were influenza (flu) cases elsewhere, it was the Spanish cases that hit the headlines. One of the first casualties was the King of Spain. Spain was neutral and not involved in the war so had a 'free hand' to report the awful pandemic that was engulfing the world.

The wearing of face coverings had not been mentioned in England when the Pandemic first came to light.

Victoria enjoyed school but little Victor was too young to attend just yet and one day, at the end of the war, she ran into the kitchen all excited and handed Emma an envelope from the school.

"Mother, there is a rhyme that children are saying at break time; can I tell it to you?"

Emma stopped washing up in the sink, turned and smiled, although she wasn't Victoria's mother, she loved that the little girl wanted to call her that.

"Yes, Vicki what is it?"

Victoria liked Emma calling her by her nickname instead of the formal *Victoria*. Victoria stood up straight and recited what she had learned.

"I had a little bird
Its name was Enza
I opened the window,
And in-flu-enza."

Emma laughed quietly as Ethel was asleep in the bath chair for the second time that day which Emma felt wasn't normal, it was happening a lot these past few days.

She opened the envelope, it read "*There will be no school until further notice due to Influenza contagions.*" Just one line with no signature. A neighbour next door but one had died of the flu as it raged through Gravesend, Emma tried to hide this event in the back of her mind, but it still hovered nearby.

As she sat at the kitchen table, again her thoughts turned to Arthur, there had been no communication from him or the war office the past four years, troops were now coming home, each day; she hoped, but still no word.

Ethel woke up suddenly, she coughed then a deep guttural sound came out like a gurgling, Emma swung round to see her struggling to breathe and turning blue.

"Mother, what is it? Can I get the doctor?"

Emma rushed over to the bath chair and felt Ethel's forehead, it was burning hot, and her eyes were rolling.

Quickly she grabbed Victoria's hand whilst little Victor was asleep in his makeshift bed having his afternoon nap. The Doctor's house was in the next street; Emma ran as fast as she could whilst Victoria's feet were almost not touching the ground trying to keep up.

She ran up the path to the Doctor's house with its black shiny door and gold door furniture, knocking as loudly as she could whilst holding a sob back.

The Doctor answered the door with tears in his eyes which stopped Emma in her tracks.

"She's gone, she's gone," it was all he could say between heaving sighs and tears. Emma could only take this declaration as being the Doctor's wife.

"Doctor, I need you to come and see my mother, she has a temperature and has started coughing really bad, please come quick!"

The Doctor looked at her like she was delivering a death sentence.

"I can't come, no one can, don't you realise we will all be dying soon anyway?"

His words cut through her like a knife.

"But please, my mother is terribly ill, she may have…" He shut the door in Emma's face before she could finish the sentence. The pandemic caused many to act unnaturally, with stress and fright.

There was no one else that could help so her slow walk back to Library Cottage, holding Victoria's hand enveloped her with thoughts of losing her mother to the influenza outbreak. Walking up the path towards the front door, she paused and gathered herself.

I won't let her know that she may be facing her own death, I can't do it, I can't.

Emma held her tears back walking into the kitchen.

Standing in the doorway, she was faced with the picture of her mother slumped in the bath chair... it was as quick as that. Another statistic. Apparently, within hours of feeling the first symptoms of fatigue, fever and headache, some victims would rapidly develop pneumonia and start turning blue, signalling a shortage of oxygen. They would then struggle for air until they suffocated to death. These horrendous symptoms could not be stopped.

Hospitals were overwhelmed. Doctors and nurses worked to breaking point, although there was little they could do as there were no treatments for the flu and no antibiotics invented to treat pneumonia.

By the end of the pandemic, only one region in the entire world had not reported an outbreak: an isolated island called Marajo, located in Brazil's Amazon River Delta. Over 50 million people died worldwide, and a quarter of the British population were affected. The death toll was 228,000 in Britain alone.

There was no money to provide Ethel with a decent burial, she was lying to rest in a pauper's grave along with many others. The churchyards were overflowing with flu victims and the hospitals the same. Emma sat in the kitchen with the children playing around her totally unaware that they and their mother were now alone in the world.

"Mother, when can I go to school?" this and many other questions were asked of Emma. Victoria had such an inquisitive mind too; Emma didn't know what to say and just hugged her stepdaughter kissing her on the head as she did. Minutes later there was a knock at the door.

Chapter 19
News

Emma opened the door, there stood a postman holding out a brown envelope. He held it out with sadness on his face. Delivering so many in the four years of the war, he rarely found anything to smile about.

Emma bit her lip to stop herself crying, he could see she was struggling.

"Miss, it seems the letter has been lost for quite a while and eventually found, it came from France."

He didn't know what else to say.

She thanked him and shut the door. Her mind raced, so did her heart as she sat at the kitchen table and opened the envelope, she noticed the date on the letter had 1914, *surely not four years since it was posted?* Emma couldn't understand.

The letter was full of love, she read and cried.

My Dearest Emma,

I don't know when you'll receive this letter, but I am sending it with hope in my heart and love for you.

In a few days, we will be sent to the Front, I'm not sure what to expect but all the boys are scared, frightened and anxious. We've heard stories already and so must maintain the courage to fight.

How is little Victoria, Victor, and your mother? I do hope they are in good health. When we said goodbye, I wanted to cry, but as a man, we must maintain the 'stiff upper lip,' my heart was crying inside though.

I'm so sorry we didn't get a chance to marry before I got the order to go to France, when I'm home we will have the most beautiful wedding my girl, and the children will have a father.

Now my sweetheart, think of me when you go to your bed, and I will do the same, I can almost feel you next to me. I'll write again soon my darling girl,

Arthur

By the time Emma finished reading the letter she already had tears running down her face, the thought of Arthur facing his fears, fighting for England and the possibility he would not be coming home, but the 1914 postmark.

How come no other letters? Is he alive or stuck somewhere and can't come home? She had so many unanswered questions until the following Tuesday and another brown envelope was delivered.

The letter confirmed her worse fears, Arthur had died on the Front in an epic battle with the Germans alongside his comrades... in 1915.

Chapter 20

New Horizons

After the war had ended and life was trying to get back to near normal particularly after the Flu pandemic, the many that had died with the Spanish Flu and all those that perished in France during the war had made a huge dent in the population. Emma needed to work to support herself and the children. Her years in service were behind her but gave her the experience she needed when she applied to become a Housekeeper in Higham, near Rochester.

The advert in the *Kent Messenger* was asking for a Housekeeper and someone with Service experience to live in. Emma hadn't thought about moving, the cottage was all she had except for the house that belonged to Alfie and that was rented out, it would mean uprooting the children, but money was money. She had thoughts of selling Library Cottage but put that aside deciding to rent it out instead, if she had to relocate, all these things would have to be considered carefully. She wrote a letter to the address on the advert, *Mr R. Southby, 29 Falstaff Grove, Higham, Near Rochester, Kent.*

No sooner was the letter posted than a new Ford car pulled up outside Library Cottage, in it was a gentleman wearing a brown suit and matching Derby hat. His moustache was neat and trimmed, Emma noticed all these things about him, his age must have been early to late 30s. She was peeking through the window to see who it was not recognising him, she couldn't help but look.

He stepped out of the car and walked up the garden path towards the kitchen door, he stood and gave two small knocks. Emma opened the door and saw the blueness of his eyes which made her blush and remembered the last time she saw eyes that blue; it was Alfie's.

"Good morning, madam. Could I speak with Emma Stedman please?" Emma almost stuttered her reply.

"You're speaking with her, and your name is?"

"Mr Ronald Southby," came his deep-voiced reply. His voice almost reverberated through Emma, she blushed.

He was a good-looking man and no denying that, she thought.

"Please come in and take a seat, I'll just settle my son in his day bed."

Emma picked up Victor and placed the sleepy little boy down.

"Mrs Stedman I..." before he could finish Emma corrected him about the status of being married. Ronald apologised for assuming.

"May I call you Emma then?" he said enquiring, hoping they could be on more informal terms in the back of his mind.

"Yes, that's fine," Emma was on her guard but equally wanted to know more about this man sitting in her kitchen.

"You sent me a letter responding to my advert, I wanted to speak with you regarding same."

His tone was slightly formal, but she felt it was sincere. Emma got up to make tea and asked him if he would join her, he accepted, watching her as she moved about the kitchen. His admiring glances were not seen as her back was to him.

Pouring the tea out, Emma listened as he gave her the requirements for the post she applied for and asked her if this were something she would be willing to take on; Emma paused.

"Your advert mentioned 'live-in' do you still require this?"

Emma was hoping his reply was *No* but almost in the back of her mind she wanted to hear *Yes*.

"Yes, that would be a requirement I'm afraid, I have an elderly mother that needs personal care."

Emma said she had looked after her own mother for many years, this was greeted with a smile.

"When can you start?" Ronald was eager as his struggles trying to juggle the house, his mother and work were weighing heavy on him.

"You haven't given me time to think about your proposal, but I need to work and have the experience you need, I will say *Yes* but will require a couple of weeks to rent my cottage out and get Victoria's school changed. Do you have enough space for me and my children?"

Emma crossed her fingers behind her back.

"Yes, there is an annex to the house where you will find all the comforts your own home has. I will expect to see you in two weeks, Emma."

With that, he got up, bid her good morning then left in his car.

Emma's mind was a whirl as she knew leaving the cottage was a wrench but there is a life ahead of her and the ability to earn money to keep her and the children. She knew it was the right thing to do.

She advertised the cottage in the *Kent Messenger*, within a few days, there were three applicants. Emma wanted someone that would look after the cottage as the possibility of having to return may come along in the future. A Mr Worthington, and his wife Enid, were very eager and provided a reference with three months' rent in advance, they were very keen indeed.

Victoria and Victor were excited by the move, they were children and didn't have the memories or the love for the Cottage like Emma. She started to pack their belongings and by the end of week two Emma was finished. The night before the move she looked out of the bedroom window once more, thinking back to her childhood with her mother and father, the happiness then and afterwards when Albert was there, the awful situation she found with him being there… and still being there. Her mother, Ethel, sadly no longer with her, and finally, Alfie drifted into her mind.

I'll never get over him, he is in my heart and always will be. She shed a few tears for her, for Alfie, for her mother then finally fell asleep.

Chapter 21

Memories

Alfie decided to visit England after the war had ended, possibly to see if his memory would be jogged and sense would return to his mind. Whilst back in Forest Lake he had managed to purchase a small weather-boarded cottage with three bedrooms, but at this time his thoughts were with England and so put the cottage at the back of his mind.

He wasn't sure where he would lay his hat but when the boat he was picked up in bought him to the white cliffs of Dover, he was thankful. He found the *Mission to Seafarers* and enquired if they could help him before he found work. As Alfie was a seafarer back on the Great Lakes, they agreed he could stay for a short time.

He settled in his room laying on the bed for a while falling into a deep sleep. Like many that returned from the Great War, he started to have flu-like symptoms just before he arrived at the Seafarers Mission and, one morning, awoke to intense pain in his chest, feeling like he couldn't breathe, he tried to get up, but it was no use, he had a fever with the pain and just lay there slipping in and out of sleep for at least two days, no one in the Mission knew he was ill and assumed he wanted to be alone. When he finally awoke, he was able to move about the room, he drank what seemed like a gallon of water and looked in the mirror.

Wow that was some kind of illness, he said to himself as he rubbed his chin bristles not knowing what caused it, but it became apparent soon after that he wasn't the only one, the flu had followed him. He felt weak but needed something to eat, managing to get some clothes on and without a shave or anything he made his way to the dining hall. Whilst there he scanned the local newspaper for jobs.

He found an advert for a cook at the relatively new *Nayland Rock* hotel in Margate. He wrote to them and posted the letter that afternoon. A few days later a letter arrived at the Seafarers Mission asking him to be there by lunchtime Friday as they had many to see but were interested in his experience due to staff shortage and the pandemic. No sooner said than done he packed what little he owned and made his way to Margate.

After a discussion with the hotel owner, he found himself renting one of the staff quarters rooms there. The sea air was pleasurable to him, there was a calmness that descended over Alfie since his time in the War. He had only sustained a deep scar on his leg, but his mind was intact, unlike many of the men, he was starting to feel better.

He found himself thinking about his life in America, the women, friends, and experiences all of which were making memories, but he had no recollection of where he came from or any previous life and try as he might those recollections were still not forthcoming.

He started work in the kitchens which were busy, and time flew for him.

One Sunday afternoon on his day off, Alfie walked along the Promenade towards the lighthouse where he sat for quite some time, the sun was warm touching his face which made him close his eyes momentarily. A young blonde woman smiled as she got closer to him, Alfie smiled back and felt the urges he hadn't felt since before the war.

"Good morning."

The words came out automatically, she stopped and turned pretending she didn't know it was him who spoke.

"Good morning to you."

He no sooner spoke again than she turned and walked back to sit on the Promenade steps with him, it took her all of five seconds. He studied her face, lips, and eyes. Then his eyes went south, she flushed as he looked up to speak.

"I'm John, and your name is?" Alfie wanted dialogue with this young lady, she felt the same.

"It's Margaret, Margaret Donnelly." Something in Alfie stopped for a moment, his mind knew a Margaret but couldn't remember why or when.

"That's a beautiful name, do you live in Margate?"

Alfie wanted to know more about her, was she married or single, did she have parents, siblings? She answered all his questions and the most important one was the status of not being married.

"I live with my parents John; I also work at the *Seabathing Hospital* as a Nurse."

The hospital was only a stone's throw from the *Nayland Rock*. She looked at him, her heart melted into his eyes.

"Can I buy you a cup of tea somewhere nearby?"

Alfie wasn't sure what to say, her beauty captivated him and his longing for the company of a woman was foremost in his mind, it had been a long time.

They walked along the Promenade towards a little tea shop near Hawley Street. A table for two just inside the door, situated in a bay window, gave them privacy, their conversation steered towards the niceties of the day and nothing else, but Alfie wanted to know more.

"John, tell me all about America and your time there."

He proceeded to tell her about his event on the *Titanic* although sketchy in places. His trip on a ship around the Great Lakes, working with Matt and what happened to Matt caused him to leave his employment. He briefly touched on time spent in Duluth and eventually how he came to be in World War I for the last year of it at least.

Margaret listened intently, she showed interest and smiled a lot as he spoke. Alfie wanted to see her again and asked if he could, she nodded.

"My next day off is Saturday John, thanks for the tea and biscuits, I've got to be off as I'm on shift tonight."

She got up to leave, he touched her hand, she smiled just before she left.

"Meet me at the lighthouse, 2:00 p.m. next Saturday?"

She nodded and agreed as she made her way out of the door.

Alfie smiled inside; he hadn't felt like this in what seemed like an eternity but next Saturday was looking good to him. As he went to work in the kitchens, he felt uplifted and certain about his future, his mind rested on the name Margaret, why? He wasn't sure, but he felt sure the answer would be in his head soon enough.

In the kitchens, he worked with three other men, peeling vegetables, washing pots and pans, it was endless work, but he was able to support himself. Part of him wanted to be back in America, it was so different to what it was in Margate.

Is it the excitement I need? Really, I just want to remember my life before New York, his mind wandered as he worked.

Suddenly, there was an almighty crash, Alfie was on the floor of the kitchen under one of the cupboards. It was top-heavy after the removal of quite a few boxes of crockery which one of the other men had done. He lay still for a long time, unconscious.

Everyone in the kitchen ran to help him, they thought he was dead but, of course, just concussed. He was taken to the *Seabathing*, Margaret was on duty.

As he was wheeled into the triage area and checked, it was decided he was to be moved to the new wing in the west of the hospital. Margaret saw him being wheeled in.

"John!" she ran over to him and stood by his bedside where the doctor was checking him over.

"What happened to him, doctor?"

She was beside herself and didn't realise that that one meeting only days ago would make her feel like she had attached to him already.

"He had an accident at work, I believe he is deeply unconscious." Margaret held her tears back and kept herself in check.

Nurses must maintain distance and not get too involved, she said silently to herself, but her heart wanted him.

Alfie was still in the land of the living, Margaret tended him at every chance she got; still, he remained in a deep unconsciousness.

Over the weeks towards Christmas, Margaret talked to him every day, every time she was near him and, indeed, on her rest days, still he didn't recover consciousness.

Then, one sunny January morning, Alfie's eyes opened. He looked around him, *where am I and who are all these people in beds, why am I here?* Alfie's memory started to return.

Chapter 22

Moving Forward

Margaret came to the ward where Alfie was and went straight over to him.

"John, I'm so glad you're awake, I've been worried for you." Margaret's general concern made him feel good that someone cared; he held his hand out to her.

Margaret took it and looked into his eyes, "Hopefully, you'll be out of here soon, John." Alfie couldn't believe it; he had been unconscious for weeks!

Over the passing days, he returned to his normal self with the nurses help and Margaret doing a wonderful job looking after him. It was time for him to leave the hospital and return to work. Margaret came to his bedside, they talked.

"Margaret, I hardly know you, yet I want to get to know you, let's meet soon for tea and, maybe, we can walk down to the beach for a while when I've been discharged." Her face lit up, she hurriedly agreed; he wanted to tell her his real name.

Alfie returned to the *Nayland Rock*; all the staff welcomed him back. His room was in disarray, but he ensured to tidy up before he met Margaret for tea, he still had yearnings for female company and was sure she would be agreeable!

His morning shift complete, Alfie strolled along the Promenade towards the little tearoom in Hawley Street, where he saw Margaret waiting outside. They went in and sat at the same little table in the bay window as before.

"Margaret, what are you doing this afternoon?"

He didn't want it sounding too formal and followed his request with a gentle grip on her arm and a smile she couldn't resist.

"John, I'd love to be with you a while longer, but it can only be for an hour or so as I'm on duty later this evening."

They both drank their tea and walked back along the Prom towards the *Nayland Rock*. Alfie took her to his staff quarters, not *The Grand* he thought, but comfortable enough. She felt a bit awkward; she had not divulged that at the age of twenty-two she was still a virgin, Alfie thought that this might be the case but later wasn't so sure.

He beckoned her to sit down on the only chair he had and asked her if she wanted another drink, she turned the drink down, her mind was a mess, and many questions were racing through it.

"Margaret, I want you, do you know what I mean by that?"

Alfie blurted the words out, not sure if she would agree or run but they were out of his lips now.

"John, I've wanted you from the moment we met."

With that, he removed his shirt, she looked at his fit and muscly physique. She had seen a naked man before but that was her secret. He walked over to her taking her hand in his, they kissed, the passion took them over. She found her clothing on the floor standing naked in front of him. He wept inside as he remembered the last time, he made love before the War, he was still a young man with needs and frustrations, he would be very gentle. They were in each other's arms for what seemed like an eternity. She cried as he made love to her, something in Alfie made him feel she had known a man before, he put it out of his mind, she fell in love with Alfie Ryan right then and there.

That afternoon, after Margaret had left him, Alfie slept with several dreams. He dreamt of a dockyard with boats, his dreams had people but no faces, he was hugged, he had a mother; he had a father. His dreams saw him toss and turn and after many hours he woke up in a sweat. When he sat on the edge of the bed the name *Margaret* came back to him with another name very distant, he could just make it out… Emma!

Chapter 23
Higham

The two weeks were up. It was time to move from Gravesend to Higham with the children plus their belongings. A car pulled up outside as Emma was dressing the children, trying to get them ready. It was the same car that arrived a few weeks before. She looked out of the kitchen window, Ronald Southby was standing there waiting for her. Emma was talking herself into keeping it formal, matter of fact and conducting herself appropriately whilst at a place of work, something she had to do in her earlier life at Lord Brockington's!

Ronald Southby walked up to the kitchen door knocking gently. She opened the door and smiled; his smile captured her. As he helped load the car, the children ran around in the garden.

"Children come on; we must go now."

Emma started to stifle tears as she knew she was leaving the cottage and its memories, she pinched herself to stop the flow.

"Emma, you won't regret working for me, you and the children will be incredibly happy indeed."

Ronald smiled to himself, *I can conduct my private life and still show I am socially acceptable with a wife and children... or can I?*

The car found itself heading towards *Higham*, a little village near *Rochester* on the outskirts of *Gravesend*, quite a famous village due to Charles Dickens who lived there at one time.

Turning into a little lane, it went a few hundred yards then on the left she saw a beautiful cottage with an annex, *this was it,* Emma thought to herself. Ronald parked the car near some trees and helped Emma with the children and their belongings to get settled in the Annex.

"Emma, my mother, and I will see you all for tea in a few hours, get yourself settled in and please join us about 4:30 p.m."

Emma nodded and hurriedly took the children into the Annex.

It was decorated beautifully; the children had their own bedrooms as did Emma. The kitchen was furnished to a high standard, and the parlour was typical Victorian, something Emma was used to. It felt homely, she knew all would be fine.

––––––––

Teatime came, Emma took the children with her to the house and knocked on the front door. Ronald answered ushering them into the Parlour. Mrs. Southby was in her bathchair at a separate table nearby, she smiled and beckoned them to sit, it made Emma think back to her own Mother in a similar bathchair.

"Ronald tells me you have no other family Emma, just the children."

"Yes, that's right, Mrs Southby; just me and the two little ones." Emma wasn't prepared to offer more at this stage as she hardly knew either Mrs Southby or her son.

"I'm glad you are with us; Ronald has struggled to manage me and the house, plus work."

Emma nodded and smiled then started to feed the children. Once tea was over, she told Mrs Southby the children have their bedtime, Mrs Southby smiled and instantly fell asleep.

That night, Emma put the children to bed and contented herself with sitting in the parlour of the Annex. There was a gentle knock at a little, white-painted wooden door next to the fireplace. It opened slowly, Ronald stood there and asked to come in for a while as he had things to discuss.

The Annex was built a few hundred years ago being used for Smugglers off the Kent coast to escape or find shelter if they were being pursued. It had a few more doors that led to the main house, Ronald was using one of them into the Parlour.

"Emma, in the morning could you start with washing and housework, then prepare the dinner? I will be going to work and shouldn't be home until about 4:00 p.m."

Emma agreed and proceeded to show him out, he stopped her. She looked confused at him.

"I have to say, Emma, I am attracted to you, I haven't had a woman in my life for an exceptionally long time and was instantly drawn to you when I first saw you at your home."

Emma's mouth dropped in astonishment as he spoke. Ronald apologised that he may be too forward. Emma reassured him.

"Ronald, shouldn't we keep this business-like? I thought I was working for you?"

He smiled and turned to go to the door then looked back.

"Emma, I'm not in a rush, I just wanted you to know how I feel, please don't be worried."

Emma let him out, shut the little door and made her way to her bedroom. It was cosy, she felt the bed, firm but with give in it. She hung her clothes near the dressing table. There was a tiny, white-painted door next to the little fireplace, just big enough to get through if you crouched a bit. She tried the handle, it appeared locked. Giving it no mind, Emma went to bed and slept deeply but not before she lay awake for a long time, the men that came into her head, Alfie, Arthur and now Ronald. She needed a father for her children, a decent, kind man that would care for her and them, *would it be Ronald?*

The next morning she busied herself with getting the children ready for school, Victoria was turning into a right little madam having the odd tantrum and Victor was starting school soon. In and out of the seasons with years slipping by, she looked back, back to the love of her life, back to Alfie, the tears sprung.

Emma made her way back to the house; it was empty except for Mrs Southby; she began to get herself busy with the chores before seeing to her employer's mother.

Time flew by, soon she found herself getting Victoria from school. She bathed the children in the huge tin bath hanging in the kitchen which reminded her of Library Cottage, she fed them, put them to bed before and went to the house where she started cooking for the Southby's.

Just as she closed the front door of the Annex and made her way to the main house, she heard Ronald's car pull up, she watched him get out. There was no doubt in her mind he was a handsome man, he had a kind face and smile, she found herself daydreaming ever so slightly.

He saw her looking out of the kitchen window, he talked to her through it, "Emma, can I speak with you?"

She ushered him into the kitchen. She wasn't alarmed at this point but felt her personal space was being slightly compromised as she could almost feel his breath on her neck.

He stood next to her whilst she started to peel vegetables in the kitchen, he stopped her and took her hand.

"I haven't been able to get you out of mind Emma; I feel such a fool for saying any of this, but I profess I am very keen on you." Emma blushed as he held her hand, she didn't pull away.

He gently put his hand around her neck and pulled her to him, he felt no resistance but a reciprocal kiss. Moving closer he held her around the waist and the kisses became more passionate, suddenly there was a shout from the parlour, upon hearing voices, Mrs Southby wanted to speak with Ronald. He left Emma flushed and shaking. She then berated herself for allowing him to get in her head and potentially her heart. Her heart was only allowed for Alfie and Arthur, but neither were there anymore. *Should I let Ronald in?* she questioned herself and, in the background, could hear laughing and talking.

She proceeded to prepare the dinner further trying to stop all the thoughts from entering her head. She rang a little bell that was sitting on the window ledge.

"Dinner is ready."

Emma took the meal into the Parlour helping to feed Mrs Southby. As she got closer to Ronald and slightly bent over, she felt his hand lightly brush hers.

Chapter 24
Comfort and Lust

Once dinner was over, Emma washed the dishes then proceeded to go back to the Annex. The Southby's were in deep conversation, she left them to it.

The children were fast asleep when she checked in on them; it was time for her to indulge herself so boiling some water in the kitchen she unhung the tin bath from its hook. She sighed heavily as she lay back in the bath, the cares of the day and what Emma had been through the past few weeks left her, she closed her eyes and fell asleep.

Suddenly, she awoke realising she had drifted for about fifteen minutes, the water was near cold! Emptying the bath and towelling herself down, she went upstairs naked, got her nightdress on then lit the candle next to the bed after putting the gas mantle out.

Lying back on the bed she had so many thoughts, mostly involving Alfie, Arthur, and the situation she now found herself in. The candle burned, she drifted in and out of sleep only to be woken by a gentle knocking on the little door next to the fireplace, it was Ronald!

She couldn't open it as it had no doorknob, he unlocked it from the inside entering the room with his chest bare which sent her stomach flipping over.

"Emma, I…" his voice trailed off as he looked at her.

She drew the covers back, almost on autopilot, she wanted him as much as he wanted her. He removed the rest of his clothing and gently lay next to her. Her heart was beating so fast she thought she would pass out with excitement… his touch was gentle, but his urgency took them both to another place that was familiar to them both.

Chapter 25

Realisation

The next morning, Emma awoke alone. Ronald had left her to sleep, possibly using the passage behind the door to return to the house. Her mind raced as she felt a flush and remembered the night before. Not meaning it to happen but glad it did.

Weeks turned into months with the children getting close, not only to Ronald but to his mother. On several occasions, she would find Victoria sitting with Mrs Southby chatting and laughing whilst Victor played in the garden with a bat and ball. It appeared the idyllic life, everyone happy, everyone getting on with their lives, Emma still had a longing in her heart, she knew it was for Alfie.

Almost on a nightly basis Ronald would visit Emma in her bedroom, making love and leaving her before dawn, she awaited the proposal of marriage, it was not forthcoming.

One night, as Ronald made his way along the passageway from the house to Emma's bedroom, he knew this clandestine way of having Emma would end as abruptly as it started if he didn't give a promise of betrothal; he formed a plan.

As he knocked gently and opened the door to her room, she wasn't undressed but lay on top of the bed waiting for him.

"Ronald, it has been months since you first visited me here in my bed, should we not make things more permanent at least for the sake of my children? Your coming and going in the night is making me feel like I'm being used. The children are growing close to your mother as am I plus they love living here."

Emma stated her case and awaited his response.

"You're right Emma, we should make it a more permanent situation. Let's get engaged."

Her ears were happy to have such news and immediately she divested herself of her clothing; he climbed into bed with other plans that night.

He left her just before midnight, Tom was waiting at the gate to the park nearby, they embraced and kissed with Ronald finding the passion intense, not like the pretend passion with Emma, he knew what he was but was powerless to deny his sexuality, Tom loved him, they spent an hour together in the undergrowth.

Emma went from feeling used, to having an engagement promised. Life would get better as she knew herself to be Mrs Southby soon. The children would have a father, money worries would cease, she already received money from the Library Cottage rental and Alfie's house but not enough to live on with the children. Another month went by, Ronald appeared with an engagement ring to keep her happy and give him time.

At the turn of the century and before, homosexuality was against the law. He was using Emma to keep the façade of being a normal healthy man but all the time meeting with Tom in a nearby park at night and usually after going to Emma's room, it was the only way he could have his cake and eat it whilst keeping his position in the bank in Gravesend.

Mrs Southby knew her son was more attracted to men than women, she kept it quiet. When he was fifteen, she shouted for him to come in for Tea one afternoon and, upon receiving no answer, she went to look for him. She found him with a boy in the potting shed at the bottom of the garden; nothing prepared her for the sight she saw, it confirmed her suspicions, it was never mentioned again.

She hoped one day he would find a lovely woman and settle down; she didn't understand that what he wanted was not the same as what she wanted.

Emma accepted the engagement ring putting it straight on her ring finger. She threw her arms around Ronald's neck hugging him; his mind was thinking about Tom that he was with only hours before.

Chapter 26

Realisation

The engagement seemed to last forever, well, to Emma anyway. Ronald kept his liaisons quiet whilst endlessly promising Emma that marriage would come soon. She hoped it would be soon, she was pregnant.

"Can we set a date soon, Ronald?"

He didn't want to hear those words as he came through the door into her bedroom.

She could smell smoke on him and knew he didn't smoke, wondering where it came from, she asked him.

"I have been with friends before coming home, as you know I don't smoke and never will, it's a filthy habit Emma."

Ronald didn't mind his liaisons in the park with men that smoked if he had their company… and attentions, Tom wasn't exclusive.

His mind raced thinking up something to keep her quiet. He said the last day in March would be a good day. Emma knew it was too far away.

"Ronald… I'm pregnant."

His mouth dropped like a stone. There was no smile or consoling or any other type of romantic and joyous outpouring from him, but he rallied to keep her on a piece of string.

"That's wonderful news, Emma; mother will be so pleased." With that, he turned around to put his shirt on, she noticed bite marks on his shoulders and his back, he went back through the door into the passage.

She felt he had another woman…how wrong she was.

Immediately he went to his mother and told her the news, she clapped her hands and smiled.

"I'm so pleased you have a woman in your life!" she said with a smile.

He bit his tongue, knowing he would always be a homosexual but, in these times, he had to maintain the concealment to live amongst society. The marriage of Ronald and Emma had been arranged which would ensure Emma wouldn't be showing her expanding waistline.

Chapter 27

Victor

Victor was growing up into a handsome little boy.

Alfie would be so proud, Emma's heart still ached every time she thought about him, Victor looked more like Alfie every day, his black curly hair and sparkling blue eyes were the constant reminders. He excelled at school and was as sharp as a tack. Emma's heart melted each time she looked into Victor's eyes knowing she would always have a part of Alfie with her.

The school Victor attended liked him with the teachers always praising him to Emma but one day all that changed. He was a quiet child and very rarely caused Emma any embarrassment or upset, he clung to her sometimes which was his way of showing he was tired or wanted attention without saying very much, Emma knew he would grow into a wonderful young man in years to come.

Preparing dinner in the kitchen of the Annex, Emma looked up and saw someone running towards the window, it was a young girl a bit older than Victoria. She opened the door, "Come quick, Victor has had an accident!"

Emma dropped what she was doing and ran with the girl to the school. Victor was in the teacher's office lying still but awake. He had broken his leg after falling from a pile of wood whilst playing in the playground.

"I'm so sorry Mrs Ryan, I took my eyes off him for a minute!" The teacher was distraught that she had allowed the accident to happen but was calmed by Emma who was not used to being called *Mrs Ryan*.

"It's alright we will get him to hospital, they can help set his leg."

Emma found herself waiting for a car to take him to Gravesend Hospital; he never made a sound on his way there but when they arrived the doctors said they did not have the expertise to help set the leg and that he should go to the *Sea Bathing Hospital* in *Margate* where the specialist for broken bones would be able to help. Emma's mind was in a mess, she would have to stay there with him, *who would look after Victoria? Would she still have a job at the Southby's?*

Leaving Victor at the hospital she made her way back to the cottage and spoke with Mrs Southby about the problem. Immediately Mrs Southby told her not to worry and go with Victor, a kind neighbour would get Victoria and she would look after her. Mrs Southby would tell Ronald that night when he came home, there was no telephone in the house.

Emma threw some clothing in a bag for her and Victor then flew out the door to the Hospital by bus to then be transferred by car to the *Seabathing*.

The journey was long, the car that the hospital had ready was not too comfortable, Victor never complained, Emma just sat holding his hand as the driver made his way towards the coast.

"I'm afraid it will take a fair few hours to get their Missus, but I'll do my best."

Emma nodded and smiled at Victor whose face was like an angel to her, Alfie crept into her mind fleetingly.

Chapter 28

Seabathing

"It's OK, young man, I have you."

After the car drew up outside the hospital, the porter took Victor on a trolley into the triage area to await the doctor. Emma gathered her bag and sat patiently with him.

"Now, Missus…?"

Emma gave the name of *Ryan* to save any further explanation. "His name is Victor Ryan."

She said with a proudness on her lips.

The porter speaking with Emma was the one that helped to bring Alfie into the hospital only a few months ago!

The Doctor came along a few minutes later and began to examine Victor.

"I'm glad you got him here Mrs Ryan, the fracture is quite bad, he will need to be in traction for at least six weeks."

Her heart sank. Away from Victoria, away from Ronald and staying in a town that she had never been to but had heard a lot about then there's her pregnancy. Emma enquired if there was a room nearby she could stay in whilst Victor recovered. Literally, a few yards outside the hospital there was a guest house that had a vacancy sign in it with one room left, she took it.

That night, after she settled in the Guest House, she went to see Victor. There was a nurse tending him, stroking his hair, and soothing him, it was Margaret!

Margaret was checking Victor's chart hanging off the end of his bed… she read the name *VICTOR RYAN*, date of birth 15 July 1912.

"What happened to you, young man?" Margaret was cheerful after Alfie had made love to her that afternoon.

Emma pulled up a chair sitting next to Victor after Margaret had fetched him some ice cream, she sang to him as he drifted off to sleep. Holding his hand for an eternity, she felt herself nodding and made her way back to the guest house soon after.

That night after Margaret had finished her shift, she made her way to Alfie's quarters, creeping along the hallway to his room, she knocked gently. Alfie answered with a smile. She threw herself into his arms, they kissed, she was his, but something was stopping him from taking her to the bed, she felt him hesitate and looked quizzingly at him.

"John, was it something I said? Did I do something…?"

He had no answer but something inside him made him think of another woman, he pushed her away as she tried to grab him. She slapped his face as he tried to hold her back. Margaret had cruel thoughts, *I'll teach him to turn his back on me*, she turned around and walked out without looking back.

Chapter 29
Recognition

The next day was more of the same for Emma and Victor, he lay in the bed with his leg strapped up, when he saw his mother, he started to sob.

"Mother why have I got to stay here? Why can't we go home? Why can't I go to school?"

All these questions were wearing Emma down, she answered as best she could. Victor settled himself once again holding Emma's hand.

Nurses were changing shifts once again and Margaret found herself in the children's ward where she first saw Victor.

"How are you doing, Victor?" she asked the little boy who smiled at her with a familiar smile, or so she thought.

"I'm doing fine, nurse."

Victor was polite, Emma knew she had taught him manners.

"Can I have some ice cream?"

Emma was amazed at his forwardness, he had seen another child with ice cream, and it was one of his favourites.

"Yes, I'm sure I can arrange something, young man."

Margaret disappeared for a moment then came back with a small blue dish and teaspoon. Victor's face lit up as he eagerly held the bowl and spoon showing the delight on his face as he took a small spoonful.

"Have you any children of your own?"

Emma spoke to Margaret to strike up a conversation as being somewhere where she knew no one it was nice to have a female conversation.

"No, I don't; I am not married."

That statement resonated with Emma; she wasn't married either but had two children, one out of wedlock, bringing up Alfie's half-sister and pregnant with another man's baby but kept that quiet for now.

"I'm sorry I didn't mean to pry but was admiring the way you look after the children on the ward. Would you like them one day?"

"I've met someone I've fallen in love with but don't know if that's what he wants."

Margaret was trying to stop herself from sobbing as she remembered the lack of tenderness that she felt with Alfie the night before as she stormed out of his room, he seemed preoccupied, and she didn't know why.

"He would be a fool to turn you down I'm sure, you are a beautiful young woman and have a lovely way about you with children, who wouldn't want to marry you?"

Emma looked back in her own world, she had loved Alfie, had his child, bought his half-sister up and then Arthur came along but thanks to World War I that love was short-lived; then Ronald, she had only just met him but now pregnant with his child and not sure of the future.

"Well, he seemed nice at first, I enjoy his company but now it appears he is distant and won't tell me why, maybe he has someone else, I don't know."

Margaret felt sadness and regret that she had given herself to someone who, she thought, wanted her.

That night, Alfie was working late in the kitchen, Margaret waited for him outside the hotel. She needed to know if her love for him was not required. Alfie finished and stepped outside.

"John, I need to know, am I to be your wife? I gave myself to you and felt it returned but now you seem distant, why?"

Alfie let her down as gently as he could, he told her he honestly believed he had someone else in his life but was still struggling with his loss of memory.

"Will it ever return? I need to know."

"Margaret, I'm having flashbacks to another life, I haven't got all the pieces of the jigsaw just yet, but I'm taking it day by day at the moment, I can't move forward until I do."

"John, that could be a long time… I'm pregnant!"

Margaret blurted it out, she wasn't really but was trying to hook him and knowing she was pregnant was a way to get him, so she thought.

Alfie stepped back and looked at her shaking his head.

"Margaret, we made love, but I made sure you wouldn't get pregnant, I was careful and there is no way you could have my child."

Alfie went to touch her arm, but she threw him off then ran along the Promenade with him chasing her, she ran to the lighthouse, paused for a moment… then threw herself in the harbour. Alfie jumped in but couldn't find her after diving more than a few times, it seemed like an eternity, the water was dark and freezing cold, he couldn't find her. There was no one else around, he was calling for help. It was dark with a high tide, men came running from nearby and dived in to help, it was no use, she was found the next morning washed up on the beach, lifeless.

Chapter 30
Recall

That morning, after Margaret's body was found, Alfie was beside himself. He thought letting her down gently would enable her to move on, unrequited love tipped her over the edge, some people can take it, and some can't, Margaret couldn't.

It was also Alfie's day off. He went to the Police station to make a statement to report Margaret's death. Sitting in an open office just off the reception area he heard Police Officers talking, "Yeah, she was a beauty, every inch a woman for sure!"

Alfie kept his comments to himself just sticking to the facts. He told them they had been seeing each other, had a tiff, she ran off along the Prom and fell into the harbour. He didn't want to say she jumped, suicide on her death certificate would be an awful thing for her parents to see, Alfie felt somehow responsible for her death.

After the statement, he went to the *Seabathing Hospital* to speak with the other nurses she worked with. As Alfie walked into the children's ward and passed some of the children in their beds, Victor was laying in his bed and smiled at Alfie, he went over to him.

"Well, young man, what bought you here?" Alfie pulled up a chair next to the bed.

"I had an accident at school." Victor was almost boasting and followed his statement up with another profound piece of information, didn't recognise Alfie as he wasn't born when Alfie went to America.

"My mother bought me here; she will be here soon, and I will get some ice cream hopefully."

"I'm sure she will be along soon," he said comfortingly.

Alfie sat for a while longer with Victor. As he sat, he noticed the name of Victor's mother on the board at the end of the bed.

Alfie's mind was in a whirl, *that name* he said to himself. He started to think about the name, how did he know an Emma, *had there been an Emma in America? Had there been an Emma on board the Titanic before she sank?*

"What's your name, son?"

"Victor Ryan."

Alfie shook and stood up, he remembered in the back of his mind, there was a Victor he knew from when he was young but no other details. When Victor said his surname, Alfie looked at him but still couldn't piece the jigsaw together, the dreams, the flashbacks… nothing was forthcoming until a woman came walking through the doors of the ward… it was Emma!

He recognised her immediately and stood up. She stopped and rooted to the spot she dropped her bag.

Alfie? Surely not, he is dead, it can't be… can it?

Time stood still for a fleeting moment. She ran over to him and then stopped, hesitating just in case. Alfie spoke.

"Emma? Emma?"

He was almost afraid to say it. She stepped toward him and stroked his hair, his face and putting her finger against his lips as he tried to speak.

"Darling man, please tell me you are him, tell me you are my Alfie Ryan."

Alfie had no recollection of his name, but he knew who she was.

"Emma is my name, Alfie? My memories of a life before the one I live now are still patchy. I can only remember back to when I was saved from a sinking ship in the Atlantic back in 1912. She knew it, it was Alfie, that fateful night took many people from their loved ones, he had survived. The only reason there was no record of Alfie was that his memory had gone after almost drowning… it was him."

Emma bent over to kiss Victor and whispered that she would not be too long but needed to speak with this man for a while. Victor nodded and carried on finishing his ice cream.

They walked and talked for some time. Emma filled in the blanks for Alfie, telling him his real name and upon that he had a question for her.

"Is that boy in the hospital my son?" Emma hesitated. She had never told Victor about his father, he had never asked but now Alfie wanted to know, she had to tell him.

"Yes, he is yours, I had him a few months after the ship went down."

Alfie put his head in his hands and cried, all these years of wondering, hoping, and never giving up the fact there may be a life he belonged to. Finally, he had a family and Emma, his life was complete, naming his son after a special man that saved him and his mother all those years ago… Victor.

Chapter 31

Unfinished Business

The Landlady at the Guest House allowed Alfie to stay with Emma whilst little Victor was recovering.

Their first night was like new love. Emma, knowing she was pregnant didn't want to tell Alfie straight away, but she had to… soon. Alfie, thinking back to the women he had had in America but being with the only one true love in his life now cancelled everything before this moment.

Slowly they went back in their minds to the first time they lay with each other. Gently he held her, kissing her deeply and caressing her body as she did his. They left their clothes on the floor of the little Guest House room as they made love crying in each other's arms.

He felt a big weight off his shoulders, to have his love with him, there was nothing more he wanted in life and, after a few hours had passed laying in their afterglow, noises outside the window of Emma's room got louder, shouts from men and a banging on the door, it was the Police!

They entered the Guest House demanding Alfie come with them. A hard knock at the bedroom door and Alfie, upon opening it, felt the handcuffs on his wrists, he was led away to the Station. Emma had no idea about Margaret, Alfie had not mentioned her, or what had transpired days before they rediscovered each other, she was soon to find out.

Margaret's parents wanted retribution for the death of their daughter and were blaming her demise on Alfie. The statement he had made the morning her body was found apparently was contested by them, the police had to follow up.

Emma was torn between going to Victor at the hospital and making her way to the police station to find out why they took Alfie away… she chose Victor as he was a child and wouldn't understand.

At the station, Alfie sat quietly as the Desk Sergeant read out the reason why he had been arrested. Alfie looked out of the window, his thoughts and mind saw Margaret's face. He wondered if he had said the wrong things, had he handled it differently would she still be alive? He only told her the truth, but it seemed she couldn't take it with her delicate nature not accepting the situation. As these thoughts were going round in his mind suddenly, he was bought back into the room.

"Come with me, Mr…?"

"Ryan," Alfie had not said his own surname since boarding the *Titanic*. Emma had told him the night before, with her love and support he felt sure everything would fall in place.

The policeman ushered him to a chair and table set up for interrogation then proceeded to question him.

"So, Mr Ryan, how did you come to know Miss Donnelly?"

The Policeman looked squarely at him waiting for the response.

"I met her on the Promenade near the Lighthouse some months back now."

Alfie had no reason to lie, he had always been upfront and honest.

Many more questions which, eventually, got down to the nitty-gritty of their physical relationship, Alfie felt uncomfortable explaining about their intimacy but if the information was required, and it helped his case then so be it. He told the Policeman everything except the fact that Margaret thought she might be pregnant.

———

Emma stroked Victor's brow; he was asleep looking like an angel. Her mind had time to take in the fact that Alfie Ryan was back in her life and after all this time she thought he was dead, she got emotional, a tear fell from her eye landing on her hand. It was hard for her to take on board the time that had gone by without him, but she feared for him nonetheless wondering what the outcome would be of his visit to the police station.

After sitting with Victor, she kissed him and left for the Police station. She was walking the two to three hundred yards then suddenly a honk of a car horn made her look up, it was Ronald!

He parked his car near to the Guest House and walked over to her. Smiling as she saw him, he quickly came over to kiss her. Emma turned from him which made him kiss her ear instead.

"I've driven all this way to see you and Victor, Emma the least you could do was greet me, I thought we were looking at the possibility of marriage?"

Ronald was puzzled why she rebuffed him, he was insistent.

"What has happened since you came down here with Victor? I want to know… now!"

He was getting angry and gripped her wrist, this put Emma on the back foot.

"Ronald, a lot has happened since I saw you last, I'll tell you all but first I must make my way to the police station."

He looked at her in amazement but calmed down when she pecked him on the cheek. Emma wanted to be with Alfie right now, Ronald could wait. She told him to meet her at the lighthouse in an hour where she would explain everything. He accepted what she said and started walking to the lighthouse, Emma carried on to the police station.

Chapter 32

Justice

Alfie was sitting in the interview room after the policeman had left, his mind was going round in turmoil. Hours had passed which seemed like an eternity to him. Emma sat in the waiting room for the outcome of Alfie's situation, she was hoping and praying that all would be well.

The policeman that was questioning Alfie, came back into the room, he bought with him good news.

"Son, you have been completely honest with us, you have nothing to hide and no motive, it appears Miss Donnelly was slightly unhinged. We went back to a report on her from two years ago, she was seeing a young man for a while and had a child by him who died, she never recovered from the event apparently."

The relief upon hearing this news calmed Alfie's mind down. The policeman said he was free to go and as Alfie walked out of the room, he saw Emma waiting for him, she ran to him.

"Why did the police want to question you Alfie? What did you do?"

Emma had lots of questions, Alfie was trying his best to answer.

"It's alright, Emma; it's all sorted now."

Alfie told her everything about Margaret and what had happened. Emma listened and was saddened to hear about her, this news bought back the memory of her own sister who had taken her life when Emma was four years old. Florence was fourteen, Ethel had had her out of wedlock after being sweet-talked by a young man who lived a few doors away. Florence got pregnant not bearing the shame of telling Ethel, so one morning down at the docks she threw herself in, they never found her body.

Outside the police station, they stood together, Emma started to tell Alfie about Ronald and the fact he was waiting at the lighthouse, as they walked together, Ronald's tale unfolded.

Alfie was sorry she had been through so much since he had been found floating in the water off the *Titanic*, sadness entered his heart, his head hung low. She kissed him, they hugged.

In the distance, they could see a figure on a bench near the lighthouse, it was of course Ronald, they approached him slowly.

"So, who is this fancy man, Emma? Some chap you picked up along the seafront?" she could see Ronald turning red whilst getting explosive.

"Ronald, this is Alfie…" As she tried to explain he got more agitated, it appeared he was ready for a fight, but of course, that didn't happen.

"Ronald, I won't beat about the bush, this is my long-lost love. His child is laying in the hospital right now, Victoria is Alfie's half-sister. There is no other way for me to convey this to you, I am being honest."

Ronald's face was still red, he was angry and upset. His ego had been dented by a woman he felt sure would be his wife and tend to his mother, he felt the ruin but didn't show it.

"So, my mother is looking after Victoria whilst you are down here with your fancy man? Emma, when were you going to tell me about it? Was the intimacy with me just a play? You're carrying my child, I won't let you take it away."

Ronald was venomous.

Alfie looked at Emma for confirmation.

His accusations hurt her. Emma told him the whole story from start to finish, he listened, turned, and walked away but not until he had uttered these words, "When you have finished here in Margate you can fetch your belongings and your daughter or whoever she is and leave my employment. When you have my baby, you will bring him to me and my mother, we will bring him up and you're to have no hand in it." He spat the words out, Emma had a trump card and played it.

"Ronald, I had my doubts about you and the men in the park, I saw your back one night and it wasn't a woman that did that plus you smelt of smoke regularly. I know full well that a man like you could not bring up a child, I will give birth to your baby and bring him up the best I can so you needn't think you will have the child for yourself or your mother!"

Ronald, went puce, *so she knew all along*, he said to himself, calming down, he straightened his tie proceeding to walk back along the promenade away from the lighthouse, Emma, and Alfie. That was the last time she saw Ronald.

Emma asked Alfie if he wanted her to give the baby up, he put his arm around her, kissed her assuring her he would treat it as his own.

They made their way to the hospital, Alfie and Emma were talking whilst Victor was eating his favourite ice cream. They sat together, it was a family scene but before it could be a real one, she had to tell Victor that Alfie was his father. Holding Victor's hand whilst she tried to explain to the seven-year-old who his father was his face wrinkled, he began to cry. There were lots of questions which she did her best to answer. Victor wanted a hug but only from Emma at this time, Alfie was not in the running for any kind of reunion with Victor at that moment so just sat and smiled; *it will all come good soon*, he felt certain.

The sister in charge came over and gave the good news to Emma, "Victor can go home at the weekend, he will need crutches I'm afraid."

The news was welcomed, Emma, however, had no home to go to. Not only was she homeless, she had Alfie with her too. There was no telephone in Library Cottage so no way of advising the tenants they had to leave, Emma and Alfie would have to rent a room until the tenants could vacate, this problem coupled with having Victoria and Victor, would make a room a bit cosy for sure. Emma had yet to face Ronald and Mrs Southby again once they returned from Margate.

Chapter 33

Back Home

Going back to the Guest House for her belongings, and Alfie's from his servants' quarters, they walked back to the *Seabathing* to collect Victor, he was still shy of Alfie but walked next to him as they went the few yards to the train station. Steam train journeys took time, it was the best transport available after the little boat service that ferried people along the north Kent coast had ceased.

As they boarded the train, Victor asked Alfie a question followed by many more.

"So, you are my father then?"

Alfie looked at him, he was his father's boy for sure, the black hair, blue eyes and smile confirmed it. Alfie didn't hesitate telling him he was, and everything would be fine from now on. As the conversation carried on, Emma looked out of the window of the train, she had so many reflections and worries, she thought her head would spin! Her one main concern was getting back into Library Cottage and letting the tenants down gently, it had only been a short time and now Emma needed to return with her family.

After leaving Rochester train station, they managed to get a taxi to take them to the Southby's and, as it got closer, Emma's stomach lurched a few times fearing the unsavoury situation ahead of her.

They were dropped off at the end of the driveway then walked to the little annex where they saw Victoria playing in the garden, she looked up and ran towards them, then stopped looking at Alfie, her face wrinkled, the tears fell for her half-brother, she thought she would never see him again, he scooped her up in his arms giving her the biggest hug. Emma, upon seeing this, had tears as well, the family was together at last.

"So, you've turned up then!" Ronald shouted from his front door before walking down to the front of the annex.

"About time, Emma, we've looked after your offspring far too long, take your belongings and leave, oh and there will be no salary owing, we will take that in lieu of money spent on food etc."

Emma wasn't surprised by this but could have done with the extra money. Alfie interjected.

"You can keep your money; we have enough thanks."

Alfie wasn't sure, he could tell Ronald had female mannerisms, *I've seen one of those types of men down at the docks years gone by… I know what he is,* his thoughts turned to the situation at hand. He was proud knowing he had saved some money whilst working at the *Nayland Rock*. Alfie helped Emma pack. It took only a few minutes to gather everything, but, just before they left, Victoria ran into the house and found Mrs Southby, she gave her a kiss and a hug thanking her for looking after her, the old lady shed a tear; it had been a long time since she had had a hug.

The Ryan's walked down toward the end of the drive; sat on a bench then proceeded to work out how they would get back to Gravesend and into Library Cottage.

Chapter 34
Library Cottage

The evening was drawing in, there was still the question of having somewhere to stay. As they sat and talked about their options, a flatbed lorry was passing by, Alfie flagged it down then spoke to the driver. He waved Emma, Victoria, and Victor to come and get in the back, their passage to Gravesend was assured.

Near Library Cottage there was a Guest House with a few empty rooms. Alfie knocked on the door of one of them. An elderly lady opened the door smiling, she told them she knew Ethel, Emma's mother, many years ago and would be happy to help. She ushered them into a room that had an adjoining room through a connecting door. Emma made the children comfortable in one room, she and Alfie had the bigger room for themselves.

The children were getting hungry, so Emma went to the landlady to ask for help.

"Do you know where we could get something to eat? The children are getting restless."

"Why? Don't be silly? I will cook you all something to save wandering the streets. Sit yourselves down in the Parlour, I'll call you in presently."

Emma felt like she had a guardian angel.

That night, after they had eaten, Emma put the children to bed closing the connecting door behind her. They were alone, she felt like a shy young schoolgirl in Alfie's presence once again. There was the experience with him that he bought to his lovemaking. He took her to heaven and back many times that night, his urgency excited her making her feel alive, she loved him above everything else, he was her life, she cried into his chest before they slept with gratitude that he had come back to her at last.

In the morning, after breakfast, Emma struggled to see how she could tell the tenants to leave Library Cottage, they wouldn't be happy, but she had to think of the children. Leaving Alfie and the children at the Guest House, she walked the short few hundred yards back to Library Cottage, it made her smile to see it and also bought a tear to her eye as she remembered her mother in happier times.

She walked up to the kitchen door and hesitated whilst knocking gently. The door opened, a small rotund lady with grey hair answered.

"Emma! How lovely to see you, please come in, what can I do for you?"

Emma felt bad but cut to the chase.

"I'm afraid I have to ask you to leave, my circumstances have changed, I now find myself needing my home back for not only myself and my children but the love of my life whom I've found by pure chance in Margate, I thought he was dead."

The woman's face dropped; she began to get upset.

"We've enjoyed living here very much and will be so sorry to leave, I guess as it's your home…"

Emma said she could stay for a week until they find somewhere else and that she wasn't too far away at the Guest House, the woman nodded then saw Emma out.

On her way back, Emma stopped near The Three Daws public house. Looking out over Gravesend Docks at the water, she remembered the first time she saw Alfie, how they smiled at each other, the moment she fell in love with him. Their first time at his home, the love she felt with him then. When she told him, she was pregnant then the sorrow of thinking he went down with the ship. Her bringing up Victor and Victoria on her own then, finally, they are all back together. She felt happy once more.

Back at the Guest House, Alfie and the children were sitting in the Parlour waiting for her.

"When can we go home?"

Victor wanted to play, Victoria was missing school. Emma pacified them both with the news that it will be a week or so. Alfie asked Emma to sit with him for a while as he had something to tell her. Her face fell as he told her about America and his life there.

"Emma, when I left to make a better life for us in America, I had no idea how things would be. My loss of memory, not knowing about any of my life before the ship went down. Trying to make my way in a world I had never experienced, feeling alone and helpless. I sought the comfort of women, made friends and some enemies but, I made a life for myself there. Now knowing who I am helped me enormously, I want to take you and the children there as I know we will have a better life."

He went on to explain further.

"In the small amount of time there, I ended up in a lovely town outside of Duluth, Minnesota. I even managed to buy a house; I'd like it to be our home."

The thought of Alfie with other women made her upset, he had no idea who he was or who she was so it was forgivable, *moving to a country I have no knowledge of and uprooting the children, could I?* she went into deep thought.

"Let me think about it Alfie, it's a lot to take in, I have been bringing up the children, lost my mother to the Spanish Influenza, found comfort with someone who died in the War and, like you, tried to move on with my life."

Alfie had tears in his eyes, he wanted and loved her so much but also wanted a good life for them. *Would Emma agree?* He had hope in his heart.

A week went by quick which also saw Victoria go back to school, Victor was still on crutches getting edgy, he wanted to go back to school too but not just yet. Alfie found employment down at the docks although his heart wasn't in it. Finally, it was time to go back to Library Cottage, the tenants were gone when Emma, Alfie and the children arrived. Emma's heart leapt; she was home at last.

Chapter 35

Farewell

"We will have to get married before we go to America, Emma." Her face lit up at the prospect of becoming legal and *Mrs Ryan* at last. For them to emigrate they would have to be husband and wife upon landing in New York along with hundreds of other migrants.

As Emma had children already it was impossible to have a church service, so they hurriedly arranged for a Registrar wedding at Gravesham Registry Office on Windmill Street. The date was set, Emma began to get excited, her only problem was what would she wear?

"Alfie, I still have my mother's wedding dress, but I doubt I'll get into it in my present state."

Carrying Ronald's baby made her stomach wide which stopped Emma from wearing the beautiful dress she had saved in a box in the attic. Then she remembered, the kind lady that lived a few doors away that had died in the Pandemic. Her husband had given Emma some of the old lady's clothes in a trunk that she hadn't really bothered to open, then, climbing the narrow staircase to her old bedroom, she opened the trunk, she peered inside. There were a few everyday dresses, finally, at the bottom of the trunk wrapped in muslin, was the most beautiful wedding dress she had seen even more beautiful than her mother's.

Carefully she removed it from the protective muslin, took her clothes off and tried it on, a perfect fit with a problem solved. Alfie had a suit that belonged to his stepfather, Victor, he kept it as one of the only things left after his death that Victor owned, he couldn't part with it deciding he would wear that to his wedding. The morning of the wedding, the children were taken to the lady that had given them a room in the Guest House, she had no children of her own and welcomed the chance to spoil them.

The sun shone for them both that morning. Emma used the old tin bath that she had bathed in many times in her life, she carefully filled it with warm water from the big kettle that had hung from the clothes airer since she can't remember when, removing her clothes and laying in the warm comforting water. Alfie came into the kitchen looking lovingly at his future wife, "Mrs Alfie Ryan." He said with a smile a mile wide and a little tear in his eye. Her breasts were floating on the water, he loved every inch of her, as she went to get out of the bath, he passed her the towel. Wrapping it around her he kissed her and held her for a long time.

"You are my one true love Alfie; you know that don't you? You, above all others forever."

Alfie felt the same way, his heart was full of her.

They got themselves ready then made their way to Windmill Street. Grabbing two strangers off the street as witnesses, Emma and Alfie were joined in holy matrimony, she used the ring that belonged to her mother.

Alfie was getting impatient to return to America, to the small home he had managed to buy and the life he had built there; Emma was slowly coming around to the idea. He could tell she was a bit uneasy about the upheaval and tried to reassure her.

"Look, Emma if we go and you don't like it, we can come back."

She didn't want to uproot the children any more than she had. Library Cottage was her home, a big decision was looming. That night as they lay together, she agreed that they would go but just for a year, if it wasn't what she wanted then they would come back. He agreed.

A Steamer leaving Southampton for New York at the end of June was booked, Alfie secured tickets for them, he felt lighter in his heart already.

"Alfie, have you told me everything about America?" further questions came, and Alfie did his best to answer them.

"Emma, yes I did have dealings with women but never married as you didn't Arthur."

Emma would have married Arthur in a heartbeat as she believed Alfie dead, but of course, World War I happened, Arthur never came home. With Alfie's comforting words and the love she had for him, she found herself on the boat in her mind already.

"What shall I do with Library Cottage, Alfie?"

He thought for a moment, "If we let it out then it would give us the money to help until I find work."

They agreed to let it out once again.

Library Cottage was rented by the time the Steamer arrived at Southampton with just a rolling six-monthly agreement in case they came back. They packed all their clothes and personal items ready for the big voyage across the Atlantic. The children wanted to keep their whips and tops but could only take clothing as the lighter they travelled the better; toys could be bought in America.

The children left school, bills were settled, the final days were getting nearer for them to go. Emma started crying the morning they had to leave for Southampton, all the cottage memories came flooding back, it was a wrench to leave it. They walked to the horse tram terminus with just a few pieces of luggage.

The journey to Southampton seemed to be never-ending, trams, taxis, where they could find one, and a short ride in a tractor eventually got them there. The children's eyes went wide when they saw how huge the ship was.

Once onboard, they were shown to their cabin, tiny with bunk beds on both sides and a small sink in between, *It'll be tight, but we'll manage,* Emma said to herself. The trip would take seven to eight days to New York then onwards to Alfie's home in Forest Lake, Minnesota across the Great Lakes. He felt sure Emma and the children would love America, it took him some getting used to, but he made his way eventually.

Seasickness visited, Emma was already having morning sickness, with Victoria being terribly seasick it made the days wretched for them all. The journey, coupled with a few small storms, made Emma's mind up that she would not be getting back on a ship any time soon!

Finally arriving in New York harbour with Ellis Island in the distance, the Statue of Liberty stood proud, she welcomed the many people who appeared like ants from the ship. The ship docking and allowing passengers off, they filed into a large holding room for immigrants to go through the motions of wishing to live and work in America. Paperwork completed, they made their way out into a huge city the like Emma and the children had never seen. Alfie felt at home straight away.

The ship taking them to Duluth was not due to depart for six hours so Alfie suggested they leave their luggage on the ship then see some sights.

It was like 'coming home' for Alfie. They walked past the *'Jane'* where he first used his new name and became *friendly* with the receptionist. They found a Diner nearby, they stopped for something to eat. As they opened the door and found a table, a blonde woman came over, she grabbed Alfie's hand.

"John, I've missed you, honey!" Emma's eyes went wide, Alfie suppressed his surprise as The Jane's receptionist was having lunch in the next booth but one! She leaned over so he could see her charms and rubbed against his arm.

"Boy, are you a sight for sore eyes!"

The feeling of discomfort was overcoming Emma, she shot a stare at Alfie. He shook the blonde off and told her he was with his family; he wished her well.

She spat at him the words of a woman scorned.

"Well, I was good enough to take to bed but not good enough to exchange the niceties of the day! Go to hell, John!"

He wasn't surprised to get this kind of response as he remembered how rough and ready she was, he touched Emma's arm to comfort her.

"It's OK, Alfie. I know you had your life whilst here before, it's not your fault."

They ate up, paid the check, and left; Emma felt sad and a bit jealous inside, and somehow insecure.

Back at the boat, they made their way to the cabin that would be their home for a few days, finding their luggage just inside the door, they proceeded to go up on deck but not before Alfie took Emma in his arms and kissed her, her stomach still flipped when he did this as it always did. On the main deck, the sights and smells assaulted their senses until the ship unmoored then left for Duluth.

The children stayed up on deck every day watching the ships and boats as their own ship sailed along towards Lake Superior. Alfie and Emma went to the cabin to spend some time together.

"Alfie, tell me I'll love my life here in America."

Emma needed comfort, Alfie needed to give it.

"All will be fine Emma; you'll love the house I have and the little town I settled in before the War called me. The children will have a good education, our lives will be richer than they would have been in Gravesend, you'll see."

He kissed her lips then her neck, she undressed, he watched her and eventually they found themselves in the throes of all-consuming passion.

Chapter 36

Home Sweet Home

The Ship docked earlier than was listed but Victoria welcomed it as the seasickness from Southampton to New York then onwards to Duluth, took its toll on her.

Coming into Duluth, the ship slowed down to a stop and docked. Gathering up their belongings Alfie, Emma and the children found themselves on the quayside waiting for a horse and cart to get them to Forest Lake. There was no other transport available, Emma liked the fact that it was almost reminding her of Gravesend way back although there were now horse trams in Kent these days.

In the distance, Alfie spotted his house, "There it is! It took me a long time to buy it, I know it's not much but it's ours together now."

Alfie felt happy seeing the house again. A little white weather-boarded cottage with a small picket fence and its gate loomed up in front of them. The stoop had a swing on it, the children ran over to it immediately.

Summer in Forest Lake is a time for enjoying life in the sunshine. A time for families to gather and have parties, play, and relax. The date, 4th July, was only weeks away.

Life was so different for Emma in America, getting the children into schools, coping with her pregnancy and being with Alfie in another life, another land, things were coming to a head.

"Alfie, I'm struggling to cope with the huge amount of changes we've all gone through, guess it's the pregnancy."

Emma sat with tears forming.

"Emma, we will be OK, we can bring up the child as ours, no one needs to know. As far as anyone outside this house is concerned, we are just a normal family." That night, as they lay in bed, Emma had questions that she hadn't asked Alfie when they found each other again, they wouldn't go away unless answered.

"Did you have other women here in Duluth, Alfie?"

It stopped him dead in his thoughts. Carefully, he chose his words.

"Yes, I did Emma, but I was single, I had no recollection of my life with you before the ship sank."

Alfie waited for further questions, they always said they would keep nothing from each other. No more questions, Emma had fallen asleep, Alfie was grateful, finally he saw blackness.

The next morning, Emma got the children ready for school, they were really enjoying themselves meeting new friends with their education really taking off. Alfie had found work in a local hotel cooking and Emma settled herself in the kitchen making dinner for the evening. There was a knock at the door…

Emma moved to open it, looking through the screen door, she could see a woman with a small girl holding her hand.

"Good morning, can I help you?"

Emma didn't recognise the woman or her child but remained polite.

"Yes, I've come to see, John?"

Emma knew that Alfie had called himself John and wondered where this woman was in all this.

"Who is asking?"

Emma's mind was in turmoil as she looked at the little girl but couldn't recognise any distinguishing characteristics against those of Alfie's.

"My name is Jenny; John and I had a relationship before he went to war. This house has been locked up since he went, I was passing, I saw lights on last night."

Emma's mind went into overdrive, had Alfie fathered a child and not told her?

"I'm afraid there is no one of that name here."

She told the woman a little white lie.

Jenny began to get upset, the child started to cry with her. "Please don't cry, I'll ask around and see if John can be found for you. Where do you live?"

Emma wanted time to think up what she was going to say to Alfie.

"In Bay View Road, about twenty minutes from here. If you can help, I would be incredibly grateful."

The woman turned around walking down the path with the child sobbing in front of her, a hint of a sneer coming over the woman's face.

Emma sat down stroking her stomach, her thoughts turned to England, *should I have stayed there? Why didn't Alfie tell me about his child?*

———————

The children finished school for the day, Emma went to pick them up. Their laughing and chatter made her smile, gradually she came out from under the cloud of discovery from the visitors. Alfie would be home in a few hours.

Chapter 37

Jenny

Alfie found himself whistling, assuring himself as he walked back from the Hotel, life seemed good for him, *I've got Emma, my half-sister and son, someone's else's child on the way but I'm OK with it, I'm happy in my world.*

He approached the cottage and spotted Victoria sitting swinging on the stoop chair, Victor was playing nearby. Looking up, they saw him, both ran to him with hugs, and, in a bundle, they made their way into the kitchen where Emma was making pastry. Alfie went to kiss her; she turned her face away. He grabbed her arm and spun her around, he looked hurt… so did she.

"What's wrong, Emma? You were fine this morning when I left, is it the baby?"

He didn't know what else to say. She blurted out the incident that morning. Alfie stood shocked with no words at first.

"I'm sure you remember Jenny, Alfie, was she another of your conquests?"

Her words bit into him; Alfie was hurt but totally understood that Emma would be too.

"I met Jenny before the war, we had a few months together, I left to join, I didn't know she was pregnant Emma believe me, I wouldn't have just left without providing for them."

Emma knew this to be true, the life Alfie had endured in Dublin, and subsequently, the hardship since said a lot about him as a person.

"How are we going to sort this problem out?"

Emma said *we*; she loved him above all else not wanting him to feel alone in the matter. He sat quietly on the sofa in deep thought. Emma got the children ready for bed after their dinner so she could sit with Alfie to try to see a way through the dilemma.

He knew Jenny would be at her mother's in Bay View Road, he'd make his way there in the morning before work.

That night, they climbed into bed, Emma became conscious of her expanding waistline, the baby was getting close. They lay next to each other noticeably quiet; Emma could almost hear Alfie breathe. He turned to face her, he quietly assured her, "Emma, I love you and this situation won't change anything. I'm not sure what to do right now but I'll sleep on it then go around in the morning before work."

She knew Alfie loved her, it was intense and mutual. He stroked her stomach as if to give her comfort, they fell asleep in each other's arms.

Chapter 38
Close Shave

It was a slow walk to Bay View Road, Alfie wasn't in a hurry to face what he knew to be a difficult situation. Finding himself at the gate, he let himself in. On the stoop was the old Irish Setter that Jenny had had from a pup, he looked up at Alfie and wagged his tail, remembering him from years ago, Alfie scratched the dog's head; he stood in front of the screen door.

Gently knocking, he could hear the footsteps of a child, *was it my child?* he thought to himself. The little girl opened the door and ran inside, Jenny was there waiting on the sofa.

"John, nice of you to visit!" instantly spitting the words out at him.

"What are you going to do about this situation John? How will it work for you?" she was venomous.

Alfie looked around seeing photos of the child then, nearby, photos of a man that had ginger hair just like the little girl's, it was Jenny's cousin, George. His mind did the math, he left for the war towards the end of 1917 just three months after he had met Jenny, how old was the girl? As he was trying to work things out, the child spoke to him, "Guess how old I am?" she stood with her arms behind her back asking Alfie again as he didn't answer straight away. He pretended he didn't know.

"I'm three and half next week, my grandma told me."

Well, Alfie was no mathematician, but a child is carried for nine months, he was with Jenny three months, it's not possible the child is his, it had ginger hair, Jenny's was blonde, and his was black.

"So, who is that in the photo Jenny?"

She looked at the photo of her daughter and then at her cousin's.

"You met George once John, I'm sure of it, he was here for a visit just before you left for the war."

It didn't take brain surgery to work out the little girl was George's. She had the same nose and eyes but was still cute. Alfie could see a dimple on her chin, George had the same. Jenny was trying to pass off the little girl as his, maybe looking for a meal ticket or maybe just wanting to cause trouble because she had a child out of wedlock. She was just about to add something else then in walked Jenny's mother, Bertha, she had always liked Alfie, she and smiled when she saw him.

"We didn't think we would see you again John, it's been a while." She was holding an ice-cold lemonade freshly made, handing it to him she said, "You've come back to live here after the war?" He nodded then proceeded to tell her about his family and what had happened to him to bring him back.

She listened intently then spoke, "What do you think of our little girl here? Susie is as cute as a button looking just like her daddy doesn't, she Jenny?"

Jenny's mother said this as she looked over at the photo on the dresser. Jenny's face was red, her mother knew all along. The child was indeed her cousin George's child. As she thought back to the night George had visited four days before Alfie had left. George had always liked Jenny, basically he forced himself on her that night after alcohol was consumed, he knew it's what she wanted too.

She intended to say it was Alfie's, but the child didn't look like any child Alfie had fathered. Jenny's mother knew what had happened between George and Jenny, she wasn't about to let an innocent man take the rap for something he didn't have a hand in. George left his handkerchief embroidered with a 'G' in Jenny's bedroom where her mother had found it… in the bed… and not clean, but never told Jenny. After his visit, he went and married a woman from Duluth not knowing he had fathered a child; Jenny never told him.

Alfie drank his lemonade and went to get up.

"Jenny is there something you wanted to say to me? My wife told me you were looking for me… and by the way, my name is Alfie… not John."

Her reply came back acidic and sickly sweet at the same time.

"Why, John? You just have yourself a lovely time here; I'm sure your wife will be keeping an eye on you for the future."

With that, Alfie got up and made for the door saying his goodbyes to Bertha and Susie. Walking down the street towards the hotel he realised he had dodged a bullet for sure. He'll tell Emma when he finishes work.

Chapter 39

New Arrival

The summer came with a blast of heat that would let you fry an egg on the pavement! Emma and the children were not used to such heat and humidity living near lakes, it bought them all down with lethargy and tiredness. Emma's pregnancy was hard for her to cope with in the searing heat and to keep cool they at least had a couple of fans then stayed in the shade as much as possible. Alfie worked in the hot kitchen of the hotel barely wearing his shirt, but it was stipulated that shirts must be worn whilst cooking food.

Emma awoke one morning after Alfie had gone to work with pains in her stomach, she went downstairs, the contractions had started, she sat on the stoop in the cool air of the morning. The baby wouldn't be long. Making her way back into the kitchen to prepare breakfast she dropped a wooden spoon she was using to beat the eggs for scrambling. As she bent to pick it up, she felt pain again, the baby was coming she was sure of it! Water spilt out from her legs which she knew to be the sign it was on its way!

Gathering the children, she told Victoria to go for the Midwife who lived one block away. The contractions were coming fast and furious as she struggled to cope with further pain.

A few minutes later, a Midwife arrived in the form of a large black woman who had helped many come into the world. She had a large smile and kindness in her eyes. Emma had hardly seen any black people since being in Forest Lake but was so pleased to see this one. The woman boiled water, got towels, and told Emma to go to her bedroom to make herself ready. Victoria took Victor outside on the stoop where they waited for Emma to have the baby. The birth wasn't easy, Emma had a terrible time with it, however, three hours later, a healthy baby boy was born. She found it strange that she didn't want to bond with the baby straight away, possibly because it was Ronald's, her mind was a mess as she didn't want to hold him at that moment then, as the baby cried, her mothering instinct told her to pick him up, the midwife smiled knowing all would be well.

Alfie came home that night finding an increase in the family population. He looked at the little boy, smiled, although not his, his thoughts were that the child did not ask to be bought into the world. Emma called the baby Arthur; Alfie was happy with that as he knew how much Arthur had meant to Emma before he died, the name Ronald was not an option.

The children came in from the stoop to look at their new baby brother, they had no idea it wasn't Alfie's, that secret would be kept between Alfie and Emma for the time being. Their smiles blessed little Arthur as they welcomed him into their lives.

The next morning after Alfie went to work, Emma took it easy with the baby, Victoria took time off from school doing all the chores whilst Victor went to school.

Life was good in the Ryan household. Victoria loved her school; Victor was growing like a weed and little Arthur was pure joy as a baby, hardly ever cried sleeping all night through, Emma was so grateful for this. Their lives were settling in Forest Lake, Emma still missed Gravesend and Library Cottage, she never told Alfie for a long time; not wanting to hurt his feelings and seeing the children having a good life, she kept it all hidden until the right time presented itself in the future.

There wasn't a day that went by that Emma didn't think of England. Some days were easier than others, some days left her in tears which she hid from the family. Homesickness was real to her but for the sake of everyone she must carry on.

Over the course of the next few years, they had the usual childhood traumas, disease, and accidents. One day Victoria came in with a piece of metal sticking out of her arm, Emma, almost fainting, managed to get her to the doctors and a small operation was performed, the scar wasn't pretty, but it meant Victoria kept her arm at least. Then another time Victor was playing on the stoop and fell up the steps, a large red and blue bruise appeared on his cheek where he had fallen on the wooden flooring. Leaving no scars, Alfie said, "His good looks won't be compromised at least!" Emma and Victor laughed at this.

Chapter 40

Depression

The headlines said it all, 'Prices Collapse on the Stock Market!'
'Wall Street panic as Stocks Crash!' *The Great Depression*, as it was called, was a severe worldwide economic recession that started in late 1929 and lasted until the late 1930's. The banks collapsed with rich and poor alike struggling, many took their own lives, it was said that bodies were *like rain* in New York as they jumped from high buildings to end their sorrow at losing everything. The impact of the Depression on Emma and Alfie's lives was immense. The Hotel closed; Alfie could not find work. With mouths to feed it was time for them to think about how they were going to cope going forward.

"Emma, I will have to go back to sea, I've got experience and can cook, joining the Merchant Navy again should at least give us money to live."

She bit her lip to stop her crying, having lost Alfie once then to find him and now to potentially lose him again was more than she could bear.

"Alfie, I can't lose you again, God knows when I will see you, I understand we have to live but I'm in a strange country with the children…"

She started to cry. He put his arms around her hugging her to him for what seemed like ages.

"We will survive this Emma, but I must do what's right for our family, I'll join up tomorrow."

———

Alfie walked to the shipping office; he knew it was the right thing to do. His experience would hold him in good stead with his heart and family in Minnesota. Later that morning, as he was crossing the road, he recognised a man standing outside the office, it was Jed! Jed and Alfie had worked on the same ship with

Matt all those years ago. Jed's smile told Alfie he recognised him too, swiftly Alfie crossed the road.

They shook hands, slapped each other's backs, had a hug knowing they had history, they were pleased to see each other.

"What brings you here, John?" Alfie had forgotten that many knew him as John. He hesitated slightly and proceeded to give Jed the short story version. Jed stood wide-eyed and in disbelief at the things Alfie had been through.

"So that's my story Jed, what's yours?" Jed motioned for Alfie to sit on the bench outside the shipping office, with sadness in his eyes he told Alfie his own sorrowful tales.

"When you left the ship, I decided to finish the voyage and make my way back to my wife, Virginia. The voyage must have been too long for her to wait."

He had a tear in his eye as he went on further.

"I walked in expecting to be greeted by a loving wife with the prospect that we may be able to have a family sometime soon. How wrong I was, she had a little boy of 18 months sitting in a highchair… he wasn't mine; he was black," Alfie was listening and nodding, he acknowledged the sadness in Jed's voice but carried on paying attention.

"I walked out of that house with nothing and never looked back, she broke my heart."

He recovered himself sufficiently to tell Alfie the next part of his story.

"I decided to go back to sea, forget what happened and move to a new chapter of my life. Think I've done most of the places in the Great Lakes anyway. I met up with this woman in Chicago and boy what a lovely woman, we made a home for me to come back to, I left her pregnant."

Alfie chuckled at this piece of personal information but kept his attention on Jed's story.

"After the voyage finished, I went back to Chicago finding her without the child. She had miscarried it three months after I'd gone to sea, her grief was too much to bear alone, yeah, you know what I'm about to tell you."

Apparently, the *lovely woman* wasted no time in securing another man, she wasn't the love that Jed thought she was.

"John… sorry, Alfie, I am a man who wants nothing to do with women for the rest of my life, I've had it."

Jed was angry and upset, Alfie touched his shoulder in a kind gesture of men who have been through a lot would do.

"That's why I'm here now Alfie, I'm signing up again as the Depression has seen no other way to earn a crust."

Jed stood up making his way to the shipping office door, Alfie followed him. They waited for half an hour before they were called to sign papers. They found themselves being taken by a merchant seaman to the dock on the lake at Duluth. The *SS Lake Splendour* was there, being loaded with provisions. They found themselves standing watching the hive of activity, soon they were to join the ship but not for another three days.

"So Jed, I'll meet you back here on Thursday, where are you staying by the way?" Jed hesitated, he had nowhere to stay but was embarrassed to say.

"I'm OK; I'll find somewhere just for a few nights." Alfie couldn't let him stay on the streets and suggested he come back with him, *Emma won't mind*, he said to himself.

They got a lift on a small horse-drawn carriage back to Alfie's house, they walked up the path then opened the screen door. Emma was sitting with Arthur breast-feeding him; Victoria was in her bedroom and Victor was outside playing catch with a baseball.

"Emma, this is Jed, I worked with him in the Merchant Navy years back before the war, he has nowhere to stay so I said he could be with us for the three nights before joining our ship, you're OK with that aren't you?" she nodded her approval. Jed eyed Emma's breasts whilst she nursed, *it has been a long time*, he thought to himself.

That night, after the children went to bed, the house was quiet, Emma made up a bed in the little room off the kitchen for Jed to use. He said how grateful he was and proceeded to get his head down for the night. Emma and Alfie went to bed laying and talking for a while.

"Alfie, we have three days together before you leave, we need to make plans in case..." he touched her lips with his finger to stop her from saying anymore.

"Everything will be alright Emma, we're not at war, my voyages will not be too long I'm sure. One thing I am sure of is that money will be provided so we can keep body and soul together."

She had a tear in her eye which he wiped away before kissing her in that way she always loved and the joyous way they intertwined before going to sleep.

Chapter 41

Voyage

The ship sailed on the tide with Alfie and Jed safely aboard. They ate and bunked together that night after their duties and introductions had been given. When Alfie awoke Jed wasn't in his bunk. As he opened the cabin door, he saw Jed come out of another man's cabin holding some of his clothing, *looks like he has been hurt too much by women and had gone the other way*, Alfie smiled to himself, he didn't blame Jed and went to turn as he saw the men kiss.

The voyage plans were to leave Duluth and sail around Lake Superior finally the ship would make its way up to Thunder Bay following down to Sault St. Marie then through to Bay City on to the Michigan coast. It never made Sault St. Marie. After the fourth night, a terrible storm was brewing, the ship was tossed about on the water like a matchstick. All hands were on deck trying to keep the cargo from going overboard and themselves.

Alfie and Jed struggled to keep on their feet, the ship was taking on water in the holds… panic was starting to rise. Life jackets were given out as the captain felt sure the ship would sink. An hour later, with men overboard, it went down to the bottom of Lake Superior with the storm still raging. In the darkness, men could be heard shouting for help or each other. They scrambled for driftwood or anything that floated. Alfie found a large plank of wood and held onto that, his mind went back to that fateful night the *Titanic* hit an iceberg then sank on her maiden voyage, he shuddered in the blackness and held on.

Jed was only about twenty feet away from Alfie and shouted out to him, not being able to see each other was difficult but they managed to keep each other's spirits up. Over the hours before rescue, Jed's voice was getting weak, the water was freezing cold, Alfie kept talking to him, after some time the response was almost a whisper. Suddenly there were lights, a ship came into view, they were being rescued!

"Jed, Jed! We're being rescued, it won't be long… Jed?"

Alfie listened for Jed's reply, there was nothing, he had succumbed to the cold, he had floated away from his mooring on another piece of driftwood, Alfie cried.

As the remaining seamen were being hauled out of the water Alfie's thoughts went to Emma and the children. He won't tell her about this event, the worry that he wouldn't return from further voyages would not do her any good, nor him. After the rescue, he joined another ship with a heavy heart that Jed had lost his life, he would have a place with Matt in Alfie's heart always.

Once the next voyage had finished, Alfie went back to Duluth to his home in Forest Lake. Emma and the children were beside themselves with excitement and were waiting for him on the stoop. Victoria had grown up overnight and Victor was a young boy growing into a man, Arthur turned out to be a delightful boy. His family, his life, made Alfie proud, over the course of the next few years since most of his memory returned, he had occasion to think back to his mother, Margaret. The awful life she had had but the love she gave him was pure. The escape to England from Dublin on that ship, the saviour of the day in the form of Victor and finally, falling in love with Emma.

The Depression went on, Alfie went to sea as regularly as he was able, life carried on, they did the best they could. One morning Emma noticed Victoria wasn't eating after she had lain the table for breakfast. She had her suspicions *but surely not Victoria,* Emma said to herself. Victoria had spent a lot of time in her bedroom over the past few months, she attended evening classes to gain a qualification as a typist, occasionally she had mentioned the teacher, a Mr Edwards, to Emma one evening. Emma's mind darted to the supposition that this Mr Edwards might be doing more than just teaching Victoria to type.

Chapter 42

Spoiled

"Vicki, can I come in?"

Emma had made her way upstairs to the room at the end of the landing standing outside the bedroom door. After trying the handle of Victoria's room, she assumed she had locked it then, with quiet footsteps across the bedroom floor, Victoria opened it, her eyes looking down to the floor.

"Vicki, I need to speak with you, I think you are pregnant." Immediately Victoria went on the defence at Emma as if she had just delivered a death sentence.

"I'm not, I'm not... I just don't feel well!"

She was denying it, but the evidence was there, Victoria had been sick in the mornings for the past couple of weeks, she had gone off her food which, was unlike her. No signs of blood for a few months told Emma another mouth to feed was entering the family! She felt so upset, she had told Victoria about men and how to be careful, but it appears her head was turned by a smooth-talking teacher with designs on Alfie's half-sister!

Victoria started to cry breaking down then telling Emma what had transpired.

When Victoria started the classes four months ago, the teacher, Mr Edwards gave her a lot of praise, he told her how clever she was, this turned her head and made her happy; he said she could have extra practice time if she stayed after class and would see to it that she got private tuition... from him only. The first few weeks she excelled but didn't stay after the classes. The third week he asked her if she would like to stay and used the excuse that another pupil was staying after class with her, feeling this to be a safe bet, she accepted.

The end of class came, she held back and waited, Mr Edwards stayed in the classroom. He was a young man of about thirty, good-looking, with a moustache and dimples, sure of himself but a predator nonetheless, Victoria was still a virgin, and he knew it! He told Victoria the other pupil had to go home but she was welcome to stay, the error she made would cost her.

He locked the classroom door saying it would be safer for her, she didn't think anything was wrong and sat at her desk with the typewriter and her lessons for practice. Mr Edwards sat at his own desk wondering how to get her alone without anyone seeing. Quickly he made up a story to get her in the stationery cupboard.

"Victoria, can you get me a red pen, blank paper, and ruler please?" She thought nothing of it then went straight to the cupboard. He was behind her in a flash! He quietly locked the door. At first, she didn't hear him enter the cupboard then a noise made her turn around, he was right behind her! She didn't know what to do, he calmly walked over to her and told her that this was special between them, she was special to him, and he wanted to kiss her.

Her mind was in turmoil, she couldn't escape as he had locked them in the cupboard, slowly he reached out to her and grabbed her, strangely, she found herself reciprocating. She wanted it as much as he did but knew it was wrong... so did he.

"This is our special time Victoria, tell no one else, promise me?" Victoria nodded as he lay her down and took her innocence. She could feel his breath on her neck and his body on hers as he became excited, she closed her eyes. What he didn't bet on was the fact that he would make her pregnant, he had sustained an injury when young which ensured he wouldn't father a child, he was wrong. She let Mr Edwards do the same thing to her many times after class, she felt special, and well, he told her she was.

Emma listened as all the details unfolded, her anger rose, she would go to the school the next morning and start proceedings. She left Victoria crying in her bedroom and quietly shut the door.

Chapter 43

Special

The morning came, Emma got the children fed and Victor ready for school, except Victoria, she was to stay at home for the foreseeable future whilst all this was being sorted out. Emma walked with Arthur to school, Victor took himself to the high school nearby. She went to the principal's office straight away making sure she delivered Arthur to Kindergarten first. Entering the school receptionist's office, Emma demanded to see the principal saying she must speak with him as the matter she wanted to discuss could ruin lives... and the school's reputation!

Quickly the receptionist allowed her into the principal's outer office. He came out to greet her noticing a distinct lack of a smile.

"To what do I owe the pleasure, Mrs Ryan?" He had no idea what was coming his way but sat Emma down across from him offering her a drink which she declined.

Emma told him about Victoria and Mr Edwards, the Principal listened intently, Mr Edwards was his nephew by marriage. He took his mind back to his own daughter that his nephew had 'ruined' when they were both twelve. He had found him on her in the playhouse at the bottom of the garden. He got a good beating out of it; his uncle saw to that. To keep the family together he never told a soul and told his nephew that if he wanted to keep his reputation then to keep quiet. His niece just thought it was playing never bringing the subject up. *A close shave there* he thought to himself.

However, this is different, the nephew has gone too far, something will have to be done.

The principal tried to keep a serious face and not let on that he knew the teacher had previous form.

As he listened to Emma, the word *pregnant* resonated in his head.

This is worse than I thought, the principal got up from his seat, Emma watched as he poured a scotch from a little table next to his desk.

"Now, Mrs Ryan, we can do one of two things here."

His mind was all about protecting the school's and his reputations, he wasn't bothered about his nephew or the ruin he would face but, to keep things orderly and together, he devised a plan.

"I will remove Mr Edwards from the school and send him away out of state. Your daughter need not see him anymore but can finish her education until the baby arrives. If she does not wish to keep the child, then I will make provisions for it to be cared for. However, if you wish me to proceed with getting the police involved, ruining your daughter's reputation, the schools, and Mr Edwards', then the choice is yours."

He left these choices with Emma to think about. It didn't take long.

"Remove him from the school, I fear for his safety when my husband finds out, there will be no police involvement, the child will be looked after by me and Victoria and you can keep your school's reputation, as well as your own, good day."

Emma had made her mind up to keep things low-key and quiet for Victoria's sake as well as Alfie's and the children. She had yet to tell Alfie when he got back from his voyage.

The slow walk home gave Emma time to reflect on what had happened in her life in such a short space of time. Life had gained some normality but with the Depression still in existence and covering the newspapers almost daily, she looked back to Library Cottage, her memories there, finding herself getting more and more homesick. Alfie was due home in three weeks.

Chapter 44

Acceptance

Alfie disembarked and, finding himself hungry, he stopped off at a little Diner near the hotel where he used to work. The booth he sat in had shiny red leather seating, the sugar dispenser producing a glow all its own as the sun hit the silver top through the window; the waitress was eager to serve him. His thoughts turned to Emma and the children, he loved his half-sister, Victoria, and was looking forward to the day he would give her away to her future husband. She was growing into a lovely woman, he felt sure she would make a good wife in years to come, little did he know that dream would be shattered.

He stirred his coffee reflecting on the course of events over the past years since they came to Forest Lake, he had no regrets.

———

"She's what?" Alfie blew up as the news of Victoria's pregnancy hit him like a sledgehammer.

"I've taken care of it, Alfie."

Emma was trying to calm him down; his anger was coupled with shame as, of all the people, he thought Victoria would have more sense.

"Who is the father Emma? I want to know; he will make an honest woman out of my sister or I'll…"

Alfie was beside himself with rage with no amount of trying to calm him down was going to work at that moment. Victoria could hear him upstairs in her bedroom, she opened the door and came down to face her brother.

"Alfie, I made a mistake, he charmed me, I wasn't thinking, I…" her words fell on deaf ears. Alfie swung round to face her, she crumpled in a chair crying. Seeing this, he immediately went over to her and got her to her feet and hugged her. *Another woman taken by a man outside wedlock, what can I say?* Alfie tried to calm himself down. *I did the same with Emma but that was different, it was love.* Immediately he sat with Victoria on the stoop outside. They sat together as he held her in reassurance everything would be alright.

That year Victoria finished her schooling then gave birth to a beautiful little girl, she called her *Maisie* after the kindly Midwife that helped to deliver Arthur some years before. Victor left school two years later joining Alfie in the Merchant Navy.

Emma consoled herself that life was some kind of 'normal' but still her mind was in Gravesend… and Library Cottage.

————

As the Depression took hold over the remaining years of the 1930s, Prohibition saw bars and drinking places shut down, alcohol flowed down the gutters, men were making *Moonshine*! Alfie was still at sea with the Merchant Navy, it paid enough to keep the family fed allowing him to look after them. Victoria bought Maisie up the best she could with Emma's help; the little girl was as beautiful as her mother. Arthur had turned into a decent young man who had a desire to be an Engineer making cars which were his passion, he studied hard, whilst Emma busied herself with Maisie, Victoria, and the intense love she had for her family… until a bombshell was dropped on the happy life they had… World War II arrived.

Chapter 45
The World Changes

The year, 1939, was a year of change for millions of people in many countries. The first half of the year was peaceful enough however, towards the beginning of September there was some unrest in Europe. When the first of September arrived, it bought the news that war had broken out with Germany. While the British and Russians struggled against the German Reich, the United States remained officially neutral and refused to enter the war… until Pearl Harbour.

Victor worked with Alfie in the Merchant Navy to work on the Lakes. When the letter came in early 1942, Emma was ashen faced, she had found the official brown envelope in the mailbox. Victor was home with Alfie staying on the shop for a further two weeks. Emma went to the post box, finding a brown envelope with Victor's name on it, she sat down.

Victor had to leave in two days' time, life was changing again; Emma could feel it and the realisation that their lives would never be the same.

Victoria came downstairs to see Victor holding the letter of drafting. Emma looked at Victor's face and saw a young boy grow into a mature man in minutes. Victoria sat beside him. Emma was crying, *World War I took Arthur away from me, I can't let another war take Victor*, her only son by Alfie.

Two days later, he gathered up his belongings, putting them in the little leather case that Emma had had since she left England. In it, she put a letter asking him not to open it until he was on his way to Europe. Victor said he would write as much as possible and followed this statement with some small talk, Emma shushed him.

"Son, you come right back to us here, don't be thinking anything else."

He nodded then left after hugging Emma and Victoria within an inch of their lives. Emma cried once more.

Alfie came home from Sea to find Victor gone to war. Days later he was commissioned aboard a steamship to move army equipment from one end of the lakes to the other. Emma's heart was left in tatters as the thought of losing one of them, she couldn't bear it, making herself as busy as possible.

The house was quiet, having Victoria and Maisie gave comfort to Emma.

In Europe, the war raged, many killed and maimed, Emma and Victoria wrote to Victor with sporadic letters coming back full of love and thoughts. Victor saw action in France. He wrote of battles, soldiers, friends he had made… and lost, how he felt and what was around him. All this Emma took in, she wondered how Gravesend was coping, *I wonder if my beloved Library Cottage is still standing?* She said to herself.

Once morning some months later, she found Arthur playing with Maisie's dolls, he was growing into a young man. She thought about Ronald and his penchant for men, it worried her about Arthur and what lay in his future.

————————

Months later, the screen door swung open and there stood Alfie! Emma was in the kitchen and, hearing it open, she ran to him, they cried together at the welcome home.

"Have you heard anything from Victor?"

Alfie was as concerned as Emma was; she hadn't had a letter from Victor in a long time. She knew sometimes it would be difficult for letters to get through and didn't want to think anything bad had occurred. She had a dream that Victor was in a boat, it was dark, she couldn't see him, but she could hear him, he was calling her… then suddenly she would awake in a sweat. This same dream kept occurring week after week, Emma would wake exhausted at not being able to get back to sleep after the terrible nightmare.

One night she turned over forgetting that Alfie was there and screamed, then remembering he was home for a short while on leave she had frightened the living daylights out of him, he hugged her, she fell asleep again until morning.

229

Chapter 46
News and Disappointment

The war raged on after Victor had joined it. In that time, Alfie clocked up quite a few voyages on the lakes, the ships were full of various cargoes and munitions, he always had work and was glad of it.

Arthur wanted to go to sea with Alfie and felt that he was of age to do so. Emma was worried that all the men in the house would be in danger, she cursed the sea silently. Arthur got accepted for the same voyage as Alfie, he accepted it gladly and joined as an apprentice Engineer.

As Arthur grew into a handsome young man, Emma knew he looked just like his father with no resemblance to Alfie, but his good looks turned heads she knew that, what she didn't know was about his penchant for other men.

The ship arrived for Arthur to join; Alfie was waiting on board. Emma went with him and waved him off. That night, whilst in his cabin he was joined by a young man with a shock of blond hair and as equally good looking as him, he stayed the night. Their embrace confirmed one thing for Arthur, he only wanted the attention of men, keeping this side of his life as secret as long as he could.

———

Emma still had a yearning to go back to England, she couldn't settle, may never settle, she wanted to see Library Cottage once more and her beloved Gravesend. Alfie arrived home after a particularly long voyage and, that night, in bed she told him how she felt waiting for the fallout, it never came, Alfie felt the same way as her. They held each other tight for some time, and, after making love decided their next move. They hadn't heard any news about Victor coming home and were fearing the worst, Arthur was still at sea.

Days later, Emma was preparing a breakfast of eggs with one rasher of bacon, rations didn't allow for any extras, she had baked some bread the day before, cut it and used the little amount of butter she had left.

Alfie felt restless, he had a feeling something wasn't right and decided to go to the mailbox. He got up before Emma could stop him, she dreamt of Victor the night before and had a bad feeling.

As he walked to the mailbox, he wondered how his son was doing, his mind didn't allow him to think the worst. He opened the letter from the War Department, he read the words, *"...injured in the line of duty... home in three months."*

Slowly, Alfie walked back to the stoop, sat on the swing chair and, holding his head in his hands, cried for his son. Emma ran out after hearing his sobs, she feared the worst then took the letter from Alfie, Victor is still alive; she joined him on the chair. After three months, Victor arrived home with a prosthetic leg enabling him to walk a few yards without the aid of a crutch.

They hid their anguish about his condition as he carefully negotiated the steps up to the front door. They all hugged for an eternity, tears of joy, tears of sadness and welcome home. Little Maisie ran over to Victor and hugged him to her, in her mind he was a hero back from the war. Hours went by with tales of events in France and the Netherlands, Victor didn't tell them all the gory and disturbing details, these incidents were to be kept in his mind and heart. The loss of his leg was just a 'matter-of-fact' incident to him, he spared them the awful trauma he went through.

Victor remembered England from his young years and the broken leg episode, *"How strange I've lost the leg that I broke."* He laughed to himself as his mind took him back in time to Margate and the *Seabathing* hospital where he discovered that Alfie was his father and how they ended up back at Library Cottage, albeit for a short time; he smiled.

It was another eighteen months before Arthur returned home from voyages. He went from one to another having only a week or so in between, keeping his secret hidden from his family, he delighted in having the attention of men in his life which he took for love until one day some months later.

Chapter 47

Recovery

Life after the war was attempting to return to normal in the Ryan household. Maisie was growing fast, Victoria had found a young man she became fond of; he was a neighbour's son back from the war who had his eye on her.

One night he came by her bedroom window throwing a tiny stone up at the glass, she looked out, seeing him, her heart leapt. She went quietly downstairs whilst everyone else was asleep. Silently she opened the kitchen door letting him in. In their haste to make love she forgot Arthur was sleeping in the little box room next to the kitchen, he heard their noises and not wishing to be found out, watched from the keyhole as they took each other to another place on the kitchen table. The neighbour man stopped after fifteen minutes of frantic lovemaking with Victoria who was straightening her clothing as they talked. They were right for each other, she felt she wanted to be with him more permanently. Arthur could hear them talking and knew Victoria had found 'the one', he just wished he could, *maybe I will once I go back to sea?*

————

Once Alfie had finished his voyages and life after the war was getting back to normal, he returned to work as a cook with a small Diner in Forest Lake, Emma kept house for them all with the homesickness still in her heart and mind. Arthur went away to sea again for a small voyage around Lake Superior.

A few months later, returning home from sea, Arthur had multiple bruises and the look of having been beaten very badly. He told Alfie he had had a fight with a man on the last voyage, he hadn't lied but didn't tell the rest of the tale. Apparently, the man found him with another in the cabin and was jealous, a fight ensued, and he came out of it worse. He was asked to leave the voyage at the next port.

Life was beginning to return to normal until Emma could hide it no longer, she must return to England and soon.

Chapter 48
Homeward Bound

With the War over, Emma and Alfie sat the children down proceeding to tell them that they were thinking of returning to England. As they talked about it, Emma's heart was light at the thought she would step on English soil once more. They tried to include Victoria in the conversation, it became apparent she didn't want to go.

She loved living in Minnesota and felt there was nothing for her and Maisie back in Kent, especially having a new relationship with the neighbour man, she was now pregnant by him but didn't know it at this time. No amount of persuading could make her change her mind; she was staying. Arthur wanted to return to sea and thought this may be a good way he could find a loving relationship whilst working out of Gravesend so was happy to go.

Emma and Alfie felt the heartache but had to accept Victoria's decision; on the other hand, the pull of England for Emma was all-consuming and, as she aged, she felt the need to be back on home-ground; the planning of a voyage back was getting closer. Carefully, they thought up their strategies, Alfie proceeded to check for a ship sailing to New York and eventually on to England, his heart was light and happy with the thought of returning home too.

A few weeks later he announced there was a steamship heading for New York through the lakes in three weeks' time; a long voyage but the first leg of their journey home to England. He decided to give the house to Victoria, it seemed the right thing to do, Victoria could provide a home for Maisie.

Victor sat out on the stoop with Arthur. Arthur was looking forward to seeing Gravesend, he was conceived in England but born an American, it didn't bother him, he also had other thoughts running through his head.

Chapter 49

Plain Sailing

The 'goodbyes' were not easy. Victoria clung to her brother and cried, there were promises of visits in the future and letter-writing, all of this was said in a moment as the time for the taxi to arrive drew closer. The tide would take Emma, Victor, Arthur, and Alfie to their new lives in England. Maisie ran to Emma and buried herself in Emma's dress. The little girl will miss her grandma and had no idea why she was being left as she was too young to understand. Emma turned to Victoria, hugged her, and told her she was loved very much, to take care and to keep in touch; Victoria nodded slowly then wiped away a tear.

Heavy hearts but joyful at returning to England, beginning their journey via New York. Arthur had eyes like saucers as they got near the ship on the quayside, there were plenty of young virile men on deck. Emma saw the way he looked, she shuddered inside as she remembered back to Ronald and his penchant for men, just for a moment she hoped he wasn't following in his father's footsteps.

It took about fifteen minutes for them to get to their cabin, but finally, they arrived, set their luggage down then went in search of somewhere to eat. Victor negotiated the decks well with his prosthetic leg, people hardly looked at him as he made his way around. The last thing he wanted was pity and just kept smiling, one young girl smiled and caught his eye. She was blonde with a beautiful figure, her eyes twinkled blue, the sight of her captivated him, stopping him in his tracks.

He wanted so bad to talk with her, but he was a bit shy having not been with a girl before, the war took care of any dalliances he thought he might have had and left his virginity intact. His yearning for intimacy had to be kept under control, his mind was uneasy, *how can I start up a conversation,* he wondered to himself. He didn't have to wait long...

Chapter 50

Stormy Water

That night, Emma and Alfie were in their bunks fast asleep, Arthur was on the top bunk, this left Victor restless in his. He couldn't stop thinking about the young girl he saw with the beautiful smile, little did he know she was in the same situation, laying in her own bunk with her parents nearby thinking about the handsome young man she saw that afternoon.

Dawn came, the family started to stir, breakfast was the order of the day. They made their way down to the room where second class passengers ate; Victor saw the girl again, they both smiled at each other. He plucked up the courage winking at her, she blushed crimson then put her head down.

I must get to see her and find out her name, he whispered to himself. Sitting at the table with his breakfast, he devised a plan.

I'll stay up on deck after everyone has gone to their cabins and see if I can meet with her, how can I let her know I will be on the main deck? His plan had a flaw, he was determined to come up with a solution. He wrote:

"Meet me at 10:00 p.m. tonight near the big funnel, Victor," on his napkin then, as he walked past her table, he dropped it next to her chair not stopping to see if she picked it up. He felt sure she would be there.

Time couldn't fly quick enough for Victor, he made sure he shaved that afternoon, looking half-decent before meeting with the mysterious girl. Emma noticed he was taking a time to groom himself and made a comment, "Victor are you going somewhere special?" she was half-laughing having an inkling there might be a young woman involved.

"Ma, I'm a grown man, I may have time to meet someone on this ship, even just for the company, don't go planning any marriage just yet!"

He said this tongue-in-cheek with high hopes that he may even get a kiss. Emma put her hand on his shoulder and patted it, she loved Victor, he was indeed

Alfie's son, the bond was strong, particularly as he looked just like his father in so many ways.

Time was getting close, Victor kept checking his watch, finally, 9:55 p.m. came and off he went, quietly shutting the cabin door behind him as Emma, Alfie and Arthur slept. Making his way to the largest funnel on the ship he caught sight of her. With a pink shawl wrapped around her, hair in blonde curls, she set his heart on fire. As he got closer, he could see she was smiling, waiting for him… just for him.

"Good evening, my name is Victor Ryan."

He said it in a formal whisper, took her hand and kissed it. She told him her name was Donna Selby and that she was travelling to New York with her parents. Apparently, they had a business there and were returning after visiting family in Duluth. Victor and Donna found some steamer chairs then sat holding hands as they talked about their histories, Victor during the war and Donna working in a Diner part-time. The time was flying by it was already 12:30 a.m., Donna began to worry she would be missed, likewise Victor. They made a pact that they would meet the next day; love was sealed for them both.

Chapter 51

Smooth Sailing

The whole journey would take a week from Duluth to New York. Emma and Alfie kept occupied as much as they could, walking around the decks, stopping to chat to people just to pass the time.

Arthur sat up on deck most days, he had already caught the eye of a crew member, a tall man with blonde hair sneaked Arthur to his cabin one afternoon; he left it several hours later with a smile.

Victor was preoccupied with thoughts of Donna waiting for her on deck so they could sit and spend time together. After three days, Victor's mind turned to the physical longing he had for Donna, he wondered to himself what it would be like to be with a girl for the first time and was worried that things may not work out when he tried to kiss her or tell her he had lost his leg in the War, she had already guessed something had happened.

On a Friday afternoon, he waited for Donna at 2:00 p.m. at the big funnel. She came floating along the deck in a beautiful cream lacy dress which displayed the top of her breasts, she was ready with a smile to greet him. He looked at the beauty unravelling before him, and couldn't take his eyes off her, she had caught him, he wanted to be caught!

Donna had never been kissed; she was eighteen years old. As they sat, it became apparent that they wanted each other and not just for discussions, the pull of them to each other was almost tangible.

Victor leaned over to her and kissed her with just a peck that was closely followed by a deep tender kiss, the likes he had never known. It set him on fire and the yearning to be with her was deep within him. She reciprocated his kiss feeling the same warmth and longing that Victor did. They agreed they would meet at the big funnel that night, his excitement mounted.

How would he tell her he had a prosthetic leg? Would she turn away from him if she knew? All these thoughts ran through his head, sadness came over him.

It was 10:00 p.m.; the outline of two figures intertwined was kept very well hidden at the big funnel. With their clothes on to keep warm, the sounds of love and longing got lost in the wind as the ship made its way through Lake Superior.

Two bodies giving in to the longing and love felt both ways saw Victor so gentle with Donna, she cried as he took her for their first time which was special and gave way to several more similar events over the coming nights, they fell in love. He told her about his leg, she never gave it a second thought and said it was nothing to worry about as she already knew, she loved him.

One Saturday evening was a grand affair when all the passengers sat together in the dining room that had its tables nearer each other this time. Instead of staggering dining times, they all sat down at the same time for their meal. Victor could see Donna on the next table, he wanted to touch her, to kiss her but this was to be held off until later that night, he ached inside.

Donna's parents smiled at him; he knew she had told them about him.

The ship was due to dock in New York in two days' time, Victor didn't want Donna to leave the ship, *I wonder if she would come to England with me?* He was already asking himself and wanting to accept that the answer would be *yes*.

That night, the two of them met and made love again at the big funnel, they held each other tight and talked for ages. He asked Donna to marry him, the answer was *yes*.

The next question was a little harder to respond to.

"Donna, I don't want you to get off in New York, please come to England with me and my family, we can get married and make a life there."

Victor had felt sure she would accept his offer and was hoping he would get off at New York with her.

"Victor, I've fallen for you and have spoken to my father about you, he wants to offer you a position in his printing business should we get married. It would provide a good income for us, please think about it."

Donna held his hand and kissed his cheek, there was a lot to think about. Victor went back to the cabin laying for hours with the thought of staying in New York, letting his family go back to England without him.

Chapter 52
Decisions

The next morning, everyone went down to breakfast, Victor was preoccupied with thoughts of Donna with that familiar warm feeling coming over him.

He knew his answer would hurt his parents, but his life had changed when he went to war, lost his leg, and returning home. He was ready for marriage and the possibility of children. *I've got to tell them this afternoon* he said to himself.

"You've only known her a few days, Victor!" Emma was beside herself with the news.

"We haven't even met her yet, at least meeting her would calm our hearts and minds, you've got to tell your father."

Just at the point of Emma making her last statement, Alfie walked into the Cabin. She looked at him and then looked at Victor, *two peas in a pod* she thought to herself.

"Son, I don't want you to leave us, but you must make your own way in the world, you've already been away at war, we missed you like hell. Can we at least meet Donna before you make your final decision?"

Victor agreed knowing that he had already made his mind up, he went to see Donna and her parents to arrange a meeting for that afternoon.

Victor approached the Cabin where Donna and her parents were, he knocked gently, they opened the door and invited him in.

"Donna my parents want all of us to meet this afternoon, can you come up to the top deck at 2:30 p.m.?"

Donna's parents were agreeable, they asked Victor if he was getting off at New York with them, he had made his mind up… the answer was indeed *yes*.

It was 2:30 p.m., the families met near the big funnel, Victor and Donna felt a little uneasy; after all, it was the place where they made love more than once, they looked at each other in recognition of their intimacy.

Emma had tears in her eyes at the thought of her son not coming back to Library Cottage, Alfie was being manly trying not to let the thought of his only son staying in America causing watery eyes.

Victor took Donna's hand and, in front of both sets of parents, asked her to marry him. There were hugs all around except Mrs Selby, she just stood there with not very much to say on the subject. Around her was happiness but inside her, there was deep, sorrowful sadness.

Emma was sorry she would not see them married but had a thought, *there might be a way.*

That afternoon Emma and Alfie went to see the Captain. It was arranged for the next day. Victor came back to the cabin after lunch.

"Victor, we've been to see the Captain, he has agreed to marry you and Donna tomorrow."

He couldn't believe his ears; he would be a married man by the time he reached New York. He flew out of the cabin but not before he hugged Emma and Alfie tightly, *Donna would be my bride!* His heart filled at the thought.

The good news was well-received by Mr Selby, but sometime earlier, Mrs Selby had gone up on deck for '*some air*', she hadn't returned. Donna was overwhelmed, she had tears and hugged Victor not wanting to let him go.

"Husband and wife, husband, and wife," she said pronouncing the words slowly, "Mrs Victor Ryan." Donna liked that.

She loved Victor and wondered how, in just a few days, you could fall in love with someone changing your life in minutes. Later that night she met him at the big funnel, she gave herself to him with love and, afterwards as they bathed in their afterglow, they heard screams and shouts from the aft of the ship.

Chapter 53

New York

"Must have slipped," said one of the crew that was trying to see to throw a life jacket over the back of the ship whilst another was holding a flare to give some light. They never found the body; it was too dark, with the water swelling, their search was fruitless.

Mrs Selby was given to 'episodes', these were a depression that she was being treated for with certain drugs; apparently, she had lost a baby in childbirth and never got over it, even though it was fifteen years previously.

Donna was beside herself with grief, she told her mother that she and Victor would get off in New York, get married and make their way in the world. This news tipped Mrs Selby over the edge of having lost a child now feeling that she was losing her daughter too, it was obviously too much.

With sadness they were married the next day by the Captain using an old ring of Emma's, then they threw a wreath over the aft of the ship lovingly put together by Emma for Mrs Selby. As many of the passengers and crew stood around the sombre event, Mr Selby collapsed on deck with grief, he helped back to his cabin. All these events before they had even touched land.

Docking around 2:30 p.m. the next day, they disembarked attempting to find their land legs. Breathing in the smells of New York, Donna and Victor were helping Mr Selby come to terms with the loss of his wife. He liked Victor and was glad of a son, his only son had died at childbirth, his recollection of that awful event produced a tear that joined others as they rolled down his cheeks.

Donna wiped her father's tears away, gave him a hug and told him she loved him and that soon he may have grandchildren. His heart became lighter at this thought, Donna was already pregnant.

The next part of the journey wasn't for another three days. Crossing the Atlantic would take a bit longer, then there was the third leg of the journey to

Gravesend and, finally, Emma's *Library Cottage*; certainly, the first leg of the journey was eventful.

They booked into a hotel near the place where their next ship would be docking, the hotel was comfortable enough, Victor and Donna had a room although they were not going to England, they wanted to stay with Emma, Alfie and Arthur until the ship arrived, Mr Selby had his home in Queens and decided not to stay at the hotel. He returned to his marital home, seeing his wife's belongings produced more tears, he kept the promise from Donna in his heart, *I could have grandchildren!* He took comfort from those words, his life before Mrs Selby decided to shuffle off the mortal coil had not been a happy one due to the grief she had and the drugs she took to cope.

Alfie held Emma for the longest time after making love that night, they fell asleep in each other's arms which they did most nights. Just down the hall, a newly married couple was doing the same; they sealed their union many times in love and passion sleeping soundly until the morning.

Chapter 54

Goodbyes

The ship arrived in port with the settlement of the hotel bill on Mr Selby, he had paid for everyone after he left home before he went to his offices that morning. Touched by Mr Selby's gesture, Emma smiled and, at breakfast, looked at her son with his new wife, Donna, who was glowing, she could see the love Victor had for her; the same way Alfie had looked at her all those years ago and sometimes still did. She remembered back to that first sight of him working on the docks, his jet-black hair, blue eyes, she was enthralled by him. Falling for him in an instant, and he for her; it was mutual. She flushed when she remembered their first night of intimacy shivering even now to think of his body on hers after all these years.

I'll love him until the day I die; I almost lost him she would think to herself often.

Finally, it was time to say goodbye. Tears flowed, hugs were tight, the final chance to tell each other they were loved. It suddenly dawned on them that the realisation of a huge amount of time may pass before they saw each other again, this bought further tears.

Victor and Donna went down to the quayside to wave goodbye, he was trying to hide his tears but didn't do a good job, Donna cried with him. When the ship was out of sight, they made their way to Mr Selby's offices.

On the bow of the ship, the sea air made Emma feel alive, she stood with Arthur until New York and the wonderful Statue of Liberty was finally out of view. She turned noticing Alfie was speaking to one of the crew that he had worked with a few years ago.

"Do you remember that voyage to Lake Michigan, John?" It was funny to hear that name again, the one he used when he couldn't remember who he was.

"Yes, I do Frank, oh and by the way, my name is really Alfie." Alfie followed the statement up with the explanation of what had happened years ago, the *Titanic* and subsequent life through World War I until the voyage he was now on. Frank listened, nodded then proceeded to divulge his own life events for Alfie to laugh at and commiserate with.

"Do you remember the ship's mate, Chuck?" Alfie nodded and laughed, "Yeah, everyone thought he was a bit, you know..." Frank nodded and acknowledged then proceeded to reveal his secret, feeling safe in the knowledge that he could do so.

"We were close, Alfie, you know what I mean by that?" Alfie knew, he always accepted that many men onboard ships sought the company of each other on a long voyage, it wasn't for him, and certainly, it wasn't for him to comment. He accepted it without prejudice.

"Frank, if you made each other happy then that's all fine with me, I have no judgement to make."

Frank nodded and smiled; he knew he could tell Alfie anything although two men together were something Alfie could never understand.

As they stood talking, Arthur came over. Frank was immediately taken aback at this young man's good looks, something stirred inside him. Alfie introduced him and the two men shook hands, slightly lingering but letting go eventually.

Later that afternoon when Frank was up on deck, he caught the sight of Arthur leaning on the rails. He studied this young man's lean body, his muscles and physique, *I've lost my reason, he has captured me*, Frank held his breath and felt a glow inside.

He walked over and spoke trying to get some idea if Arthur was *his kind of man*. He knew in an instant as Arthur turned to him asking for a light, they cupped hands to stop the match from going out, slowly they looked into each other's eyes, silent words were spoken.

"So, tell me, Arthur, what is your line of work?"

Frank listened as Arthur told him about his voyages on the lakes, all Frank could do was imagine Arthur beside him, kissing him. Frank mentioned he had his own cabin. Knowing him only minutes, Arthur felt sure this liaison was something he wanted from an older man as he had only been with men around his age, it felt school-boyish every time. Something was pulling him to be with Frank, he couldn't put his finger on it, *was this love?* It seemed a different feeling to the one's he felt all the other times.

"Arthur, would you like my company, I know I'm older than you, but I think we have something in common?"

Frank was sure this is what Arthur wanted, it had been an exceptionally long time since he had enjoyed the company of a man and one who excited him as Arthur did. Looking around to make sure the coast was clear, they went to Frank's cabin, slowly they divested themselves of their clothing and quickly found themselves in each other's arms. They kissed, deep and hard, their love blossomed as hours went by with the two souls finding love under unusual circumstances.

So, this is love, Arthur, you've found it, at last, he had this wonderful thought running through his mind as he lay with Frank once more. The tenderness from Frank gave Arthur such a wonderful feeling of love and acceptance, he was the happiest he had ever been. They kept their liaison quiet from everyone else on-board ship, homosexuality was still against the law, Arthur didn't want his family to know his secret. At every opportunity, Arthur went to Frank's cabin through the whole of the voyage, his heart was light, Frank knew the love he had been seeking for such a long time had arrived at last, he kept his failing health a secret from Arthur and just enjoyed the moments they shared.

Chapter 55

Homeward Bound

Up on deck, Emma and Alfie spent a lot of time talking about the home they left, the children and the next stage of their lives back in Gravesend as the ship made its way across the 'pond' as many called the Atlantic Ocean.

The ship was huge. They walked around its decks for exercise over the days, passing fellow passengers who nodded or said, *good morning*. Each night in their tiny cabin, with Arthur, they would talk and plan. Arthur had other plans but kept quiet about Frank.

It seemed like an eternity until reaching England, the days dragged, but at last, the ship stopped at Liverpool first then Dublin and finally Southampton. As they queued to disembark, Frank pressed a small piece of paper into Arthur's hand with his address.

Be with me Arthur, here is my address; Frank had a tear in his eye, he wanted Arthur in a way that they could be together outside the eyes of the law. The village where Frank had grown up would give him the opportunity for privacy, his parents had left him a big house at the end of a private lane many years ago, this would ensure no prying eyes. Arthur agreed and said in time he would make his way to Frank once everything had settled in Gravesend. Frank smiled hugging him before Arthur left the cabin.

On the Quayside, Emma, Alfie, and Arthur collected their luggage making the journey by bus and tram. Their faces dropped when they arrived at Gravesend. Sheer devastation from the bombing of World War II was heart-breaking, Gravesend particularly was bombed regularly and, as a port, it was a target by the German Luftwaffe.

Emma cried as she remembered people she knew and the houses they lived in flattened by bombs, her mind darted to *Library Cottage*, when she left it to go to America, it was rented out. Her face fell as looming up into the distance was a ruin; *Library Cottage* had been raised to the ground. Her heart broke, she collapsed at Alfie's feet sobbing.

My Library Cottage, she uttered as she wiped her eyes, *Why? Why?* Emma felt it personal, but of course, it wasn't; it just seemed like it. They picked their way over the rubble that was the kitchen, the old tin bath was still intact of all things. She stood in the garden, blinking a few times, then realised that the skeleton of a hand was poking out of the earth, *Oh my God, it's Albert's!* she said to herself, wondering if Alfie had seen it. He hadn't, he was busy with Arthur reviewing the rubble for anything they could salvage. The sight of the skeletal hand took her back to the kitchen with the knife in her hand.

She quickly covered it over with some earth and stones she found nearby. Albert was a secret she never divulged... even to Alfie.

As they stood reviewing the situation, it dawned on them that they didn't have anywhere to stay that night. With no home and nowhere to sleep, Emma had an idea, she wondered if the old lady with the Guest House might have a room a few roads away. Mentioning this to Alfie, they started the few hundred yards walk to the road she lived in but when they arrived, they not only found her home gone but the whole terraced row had been wiped out!

What will we do? Emma was at a loss but quick thinking by Alfie came to their rescue.

"I wonder if any of my old neighbours are still alive, Emma?" Quickly they walked to where Alfie used to live before meeting Emma; the terraced house was still standing but occupied and the neighbouring houses also had lights in windows.

The house next-door-but-one had a bicycle outside, Alfie knocked on the door, an elderly lady came out to greet them. It was the neighbour, Mabel, who used to look after Victoria and Victor years ago! When she saw them, she cried, everyone had a hug. She looked at Arthur and even gave him a hug too.

"We've got nowhere to go, Mabel; have you got a room spare just for the time being until we find somewhere to live?" Mabel smiled, beckoned them in and gave them her bedroom with a box room for Arthur, she slept on the couch and wouldn't hear of them not taking the rooms.

She smiled as she assured them, "It's just for a while, please don't worry, it's fine." Making a pot of tea, she bought out some scones, jam, and cream that she had made that morning. They were all tired after the long journey to Gravesend and finally gave in for sleep.

Emma and Alfie slept fitfully until daybreak. She got up whilst Alfie slept, *I'll take him up a cup of tea,* Emma said to herself. She walked into the bedroom, he was awake, he threw back the covers, it was clear to see he had missed her physically, he beckoned her to join him, her heart leapt, it had been a long time since the ship…

Chapter 56

Employment

They all needed employment; jobs were difficult to find. Alfie went down to the docks where most of the bombing had taken place. There was an old shipping office still standing with a rotund middle-aged man inside, Alfie found himself going up the tiny wooden stairs which seemed a bit worse for wear, he gripped the handrail as he steadied himself.

Opening the paint-peeled door, he stepped in, "Good morning son, how can I help you?" The man with a handlebar moustache was sitting behind a rickety old desk that had seen better days, he smiled at Alfie.

"Have you any crew jobs?"

Desperation made Alfie happy to fill any vacancy.

"Well, I need a Cook, a ship is due in four days for some long voyages, can you cook, son?" The man felt sure the answer would be *no*.

"Yes, I can cook, and I'm available immediately."

The job was Alfie's. Slowly he made his way back to Mabel's house where Emma was helping prepare dinner.

"Good news, Emma," she turned to face him with a smile that changed as he delivered the bombshell.

"It's cooking on board ship again, but the voyages are long."

Her face dropped but she knew they needed money coming in.

Arthur came down from his room, Emma turned to face him, *he looks so much like his father,* she had the constant reminder of Ronald through his son, but it wasn't his fault.

The ship was due in four days, Emma and Alfie had that time to be together at least. The last night, before joining the ship, Alfie made love like it was his last night on earth. Emma wondered what had gotten into him, his lovemaking took her breath away, she lay awake afterwards with so many thoughts going through her mind.

The morning came soon enough, Alfie started to pack for his voyage.

"Before I go, Emma, I want you to know I love you and our children, our life together hasn't always been easy but the love we've had for each other has helped us get through. I'll be home soon enough; Arthur is here with you and Mabel too."

Emma's heart felt empty already, she cried into his shoulder as they held each other, he kissed her one last time, he left and walked down toward the docks.

———

Emma needed a job, any job, she found herself walking down to Perry Street where many of the shops had been bombed. There was one though, the old bakery; as she looked through the window, she could see only a few loaves left, she already had the experience of making bread as Alfie had taught her over the years back in the USA, she popped her head in to see if there were any vacancies.

"No Love, sorry, there's just enough work for the two of us."

The women behind the counter were protecting their jobs, she knew it was futile to go on any further. Walking down Perry Street, she remembered her cleaning experience with the Brockington household and all the memories that went with that, good and bad; *I wouldn't go back there but maybe there could be other jobs I could do with my experience?* Suddenly, Emma had an idea. She quickly spun around and returned to the bakery in Perry Street. She did a deal with the two ladies, it became her sole source of income but the wares she made were welcome, and it would keep the wolf from the door, jams, marmalade, and pickled eggs!

Chapter 57

Industrious

After a few weeks at Mabel's, Emma started her search for somewhere else to live as things at Mable's were getting a bit cramped. She went through the *Kent Messenger* finding a little tied cottage in Higham for rent, *Bendigo Cottage*. It was once the old bakery. She dropped what she was doing and took the bus to Higham, stepping down from the bus, she walked the few hundred yards from the Sir John Falstaff public house then down the little lane towards the cottage. There it was, its front door in the middle and a window on either side, *it's perfect!* She loved it straight away and knew Alfie would when he got back from the sea. Emma was beside herself with joy and just needed to tie the loose ends with the Farmer a bit further down the lane.

As Emma walked towards the farmhouse, she noticed Walnut trees on her left along the small lane, *I could make pickled walnuts too.* The Farmer came out to greet her, she stopped in her tracks as the farm geese started to spit and hiss at her; at this point, the Farmer showed them his boot, they dodged him quickly. The geese hurried away as she walked up to the door.

Emma followed the Farmer to the other side of the cottage, he bent down as the door was only high enough for someone five feet or so to gain entrance, the stairs were narrow. She walked in behind him, the bread ovens were still there, three of them with little metal doors, she smiled thinking how Alfie might like to bake bread again.

As she turned to go back outside, the Farmer followed her, she was not aware, but he watched her as she climbed the tiny stairs, he was right behind with designs in mind.

The Farmer was agreeable with rent in advance looking forward to having the cottage inhabited, particularly by a lovely looking woman like Emma. She was so pleased to be able to have a home for Alfie to come back to and for her and Arthur to live in. Once back at Mable's she told Arthur and Mable about the cottage and how much Alfie would love it, Arthur feigned interest as his only concern was to be with Frank as soon as possible.

Mable and Emma hugged for a long time, Mable had enjoyed having the company, Emma promised they would see each other occasionally for tea. A few days later, as she wiped away a tear, Mable waved goodbye to Emma and Arthur then watched until they were out of sight.

From the cottage, Emma made jams, marmalades and pickled the locally grown walnuts, she had never done this before but quickly learnt the art as well as baking cakes, pies, curing meat, all these skills she got from Mrs Dawson the housekeeper at Lord Brockington's all those years ago. From these labours, she managed to make ends meet and pay the rent.

After looking for work with no luck, Arthur came home to Emma with news that he had a job in a village about twenty miles away. It was the cover to enable him to be with Frank; he missed him every day. It had been too many months and, finally, he couldn't wait any longer. There was little work in Gravesend for anyone, life was hard whilst the town tried to build itself back up after the decimation of the war. He was sure the distance between Higham and Sittingbourne would deter Emma from wanting to visit, he couldn't tell her he was homosexual, it would break her heart so he said he would come regularly to the cottage to see her knowing she was on her own rather than her visit and discover his life with Frank. *No one must know,* he said to himself, *I can't even tell my own mother, it would break her heart.*

She was sad to see Arthur go. *How things have changed since leaving Forest Lake*, she thought. *I left with family and now find I am alone in a cottage looking after myself.* Emma's thoughts turned to Alfie and the knowledge he would be home by the end of October; it calmed her mind.

In his mind, Arthur knew that his *persuasion* as he called it, was not the norm but he felt the pull of a man rather than the attentions of women, there had been many that had wanted that from him, but his eyes were only for his own sex. Arthur told Emma he found a room near his 'work' it would save money to be close by rather than commute every day, Emma accepted this without question.

He packed his things and left, hugging Emma, knowing Frank would be waiting for him, his heart was light, finally happy in the recognition that he would be with someone that he loved and who loved him in their own 'special' way.

Chapter 58

Sittingbourne

Sitting on the train, as it chugged along, Arthur looked out of the window with his heart warming at the thought of Frank. He watched the beautiful Kent countryside go by and had heard Kent called the *Garden of England* by many. His thoughts turned back to Frank; in a few hours, they would be in each other's arms. His mind took him back to the cabin on the ship where their love carried them to another place, a safe place.

All Arthur had was the scrap of paper Frank had thrust in his hand as they left the ship, he took it out of his pocket and read it again *29, Blackbird Lane, Sittingbourne, Kent.* He looked out of the window and smiled, *not long Frank.*

It had been almost three months since they found each other; he relived their clandestine meetings in Frank's cabin, how Frank had held him in a tender embrace; the train got nearer, Arthur's heart skipped a beat. As an older man, Frank had been in the world a whole lot longer than Arthur, but Arthur liked the maturity Frank bought to their liaisons, as his mind wandered, the train arrived at the station. He found himself on the platform with his bag, his heart was full and happy as he made his way to the address on the paper.

The lane was long with trees hanging down over it giving it shade, a brown rabbit darted in front of him suddenly and the birds whistled away as he strolled along. Finally, in the distance, a huge Manor house came into view. He stopped and stood wide-eyed at the size of it. *This must be 29 Blackbird Lane?* he said to himself, so hoping it was.

The gravel crushed under his feet as he walked about 50 yards to the front door. It was a heavy, Oak Tudor-style one that had black door furniture. The huge knocker was in the shape of a lion's head, he gave it a hefty knock and waited.

It opened slowly, there stood a young woman of about thirty, she looked at Arthur in puzzlement.

"Can I help you?" Arthur didn't have a clue who she was but was polite in his response.

"I'm here to see Frank, he invited me to stay with him." She looked sad at the mention of Frank's name.

"You're too late, I'm afraid, he died four weeks ago, he had a heart attack in the garden, I'm his daughter, Angela." Arthur's jaw dropped, his eyes filled with tears, the awful news killed him inside. He told her how they had met whilst on the ship sailing back from New York.

She said her father had spoken about Arthur to her and if something happened to him, she was to give him something, she held out a little box. The box was tied in waxed brown paper, Arthur opened it, inside was a gold ring and a note which read:

If you are reading this, it will mean I am gone. You made me happy Arthur, just for those days we spent together, I want you to keep this ring as a reminder of my love for you, Love always, Frank.

He cried as he read it, the tears fell, his lip trembled, Frank's daughter handed him a handkerchief; his heart was broken. She went on to tell Arthur that her father knew he was ill back in New York and came home to die. Arthur thanked her for the information and the ring then left.

He stumbled back down the lane to the station, tears staining his face, falling onto his shirt, he didn't care. His mind was cruel, it took him back to Frank's arms in the cabin, there he let it stay.

Chapter 59
Love Lost

Making his way back to Higham was the first thought in Arthur's mind as he left Frank's house. Then something stopped him, *my mother doesn't know of my homosexuality, of my love for Frank, I can't tell her… I just can't.* Arthur wasn't ready to tell the world of his secret and in his heart, he knew he would never find the love again he had found with Frank.

He didn't alight at Higham station when the train arrived, he carried on to Gravesend. Slowly, he walked down to the docks to The Three Daws public house then sat looking out over to the Essex coast from one of the windows, double scotches were lined up all with thoughts of Frank. His heart was indeed broken, tears were relentless.

The next morning, Emma was busy preparing her pickles and jams as usual when there was a gentle knock at the door; it was the Farmer with news for her.

As the Farmer said the words, Emma only heard *dead, docks,* and *Arthur.* Apparently, the news unfolded that a young man had been washed up on the mud banks early that morning, it turned out to be Arthur. She passed out with shock. The farmer picked her up laying her on her bed, he went to the farmhouse to get some strong brandy and, as she came round, he gave her some in a cup of tea. She couldn't take the awful news in.

"Oh my God, I can't believe it, he was only going to his new job yesterday, how could this have happened?"

Emma cried for her son. The Police had found Arthur's wallet in the *Three Daws,* looking through it they found his address and saw that he lived in Higham at the cottage. They bought his belongings to the Farmer who said he would give Emma the news, the wax-covered box was intact.

Putting his hand in his pocket, he gave her the box, inside it was a gold ring with the note. She read it and realised that Arthur was indeed his father's son and that the penchant for men had taken him away from her. How did she not know about Arthur's persuasion? *He did have a girlfriend when we lived in America,* but as she started to put two and two together, she remembered how Alfie's friend looked at Arthur sometimes, the penny dropped.

The Farmer hung about in Emma's bedroom as if he were waiting for further orders or some kind of agreement. She got up and went to the door, he put his arm across it so she couldn't leave the room. Emma turned to him, "I have just lost my son, how dare you!" she spat in his face with such venom he removed his arm and left the cottage; she was furious; no one was going to hurt her or take advantage of her in her hours of grief or indeed at any time!

Chapter 60
Hello and Goodbye

Emma kept herself occupied after the news of Arthur's death. There were still a few months to go before Alfie was due back and, in her sadness at the loss of Arthur, she began to think of her other children, Victor, his wife and Victoria whom Emma always thought of as her daughter although Alfie's sister.

A few days after Arthur's death, an envelope plopped on the doormat; it was a letter from Victor. The postmark was quite a few weeks old but that didn't matter, she was hearing from Alfie's son whom she loved just a little bit more than she had the others although none of them knew it. She opened the blue envelope with its chevrons of red and dark blue around the edges.

Dear Mother, I have the greatest news! Donna and I are to be parents soon. We wanted you both to know straight away as soon as we heard the news from the Doctor. We are over the moon about it and look forward to having our own little family at last. How are you both and how is Arthur? Has he managed to find work? What are things like in Gravesend for you?

As she read through to the end of the letter, her eyes filled. All these questions with information about a baby in the family soon touched Emma but the one that really did was the mention of Arthur, she cried after reading the letter. In her haste to keep busy whilst holding her head above water, she had only written one letter to them since coming back to Gravesend.

She stopped what she was doing, writing several pages, mentioning the loss of Arthur, the cottage, the farm and how she missed them all. The next day she went to the village post office sending the letter on its way.

Arthur's funeral still needed preparations, her heart was so heavy with his loss she just dragged herself around. There was only her and Mabel attending the funeral that afternoon, Arthur was buried in a pauper's grave at St. George's.

After the funeral, Emma, dressed in black, went back to the cottage. She carefully removed her clothes and redressed in her usual day dress with an apron, all this totally unaware that the Farmer was watching through the window. He and his wife had not spoken for a long time, but he didn't want to give up the farm if they separated so just carried on in a loveless marriage with no intimacy, it was common.

Emma came out into the kitchen to make a cup of tea; she left the door of the cottage open as the sun shone that day. The Farmer knocked and walked straight in, *I own the cottage and don't have to knock* he said to himself. Emma was surprised, she stepped back as he came in.

"How was the funeral?" he asked in a gentle manner seeming sincere to her.

"A sad affair with hardly anyone there except an elderly friend and myself." Emma didn't want to talk about it, but the farmer had been good to her.

"When is your husband home?" He had designs on her she felt, she was hoping this was all innocent.

"End of October his voyage finishes, I love my husband very much." She added the declaration of love just to see his reaction, there wasn't any, he turned to leave but before he did, he told her he liked her and if ever she found herself 'lonely' at night she was just to put a candle in the window. Emma knew exactly what this meant, she came back with this reply, "I may be alone, but I am not lonely. The love I have for my husband keeps me going, there is no need for solace in anyone else's arms thank you." With Emma's words in his ears, he turned and walked out.

Chapter 61

The Wait

And as the morning sun shone through the kitchen window in Higham, Emma started the preparation of the preserves, pickles, and sweetmeats to be made for the day. The Bakery in Perry Street agreeing to take Emma's wares for sale ensured she kept body and soul together with her heart light, it was filled with the thought that Alfie was just a few weeks away from coming home. She knew the news she would give him would be bittersweet, Arthur had taken his own life and a new life just starting on the other side of the Atlantic in the form of their first grandchild.

She was happy that morning, the Farmer didn't even stop to talk anymore which he always did each morning on his way to the market, Emma was quite happy with that, *I can do without his attentions*, she said to herself as she screwed another lid on a jar of apple chutney just a bit tighter than she normally would.

All the work throughout the day in the kitchen made her weary, she wondered if she was starting to feel the years with the events that had shaped her life. She looked out of the kitchen window and watched the farmer's geese waddling down the lane squawking as they moved in a little group, she smiled at this sight and yawned.

Later in the afternoon with a cup of tea, she settled down in the little padded armchair near the fireplace, putting another log on the fire as it was starting to turn chilly, the embers glowed, it gave her peace and comfort. She sat back and fell asleep, she dreamt; dreaming of the first time she saw Alfie down at the docks whilst taking her mother for a walk. The first time they kissed and the first time she had lain with him, the heaven they both lived in would be theirs once more, *soon my love, soon*. At around 2:30 a.m., Emma awoke suddenly in the armchair; she looked around her; all she could hear was just the quiet tick of the little mantle clock; the fire had all but gone out, bed beckoned.

The next morning she walked to the bus stop at the top of the lane, feeling on top of the world. Soon, her husband of many years would be home, she felt sure that the cottage business she had going would be a way that prevented Alfie from going back to sea. *Maybe he could learn to make chutney?* she said to herself laughing as she walked.

The little brass bell rang over the door as she entered the shop, the two women who ran the bakery turned looking at her like they had seen a ghost. They looked at her face seeing a happy smile, it was this face that told them they knew she wasn't aware of the awful news that came in that morning... a ship out of Gravesend had been sunk on its way back from South Africa by an old landmine that was floating loose from its moorings on the water from World War II; all crew lost. They didn't want to be the ones to tell her, they had an inkling that Emma's husband was on board. *Maybe she will find out a different way?* They kept their thoughts to themselves, paid her and said goodbye.

Emma was on her way down Perry Street, and, for some strange reason, she diverted to the docks where she used to go with Ethel in the bath chair and where she first saw Alfie. She looked at the Essex coast towards Tilbury with a smile, *he'll be home soon*; she could see Alfie's face in her mind. Wondering when the ship was due to dock, she made her way to the little wooden office to enquire.

As she opened the door the same man that had spoken to Alfie only months before stood up abruptly.

"Good morning, I'm Mrs Ryan, when is the *Thames Star* due to dock please?" You'd have thought she asked him to chop his hand off by the look on his face. He hesitated; *she didn't know.*

"Please sit down, Mrs Ryan." His request was sombre; she looked puzzled by his sad face.

"There is no way to sugar-coat this awful news I'm about to tell you, but the *Thames Star* was sunk by a floating land mine off the South African coast, all crew were lost. It has been confirmed by a passing ship."

She stood, eyes wide with shock, she felt her head swim then finally blackness. The shipping office man was waving smelling salts under her nose as she came to. Helping her up, he could see no tears, he tried to speak with her, but his words fell on deaf ears, closely followed by the shaking of his head.

Suddenly, Emma shouted back at the man "I'm waiting for Alfie!" she scrambled up, straightened her dress, then flew down the steps to the little waiting room at the end of the pier where the ships usually docked.

She spent the rest of the day in the Terminal watching ferry passengers coming and going. Emma never moved, as the sun started to pale and darkness grew, she lay on the little wooden bench falling asleep.

In the morning, as the sun peeked in through the little window of the waiting room, she sat bolt upright but never moved after that, she watched a stream of people coming and going. Finally, an elderly lady stopped asking her if she needed help, "No, I'm fine really." Emma was sure the man in the office had made a mistake, just like the time when Alfie should have gone down with the *Titanic. It was all a mistake surely?* The lady bought her a cup of tea which she was grateful for.

Hours went by, ships sailed past, the Ferry bought more passengers over from Essex and Kent then back to Essex. As darkness fell again, she went outside to feel the wind on her face, she turned to look across the Thames toward Tilbury, seeing the twinkling lights she whispered his name, tears fell from her eyes, followed by blackness.

———

The next morning, as the Gravesend ferry docked with a few passengers alighting, they suddenly stopped in their tracks, looking in shock, they saw the body of a middle-aged woman lying on the mud bank near the jetty. One of the crew made his way down the ladder that was fixed to the wall to see if he could help, he shook his head to the others on the ferry… she was gone.